OFFSIDE

KELLY JAMIESON

To Sue Ellen Gower — you are so much more than an editor. You are a mentor who has taught me so much, a cheerleader who wants me to succeed, and a partner in my writing. I can't thank you enough for all you have done for me.

I also want to thank my all readers who loved my Heller boys as much as I do, and kept asking for more!

CHAPTER 1

Things were finally going right for him.

After working his ass off, sweating, groaning through the pain, pushing his body hard, he'd never been in better shape. He was getting closer to being ready to play again.

Matt grinned as he stood in front of his closet trying to decide what to wear.

A suit probably wasn't necessary, but a business meeting required more than just jeans, so he pulled out a pair of dark dress pants and a button-down shirt. He rubbed his jaw while looking in the mirror and decided against shaving. Once dressed, he grabbed his wallet, cell phone and keys and headed out the door of his luxury beachfront apartment.

This place felt more like a hotel than a home, but it was close to the beach with a great ocean view through a whole wall of windows, and had a huge pool and full gym, so it worked for him.

He took the elevator to the underground parking garage where his Porsche Boxter was parked, the sweet new ride he'd treated himself to when he'd moved to Santa Monica to play for the Condors.

There'd been a while when everyone had been afraid he was never going to walk again, but he'd been determined that was not going to happen. He'd busted his ass in rehab, but it was all worth it.

His mood lifted even more once he was cruising through Santa Monica traffic with the top down on his Boxter, blue sky and sunshine overhead, palm trees lining the streets. He hit the freeway but it didn't take long to get to the Santa Monica Coliseum. The Condors Community Foundation's offices were located in the Coliseum along with the offices of team management. He entered and walked down the hall, pausing to greet team owner Steve Holbrook outside his office. Steve was a hockey legend, one of the greatest players ever, who'd bought the Condors about ten years ago after he retired. Of course, every time he saw Steve, Matt couldn't help remembering the conversation they'd had eight years ago, when Matt had been newly drafted and trying to make an impression at summer development camp. The conversation about Steve's daughter Honey.

But that was a long time ago.

Thinking about Honey just pissed him off, so he didn't.

He said hi to a few other office people, including General Manager Rudy Thomas. Then he headed to the boardroom where the meeting was to take place.

"Hey, Matt." Trent Maitland, Executive Director of the Foundation greeted him. "Grab a coffee if you like. There're donuts too."

Matt poured a coffee from the carafe set up on a sideboard, then moved to find an empty seat at the board table. Some general chit-chat ensued as they waited for everyone to arrive. The boardroom wasn't exactly his comfort zone, but whatever.

He leaned back in the leather chair and sipped his coffee, turning his head at the next person to walk into the room.

Then his coffee stuck in his throat and he choked as Honey Holbrook took a seat at the table.

Dressed in a black business suit, blonde hair pulled back into a low ponytail, she calmly set a leather-bound portfolio on the table, opened it to reveal a pad of paper, and picked up a pen. She tucked a piece of hair behind one ear and smiled at the people at the table. Then her eyes fell on him.

Big brown eyes went wide and the smile faded as her pretty lips parted.

Matt was ninety-nine percent sure his own eyes were as bugged out as hers, especially since he was still coughing on his coffee. Fuck.

They stared at each other for what felt like about a year. Heat swept up from beneath Matt's shirt and into his face. Honey's cheeks grew pink, probably equally as warm.

"Okay, I think everyone's here," Trent said. "Let's get started. You all know Matt Heller."

Matt struggled to get control of his breathing and smiled and nodded at everyone as they all made noises of acknowledgement.

"And..." Trent looked at Honey. "You all met Honey this morning."

More smiles and murmurs of agreement went around the room, but this time the smiles were tight and the murmurs uncomfortable. Matt watched Honey. She still smiled, but her fingers tightened on the pen she held.

"Matt, Honey Holbrook," Trent completed the introductions, not knowing no introductions were necessary. "Honey has just joined the Foundation as a Programming Coordinator. Dulcie will be going on maternity leave in a few weeks..."

All eyes swung to a very pregnant woman at one end of the table. She grinned.

"The plan is for Honey to help out when Dulcie's on maternity leave."

Wait…what? Honey was taking over for Dulcie? So he was going to be working with *her*? With Honey Holbrook? *Fuck me.*

Matt's eye connected with Honey's again with a hard jolt. He saw her throat move as she swallowed, her smile getting tense at the corners of her mouth, her eyes shadowy.

Yeah, no doubt everyone in the room knew her. Everyone in the fucking country…no, make that continent…knew her from her wild escapades. Of course, she'd been out of sight for quite a while now. Honestly, Matt couldn't remember the last time he'd seen her name come on up Twitter or Facebook or any of the gossip blogs or tabloid magazines. Had she been in hiding, or what?

She looked thin. Her cheeks were hollower than they used to be beneath killer cheekbones. She didn't have a lot of makeup on, unlike many of the photos he'd seen of her over the years. And for sure she was wearing a helluva lot more clothes than some of the photos he'd seen of her over the years. The black suit might have been respectable and busi-nesslike, but there was no hiding the fact that she had a killer body beneath it—full breasts, slim waist and hips, and legs that went on forfuckingever.

Christ. He couldn't work with her. For one thing, she was a spoiled little rich girl who had no idea what real work was. For another, they had…history. History that had not ended well. Jesus.

He couldn't take his eyes off her hands, for some weird reason. Her fingers were long and slender, nails short and unpolished, no rings. She kept playing with the pen, which he couldn't help but think showed some nerves. Otherwise, she seemed calm, a poised smile firmly in place as she listened to the conversation.

Which he was not doing. *Pay attention, dickhead.*

Trent was still talking. "So, Matt's been doing a few things for some kids' charities since he hasn't been playing, and we're just getting going with a partnership between the Foundation and a local school."

"Yeah." Matt dragged his gaze away from Honey's hands. "I like kids. It's awesome to work with kids who don't get to play sports much. Also, when I was in the hospital I got talking to some kids there, and it would be great to do some work for the Children's Hospital."

"I was thinking about that too," Honey said. Her voice made his balls tighten. Soft, a little husky, so fucking sexy.

"Honey just started today," Trent said. "We'll have to give her some time to get oriented."

"I've been working on getting up to speed on all the various organizations the Foundation partners with," Honey said. "There are some really great ones."

Matt caught the eye roll of one of the guys sitting at the table. Yeah, that was pretty much how he was feeling too. How much time was going to be wasted because she had no clue what she was doing?

"Of course, I didn't realize that Matt was going to be working with one of the groups that we're looking at partnering, but I've shortlisted a few local youth organizations and community groups that I think would be great for us to support."

The guy leaned over to the woman beside him and whispered something to her. She grimaced and nodded and whispered back to him.

Matt shifted in his chair. Hell, that was fucking rude when Honey was talking, even if he too was doubtful of her contributions there. Her gaze slid to them, then back to the group at large, her voice faltering only a little. "I also have some ideas for some fundraising events. It would be awesome if we could get not just Matt, but some of the other players to attend to raise the profile of the events. I think I have some connections that would be very valuable and help in our fundraising efforts."

"No doubt," someone at the table muttered.

Matt watched as hot color flooded Honey's cheeks. With a jerky movement she tucked that same strand of hair behind her ear again then resumed turning the pen over and over in her fingers. Still she smiled. But yeah, she'd overheard that comment.

"Honey," the guy who'd been whispering drawled. Who the hell was he? Oh yeah, Aaron Bukowski, Programming Director. "What qualifications do you have for this job?"

The question everyone was thinking, including Matt.

Honey stared back at Aaron and blinked. Then she lifted her chin and said, "I graduated from Berkeley with a BA in Social Welfare. I did field work with Golden Gate Children's Hospital, the Boys and Girls Club, and Bay View Middle School. My education combined with my field work and my personal experience and connections should be a valuable asset to the foundation."

Whoa. Matt leaned back in his chair. Then he gave his head a shake. Was this really Honey Holbrook?

A degree in social welfare. So that's what she'd been doing for the last few years. Huh. That was a bit of a shocker.

"Personal experience," a sarcastic voice whispered somewhere. "Yeah, right."

More color washed her face and Matt saw her knuckles go white gripping the pen. Her smile appeared genuine, but he could see the tightness in it. He might've been the only one at that table who could see that, though. Because he'd seen her genuine smiles. A long time ago. But still...

When Honey really smiled, the whole fucking world lit up.

∼

Honey's insides tightened and her heart thudded hard in her chest. She worked to keep her face composed and pleasant. Why had she thought she'd walk in and everyone would be happy to have her there? Why hadn't she anticipated that her past was going to come back to bite her on the ass?

And that totally included Matt Heller. She had in no way anticipated seeing him there this morning. Or working on a project with him.

She ignored the whispers and snide comments she couldn't help but overhear and continued talking about her fundraising ideas and the list of charities she was going to be checking out to see if they'd be suitable to work with—the Foundation had criteria, of course. She fought to keep her voice steady and a smile on her lips.

"Honey," Trent said with a patronizing smile. "Don't worry about jumping into things yet. You can just take your time learning the ropes here."

She paused. Was she making a fool of herself?

"I think expensive charity events for rich people have been overdone," Celina, another Programming Coordinator, said dismissively. "We've been doing them for a while now. The Sweet Affair gala has been dying the last few years."

Honey lifted her chin. "That may be, but the reality is, this is Los Angeles, and there's a lot of wealth to be tapped into. I think I can tap into some connections and hopefully renew interest in the event. But there are other events we can discuss as well. There are ways we can raise money and at the same time raise the profile of the team and the sport of hockey."

"Working for Daddy," someone whispered. At least she was pretty sure that's what she'd heard.

She directed a cool gaze to Aaron with his hand over his mouth. "Excuse me? Did you say something, Mr. Bukowski?"

His eyes narrowed but he dropped his hand and gave a short laugh. "No. Not a thing."

"Oh, I thought I heard you make a comment about my father."

The air in the room went very still.

Honey pulled in air through her nose and sat up straighter. "Perhaps we should just get that out in the open," she said pleasantly. "Yes, my father is Steve Holbrook. Yes, he owns the Condors. Yes, he's the chairman of the board of directors of this foundation. Yes, I got this job because of him. But I *am* qualified. And you *do* need someone to replace Dulcie. So perhaps we should just get past that and get on with business."

She'd been trying to avoid looking at Matt this entire time, but now she swept her gaze around the table. He sat there looking as dumbfounded as everyone else, his mouth open. Then he grinned.

She blinked.

"Great idea," Matt said, leaning forward with his elbows on the table. "What are you thinking about doing with the kids' charities?"

For a moment, all she could think about was how freakin' gorgeous he was. His dark shirt stretched across big shoulders. His thick brown hair was cut short, his square jaw shadowed with beard stubble, and his dark eyes focused intently on her with a warm gleam in them. His smile tugged at something inside her. Attraction.

She also felt gratitude that he'd been the one to refocus on business after her little speech. She took a breath and forged on. "That depends on a few things."

These were things she was passionate about, so it wasn't difficult for her to lay out all her thoughts and ideas. She tried to ignore the cool reception she was getting.

She hadn't really been prepared for that and was now

kicking herself. Why hadn't she realized people were going to look down on her? She'd been trying so hard to put her past behind her. Now they thought "Daddy" was giving her a job, probably just to keep her out of trouble.

Maybe she should have turned down Dad's offer. Taking his offer of a job and the deposit on an apartment now seemed like a big mistake. But she'd heard stories of graduates who couldn't find jobs, or ended up making sandwiches at Subway, and she'd been scared. She'd done well in school and in her field work, but sometimes she couldn't imagine who would actually hire her. For real.

So here she was.

And here was Matt.

Ignoring the rude attitude from others was hard, but ignoring Matt was…impossible.

She couldn't do this. Despair washed over her. She was going to have to quit this job before she'd even got started. But she had to get through this meeting.

Finally the meeting ended. She rose from her chair and hugged her leather folder. She forced herself to meet Matt's eyes as he spoke to her.

"So I guess we need to set up another meeting. Just the two of us."

Clearly that idea did not make him happy. Her insides fluttered wildly.

She stepped aside so others could pass behind her to leave the room. Trent paused next to her. "Come to my office when you're done here."

"Okay." She mustered up a smile. She'd tell him then. She'd tell him she couldn't do this and had to quit. She had no idea what else she'd do, but she'd find something.

Then it was just her and Matt left in the boardroom.

"Um," she said about his comment on meeting again. That

wasn't going to happen. "Probably we should include Dulcie until I get up to speed."

He nodded. "When? Tomorrow?"

"There's no rush…"

"I know," he said impatiently. "But there's no reason not to get moving. I'm not playing right now, if you didn't know, so I have time to do these things."

She did know he wasn't playing. God, the whole world knew after the horrible hit he'd taken months ago, even people who didn't Google-stalk him like she might have once or twice or sixty times over the last few years.

"Let me check with Dulcie," she said. "Can I give you a call…?"

"Let's talk to her right now."

"Sure. Okay." They walked out of the boardroom and she led the way through carpeted office cubicles to Dulcie's at the back against a window.

They made arrangements for a meeting the next morning, and then Matt left with a smile for Dulcie and a hard, curious look for her.

She resisted the urge to press a hand against her belly as she stood next to Dulcie's desk.

She blinked a few times then turned herself to go back to her cubicle. She had to put Matt Heller out of her head and focus on business.

She used the ladies' room and freshened her lipstick, then back at her desk she logged onto her computer to check email. She had none. She grabbed her leather folder and a pen again, and hiked down the hall to Trent's office.

She gave a knock on the open door and he looked up from his computer. "Hi, Honey. Come on in."

She entered the room. He had a window that overlooked Santa Clara Boulevard. A palm tree just outside swayed gently in the midday breeze, sun gleaming off the green fronds. "Door open or closed?" she asked, pausing.

"Open's fine. Have a seat." He nodded to the round table in the corner of the office and she pulled out a chair and sat. She opened her folder.

He joined her at the table.

"I'm sorry about this morning," she said, right off the hop. "I don't want to cause problems here."

He sighed. "I'm sure you don't, Honey."

"I really think I can contribute."

"Look," Trent said. "Since we're being frank here, I agreed to this because your dad asked me to. I don't have much choice here."

Her heart dropped to her toes.

"I did have concerns about your reputation and the impact that could have on the credibility of the foundation, but on the other hand, anything that gets us attention and hopefully puts money in our coffers to do the work we want to do is a good thing."

Of course he had his doubts. Who could blame him? But she lifted her chin. "I intend to do my very best to make sure that happens. I'm not the same person I was a few years ago."

He gave her what she interpreted as a doubtful look, but he nodded. "Sure. But don't worry about getting involved in things right away. Take your time. Dulcie will give you some things to look over."

"Okay." She nodded. "But I'm eager to get to work."

"Well. We'll just see how things go."

She gazed back at him, resisting the impulse to frown at his non-committal response, instead shaping her mouth into a smile. "Sure. Great."

She returned to her desk, and sat there for a moment. That hadn't gone so well. She didn't exactly feel like a valued member of the team. But she had so much to contribute! Ideas! Connections!

Shit.

"Hey, Honey." Dulcie appeared beside her desk. Then she laughed. "That sounds funny. It sounds like I'm calling you honey, like an endearment."

Honey smiled. "Yeah. I know."

"What's your real name? Or is that it?"

"My real name is Honoria." Honey grimaced. "I thought about trying to start using it, but honestly, that's just a ridiculous name. So Honey it is." She gave Dulcie a bright smile.

"It actually suits you," Dulcie said. Honey spent a few seconds searching out any hidden insult in that, but Dulcie continued, "So, Trent told me not to give you too much work to do. He says you can spend your first day going through some files."

Honey blinked. "Oh. Okay, sure."

"Trent doesn't want to overwhelm you."

He didn't want her to actually do anything. She'd suspected that and now she was sure of it. "I'm here to work," she said quietly. "They're paying me to do a job, and I want to do it."

"Of course." Dulcie nibbled her bottom lip. "But it takes time to get to know the organization. Come on, let's get some coffee and get started."

Dulcie sat Honey at her desk and gave her some files to look at, but it only took Honey about half an hour to go through them and she wasn't sure what the point of that had been, since she'd learned nothing.

She sat there for a few minutes, a sick feeling burning inside her. So. Dad had gotten her this job, even though they hadn't wanted to hire her, but since they pretty much had to, they were going to pay her to sit at a desk and look busy.

The corners of her eyes stung and she blinked hard.

This wasn't what she wanted. She'd thought this was going to be a real job, where she'd use her education and skills, as she'd told them in the meeting. She really was qualified. She wanted to contribute and have a feeling of accomplishment.

She didn't have to show the world that she was a different person now, because she understood now that the rest of the world didn't matter. But it mattered to her.

CHAPTER 2

A couple of guys with injuries were already there working with athletic therapists Buck and Rob when Matt arrived in the dressing room for practice. A few months ago, after that massive hit into the boards that could have ended his career, he would've been one of those guys. Now they checked in on him about how he was feeling after skating last week with the team for the first time. He was happy to report he felt great, no post-concussive symptoms at all and his neck was fine. Sure, there were always minor things, sore muscles, but overall he felt solid. He changed into shorts and a T-shirt and climbed on a bike to warm up while other guys started showing up, some getting some ultrasound to loosen up their muscles, some getting minor things checked out, others getting help with some stretches.

Buck and Rob were great at their job and Matt had faithfully done everything they and the medical professionals had asked of him during his rehab, everything and more. This was his career and being in good enough shape to play was everything.

As he pedaled he couldn't help thinking about Honey Holbrook. Shit. How the hell had this happened?

She was still fucking gorgeous. He couldn't stop his mind from going back eight years to the time they'd spent together when he'd attended the Condors' development camp that summer. After the week-long camp, he'd decided to stay in California because of her. He'd been out of his element—a kid from a small Canadian city who went to school in North Dakota, spending time in Los Angeles hanging out with Honey's mega-wealthy friends, partying and doing wild and crazy things, even though some of those things he had to admit had made him uncomfortable. But she'd been pretty and sexy and fun, and wow, the chemistry between them had been red hot.

Christ. He couldn't be distracted by her. He had a career to get back on track. He'd been working his ass off and wasn't going to let her pretty face and hot body divert him from his goal. He pedaled harder.

The practice went well. After a win last night the mood was always lighter, with lots of joking and trash talking and Matt was right in there, despite still wearing the orange no-contact jersey. He liked to try to make things fun. When the team was losing, that wasn't always easy, and sometimes the fun aspect of what they did got away from them. But they were all there because they loved hockey and focusing on that was better than focusing on the negatives.

Not that there wasn't anything to work on.

Despite the win, their power play had not rocked, so coach Kris Radnor had them working on that, trying to create good point shots and puck movement. He spent time explaining plays and drawing diagrams on the white board. "We've got to simplify it. We've got to have better convergence on the puck and on the net. We gotta make sure when we get an opportunity to shoot the puck that it's getting off our stick fast and getting to the net."

While recovering from his injury, Matt had been watching home games from the press box. Watching from above gave a whole different view of the game and he'd seen a few areas the team could improve on—puck movement, player movement not being so stagnant, getting pucks to the net, having a better net-front presence—which he'd shared with Coach. He was glad Coach had been interested in listening to what he'd had to say.

Then they got down to running drills. Coach kept stopping them in the middle of plays, explaining how they could put themselves in better position, and then resuming the drill.

"Keep adjusting your angles based on the passes being made," yelled goaltender coach Bob Purcell to goalie François Letellier. "And square your body more to the shooter."

Matt focused on a quick release, and put the puck in the net several times to Frankie's annoyance. That just made Matt grin.

They ended the practice with a shootout competition that had lots of cheering and jeering. When Matt rang one off the crossbar, he deliberately fell to the ice and slid gently into the boards to hoots of laughter.

He left the ice sweaty but exhilarated. Some media guys were hanging around, including Dan Jasper from ESPN, wanting to talk about when he was going to play. That was a question he couldn't answer, but he spoke to them for a few minutes then cooled down with more time on the bike and stretching. He wasn't fond of stretching but had come to see how important it was in preventing injuries.

After a shower and dressed in his street clothes, he lounged around in the dressing room listening to music and shooting the shit with some of the guys.

"Hey, wanna come to my place and swim this afternoon?"

he asked teammates Joe Barzetti, Chris Dobie and Niklas Berglund. "Bring some beer."

So later that afternoon, that was where they were, lounging around the pool at his apartment building. Matt made himself work out before he kicked back with a beer. After a punishing round of laps, he climbed out of the pool dripping water all over the pool deck and walked to where he'd left his towel on a chair. His three buddies and teammates already lounged there in the sun, beers in hand.

Matt rubbed his towel over his wet hair and reached for the can sitting by his chair.

"How many laps did you do?" Joe asked with amusement.

"Lost count," Matt said. "Fuck, that felt good." He loved swimming. "You should try it. You need to work out and keep your svelte figure. You're getting love handles."

"Fuck off, I am not." Joe tipped his face up to the sun, his dark complexion now even more tanned.

"I was reading the other day that love handles are a hormonal thing," Dobie put in.

"Huh?" Joe turned his face to Dobie. "What the fuck? Hormonal?"

"Yeah. Swimming won't get rid of them. You gotta do a different workout to produce the hormones that will help get rid of fat there."

"I don't have fuckin' love handles," Joe said.

Niklas reached out and gave Joe's side a pinch. "Oh yeah, you do, man." Joe jerked back from his touch and shoved his hand away.

Matt grinned and guzzled down his beer. "Ugh. This is warm. Toss me a cold one from the cooler, Nik."

The blue-eyed blond Swede unzipped the top of the soft thermal bag they'd brought down to the pool, reached in and then lofted a can toward Matt. Matt caught it easily, the aluminum cold and wet in his hand. He popped it and gulped.

"If you're insulin resistant, you'll store your fat as love handles," Dobie continued.

"Our resident fitness expert," Nik commented.

It was true. Dobie read a lot about health and fitness and was a workout fool. But that was cool, because Matt had learned a lot from him. He'd lost a shit ton of weight after he'd been hurt and he had to work hard to keep muscle on. Six foot three and a hundred eighty pounds was pretty damn puny by NHL standards. Sure, there were a few guys under six feet and two hundred pounds, some damn good players. But he could battle better in the corners and take out some bodies when he had a few more pounds on him, and he tried to keep his weight over two hundred.

For some reason a memory of talking to Honey about that eight years ago flashed through his head. Shit.

Now he was thinking about Honey again. He leaned back into the lounge chair and closed his eyes against the bright sunshine.

He hadn't expected that to happen when he'd walking into that meeting room. Honey Holbrook back in his life. Honey looking all professional. Honey being attacked by a bunch of jerkoffs. He sighed.

"What?" Joe said to him.

He cracked open an eye. "What what?"

"Why the big heavy sigh?"

"Nothing." He paused. "You guys know Honey Holbrook?"

They all made noises.

"Oh yeah."

"Who doesn't?"

"Big time trampy trouble."

Matt frowned. "She's not a tramp."

"Are you fucking kidding, man? Have you *seen* some of the pictures of her?"

Yeah. Sadly, he had.

"Heimdall got traded away by Daddy when he fucked around with Honey."

Matt's scowl deepened. "Heimdall? Seriously?"

Joe shrugged. "Yep. She's been with a fuckin' million guys. She stayed away from hockey players after that, but rumor has it she slept with most of the Dodgers."

Matt's gut clenched and his fingers tightened on his beer can.

"Why'd you ask?" Dobie said.

Matt took another mouthful of beer before he replied. "She's working for Condor Community Foundation now."

"Huh."

"No shit."

"They gonna use her as a poster girl to raise money?" Joe asked. "That could definitely work. Put her in a skimpy swimsuit or something…no question she's hot as hell."

"Killer rack," Nik agreed.

"I'd tap that in a heartbeat," Dobie said.

"Shut the fuck up," Matt snapped.

All heads turned to look at him. Silence.

"Uh dude…what's up?" Joe asked.

Matt scowled at his beer again. "Nothing."

They all gave him skeptical raised eyebrows.

"What?" he snapped again. "She was at a meeting this morning."

"Dude! Fucking A! You want to tap her too!"

Christ. What would they say if they knew he already had? Years ago. But still.

"Stay away from her," Joe said. "You don't want Steve Holbrook coming down on you because you nailed his daughter."

"Jesus," Dobie said. "She's what…twenty-six?"

"Twenty-seven," Matt said.

They all looked at him again.

He shrugged.

"My point being," Dobie continued. "She's an adult. Her dad can't go around getting rid of every guy she sleeps with. If he did, there'd be no major league baseball in L.A."

"There's the Angels," Nik offered.

Dobie waved a hand. "Like I said."

Joe guffawed. "I don't know," he said. "There were a lot of stories about how upset Holbrook was when she was putting half naked pics of herself on Facebook, and she was over twenty-one when that was going on."

"Ha," Dobie said. "She's supposedly the reason Holbrook's hair went gray."

Matt sucked in a deep breath. None of this was news to him. But Honey's uh…colorful past wasn't something he really wanted to think about. "She's apparently reformed. It's a serious job. She got a college degree."

"No shit?" Joe said. "She still hot?"

Matt's mouth twisted. Oh yeah. "Smokin' hot," he admitted. "Even wearing a suit."

"A suit? Jesus!"

Yeah, yeah. They were all probably picturing that photo shoot of her in a barely-there bikini—or half of it, anyway— that had been in *Mustang Magazine* years ago.

"I guess I'm gonna be working with her on this deal they set up with the school. Possibly other stuff."

"I do charity work," Joe said. "Why don't I get to work with her?"

Because she's mine.

Whoa. Where the fuck had that come from? He didn't even *want* to work with her. She was brand new, inexperienced, spoiled rotten and…fucking gorgeous.

Matt set down his beer. "I need to swim more." He tossed aside the towel, strode to the pool and dove in.

The cool water closed over his head and he did a few slow breaststrokes until he broke the surface. Then he rolled onto his back and began to backstroke the length of the pool. He never should've mentioned Honey to these guys. They were all pigs.

He was strangely unsettled by seeing Honey again. It was fucking weird. When they'd met back when he was twenty and she was nineteen, they'd been hot for each other like nothing he'd ever experienced, despite the fact that he'd been pretty fucking horny as a kid and had experimented with all kinds of shit. They'd both been…adventurous, might be the word. They'd had some crazy fun. But they'd also had other times together, talking and laughing and doing normal things like riding the Ferris wheel at the Santa Monica Pier.

And he'd felt that heat again, today. She was beautiful. She was sexy. She was…interesting.

Nah. He was just curious about her, about what had happened and how she'd ended up going to Berkeley and now working for a big non-profit organization.

He and the guys had had the pool to themselves for a while, but as Matt hauled himself out of the water again, three women emerged from the apartment building. His eyebrows rose, taking in their bikinis, all three of them damn fine.

He sat again and grinned as the other guys checked out the girls, and they in turn sent flirty smiles back as they arranged themselves on lounge chairs in the sun.

"Would you ladies like a beer?" Nik called to them.

They exchanged glances, and one then replied, "Sure!"

Chairs were moved and arranged closer and their group of four became seven.

"I'm Bryn," the woman with long dark hair introduced herself. "This is Lissa, and this is Karin."

The guys offered up their names.

"What do you ladies do for a living?" Joe asked, leaning back with a smile on his tanned face.

"I'm an entertainment lawyer," Bryn said. "Lissa and I both work at Warner Brothers. She's a production assistant. And Karin's an actor."

Of course she was. Matt smiled too.

"And you guys?" Karin, the blonde, asked.

"Hockey players," Joe said. "We play for the Condors."

The girls' eyes widened, and Matt wanted to shake his head. He'd seen Bryn around the building before and he was ninety percent sure she knew exactly what he did for a living.

"No wonder you guys are so big," Lissa said, batting her eyelashes.

"And in such great shape," Karin added.

Yup.

The girls ended up having dinner with them. Bryn kept eyeing Matt but he politely kept his distance and she turned her attention to Joe. The other two paired off as well, and by the end of the night, Matt was the only one going home alone.

Which was fine with him.

CHAPTER 3

Honey opened the door to her apartment, closed it behind her and let out a huge sigh. God.

Her first day at the new job hadn't gone quite like she'd planned.

Not only had she not anticipated the animosity she'd encountered with her co-workers, she sure as fuck hadn't anticipated meeting up with Matt Heller.

She dropped her purse on her small kitchen table and headed into her bedroom to change.

The apartment was tiny, but it was hers and hers alone. She hadn't had a chance to do much with it yet, but now she'd started her new job she'd be able to buy some things to make it nicer.

There was a time in her life when she would have turned up her nose at this little one-bedroom apartment with fake hardwood flooring and fake granite countertops in the tiny kitchen. There was a time she would have laughed at the thought of living somewhere like this, on 6th Street in Santa Monica. Having grown up in a huge house on six acres of property in Thousand Oaks, this was not just a step down, it was several stories down.

But that was okay.

She hung her skirt, jacket and blouse in her small closet and pulled on a pair of drawstring yoga pants and a T-shirt, then padded to her kitchen to search out dinner. Eating alone was no fun.

She opened the freezer and eyed her selection of Lean Cuisines. Whatever.

While one was heating in the microwave, she poured herself a glass of white wine and sorted through some mail. Then she sat at the small table and ate the chicken and pasta dinner while she flipped through Newsweek magazine.

But she wasn't really reading the articles. She was reliving her day.

She needed to figure out what to do about this job that wasn't really a job. Was she going to play along and sit there and look pretty for the next four months? Was she going to quit?

She finished her meal and glanced at the time. Her neighbor Farrah Bedros was bringing her daughter Mia over in about fifteen minutes so Honey could babysit her for the evening. Honey turned on the television and flicked through channels, pausing at Dan Jasper on ESPN talking about the Condors and their chances of making the playoffs this year.

Fucking hockey.

She emitted another long exhalation.

And she'd ended up working for a fucking hockey team. Well, not exactly. For the Condors Community Foundation, the charitable arm of the California Condors. You couldn't get much closer to the team.

She leaned her head back against the couch. She'd made so many mistakes in her life. The therapist she'd seen had helped her understand why, but even so, she still felt shame wriggling inside her whenever she relived her past. But that was another thing she had to get over—the guilt and self-recrimination.

This job was so important to her, a chance to prove that she'd shed her past and grown up. And now it turned out to be not what she'd thought. Damn.

On television, Dan was now interviewing Matt Heller, all sweaty and gorgeous after their practice earlier.

She sat forward involuntarily.

Matt.

She'd tried to avoid Matt or any mention of him for the last eight years. Avoiding him hadn't been that hard, seeing as he'd been shipped up and down from the minors to the NHL and back again, then traded to another team. When he'd signed with the Condors again last year, she'd been away at college, but shortly after signing with them, he'd been injured and out for the rest of that season. Injured bad. Now he was back, apparently almost recovered from his injuries, skating with the team, and the media was all over him.

When he'd been hurt last year, she hadn't been able to ignore it. She'd watched the news stories in horrified fascination, like watching a car accident, her stomach hurting at seeing him carried off the ice on a stretcher.

She hadn't been able to avoid him in the meeting that morning either, and it looked like if she stayed with the Foundation she'd be working pretty closely with him.

She gazed at his image with disturbing fascination.

Matt. He didn't look much different than he had eight years ago, bigger and more solid definitely, his face settled into more mature lines, but still boyish—square jaw, chin dimple, dancing eyes.

Memories flooded back, the weeks they'd spent together that summer eight years ago. She'd already been in trouble then, even at nineteen years old, partying too much, drinking too much, doing wild things. Her stomach clenched and she reached for a cushion on her couch to hug as she stared at Matt talking.

Smart, well-spoken, charming. The smile he flashed would make a fan out of anyone. He knew hockey, he knew how to talk about it, he was passionate about it. He was self-deprecating, not an asshole at all. A good guy who was popular with everyone—fans, teammates…her.

Her heart squeezed remembering how she'd messed things up with him. How he'd messed things up for her. For a lot of years she'd been angry and resentful about that. Blamed him for her downward spiral. Now, she couldn't really blame him.

The knock on her door startled her and she clicked off the TV and jumped up to answer it.

Mia and Farrah entered. "Hey, Honey," Mia said. "Are you going to do my nails tonight?"

"Sure thing, sweetie, if you want."

"Thank you, Honey," Farrah said, dropping a small backpack on the carpet. "I'll be home by ten."

"No worries. Happy to help." A single mom Honey's own age, Farrah worked two jobs to support herself and her eleven-year old daughter. Honey had recently ended up spending "girls' days" with Mia, when Farrah had no child care and Honey hadn't started her new job yet. Honey wasn't sure why she'd made the offer, but Farrah had been so grateful and Mia was a good kid, just not quite ready to be left on her own.

A few hours later, Honey looked down at the small toenails she'd just painted Strawberry Margarita pink. "There," she said, screwing the cap on the bottle tightly. "Beautiful."

Mia sat on Honey's couch, thin little legs stretched out in front of her, feet on the coffee table, pink foam spreading her toes. "I like it." She flashed Honey a smile. "Thank you, Honey."

"You're welcome." Honey smiled back. She cast a quick glance at her own toes, which Mia had painted Cha-Ching Cherry, and tried not to wince. The polish had wandered off the nail onto her skin in more than a few places, and her left big toenail was bumpy. Not like the salon pedicures she used to get. Ah well. She'd wear closed-toe shoes to work tomorrow.

Honey liked kids, but didn't know much about them and somehow she and Mia always ended up doing manicures and pedicures and facials to pass the time. Which probably wasn't doing Mia any real good. Why that mattered, Honey had no idea. She was just helping out a very new friend, really an acquaintance. Why did she have this feeling she should be taking Mia to museums and art galleries, doing crafts or something educational and mind expanding? Mia wasn't even her kid.

"Next weekend we'll go to the Aquarium."

"Yes!" Mia bounced on the couch. "The pier!"

Oops. That was probably a wrong move. Mia was undoubtedly thinking about the Ferris wheel and roller coaster and junk food at the Santa Monica Pier.

Whatever. Kids needed to have fun too. Right? Right.

"I want to shave my legs," Mia announced.

Honey blinked. "Oh. Really."

"Mom says I don't need to, but I want to. You'll show me how, right, Honey?"

Honey pursed her lips. "Um. That's up to your mom, sweetie. If she says no, then I'm not going to go against that."

Mia gave her a pout. "I thought you were cooler than my mom."

"Are you kidding me? Nobody's cooler than your mom!"

She leaned over and gave Mia's waist a tickle. "Moms are the best!"

Mia giggled even as saying those words made Honey's chest hurt, but she kept her smile firmly in place. God, she wished she had a mom like Mia's, a mom who loved her so much she'd do anything for her, who loved her no matter what.

But that was all old shit in Honey's life. She was starting over.

"My mom will let me shave my legs if you ask her," Mia said with a sly smile.

Honey had to laugh. "It's a good thing you're cute."

Mia grinned.

A loud knock on Honey's door had both their heads turning, and Honey hopped up to answer the door. "Hey, Farrah," she said, letting Mia's mom in. "How was work?"

"Hell." Farrah shoved her long dark hair back off her face. She looked at Mia and smiled. "Hey baby, how's it going?"

"Good! Look at my toes! We did pedicures." Mia lifted her feet and wiggled her toes.

"Nice!" Farrah shot Honey a grateful glance. "Get your stuff and let's get home. It's past your bed time."

Mia and Farrah shoved a few things into Mia's backpack and Honey stood in her open apartment door watching as they let themselves into the unit across the hall. She gave them a wave and a smile then closed her door.

She moved back into the living room and gathered up the things they'd used for their pedicures, her manicure set and bottles of base coat and polish and top coat. Mia had hobbled across the hall still wearing the toe separators, but she'd get those back. She put things away in her bathroom, the only bathroom in the small apartment.

She should get to bed too. But the tightness of her

stomach and the way her mind kept replaying things told her she wasn't going to be able to sleep just yet. She still hadn't decided how she was going to handle things in the morning. So she pulled out her yarn and knitting needles and settled on her couch. If there was ever a time she needed the comfort of knitting, it was now.

Her needles and fingers moved rhythmically as her mind raced. She should quit this job. Working with people who hated her was not exactly fun. Yes, they'd judged her on her past and who she was, and she fucking hated that. But she also hated that she might be causing problems for an organization that did a lot of good. She did not want to mess things up for them.

And if it wasn't going to be a real job, what was the point? She could quit. Surely to god she could go out there and pound the pavement and find something that was real, something she could be proud of.

By the time her mind was calmer and she felt more settled and ready to go to bed, that was her plan of action for the morning — quitting.

But by morning, things didn't seem so black and white. Maybe it wasn't so bad. Maybe they really were just trying to ease her into things on her first day and not overwhelm her. Today she would work hard at figuring out everything she needed to know and showing people that she was there to really work. She'd give it a little more time.

And she had that meeting with Matt Heller.

Which had nothing to do with her decision.

She and Dulcie spent the first part of the morning reviewing the projects that Matt was working on in preparation for the meeting with him. Honey had a lot of questions, but Dulcie's answers were brief, meaning Honey had to ask more questions, which led to Dulcie frowning and looking at her watch.

"I'm sorry," Honey finally said. "I can tell my questions are annoying you. I know you're busy. I'd really like to learn so I can help you."

Dulcie sighed. "I have so much to do before I leave on mat leave."

The foundation had a number of existing projects that were well-organized and which Honey felt would be easy for her to step into in Dulcie's place. Well, relatively easy, once she got to know them all. When it came to finding generous corporate donors to sponsor some of the events, ideas were popping into Honey's head as she looked over the list of past years' sponsors.

"When is your baby due?" she asked Dulcie.

"In about a month. But I'll be going on leave in two weeks."

Ack. Honey'd been hoping that before Dulcie left she'd be able to learn enough to step into her shoes and show everyone she could really help out. That wasn't very long.

"And when do you plan to come back?" Honey asked.

"I'll be taking my twelve weeks of maternity leave."

Honey nodded. Even though they apparently had no intention of her actually filling Dulcie's position, she was making that her goal. They might not have any faith in her abilities but she was going to show them. The temptation to quit still lingered, but she had a stubborn streak that was being riled up and dammit, she was not going to let them push her into a corner. So she had two weeks to learn as much as she could before Dulcie left and then three months to prove to them she could do the job. No pressure at all.

Matt walked in to the office just as she was walking back to her cubicle with a coffee from the small kitchen/break room. He smelled like shower gel, his hair damp, face still a little flushed. Her heart skipped a beat at his presence, filling the room with his size and big smile.

"Hi," she said. "I'll just let Dulcie know you're here. Um…would you like some coffee?"

"No thanks. Don't drink coffee."

"Anything else…juice? Water?" She wasn't sure if they had juice, but they had a water cooler.

"I'm good. Just drank a few gallons after practice."

"Okay. Have a seat. We'll be right with you."

She hustled down the corridor toward Dulcie's cubicle, her spiky heels muted on the carpet. She could hear Dulcie's low voice as she approached.

"She's driving me crazy with all her questions," Honey heard. "Oh. My. God. Why did Trent saddle me with her when I'm trying to take care of stuff before I go?"

Honey paused, her insides seizing. Heat washed down over her and her fingers tightened on the paper cup of coffee she held. She blinked unseeingly as another voice responded, "Let me know if there's anything I can do to help. Maybe we can keep her busy sorting paper clips."

Celina, the other Programming Coordinator.

Honey closed her eyes briefly then drew in a big breath. "Hey, Dulcie," she called out, moving her feet forward again. She stretched her lips into a smile and moved into the opening of Dulcie's cubicle. Celina half-sat on one side of the L-shaped desk and Honey caught the flash of something that might have been guilt on both their faces as they realized she'd been so close while they'd been talking about her. She lifted her chin, keeping the smile in place, but the tension in the air clearly told her they could tell her smile was fake and they suspected she'd heard them. "Matt Heller is here for our meeting."

"Oh, great," Dulcie said quickly, swiveling in her chair to reach for some files on her desk. "We can go into the boardroom."

"Okay. See you there."

Honey returned to her own desk for her paper and pen then headed back to the reception area where Matt sat on one of the small chairs, dwarfing it. Nerves jittering now from seeing him and from the conversation she'd just overheard, she struggled to keep her composure.

"Come on in to the boardroom," she said. "Dulcie will be right with us."

He followed her down the hall and she was acutely aware of him behind her as she walked on her high heels in her snug pencil skirt. She led the way into the boardroom and gestured for him to have a seat. He threw his big body down into a leather chair.

"How are things going?" he asked. "Second day on the job, right?"

"Right. Things are going great." She flashed the biggest smile she could. "I have a lot to learn, but I'm super excited to be here."

His gaze moved over her face and she had the feeling she might have been a little too enthusiastic in her response. She certainly wasn't about to tell him the truth. God. She caught Dulcie entering the room from the corner of her eye and said, "Dulcie's helping me out and being so patient with all my questions."

"That's good," Matt said.

Dulcie took a seat and Honey looked at her and caught the flicker in her eyes. Honey smiled at her again. *Bitch.*

"So," Honey said brightly. "Let's get to work."

They spent the next hour focusing on which charitable group Matt wanted to work with and what he was willing to commit to.

Honey wasn't going to let Dulcie shut her out of this and kept politely interjecting, offering to look after specific tasks, and with Matt there Dulcie really couldn't cut her out without it looking odd. By the end of the meeting Honey had an actual to-do list and Matt's phone number and email address so she could touch base with him at the end of the week.

She felt marginally better when she returned to her desk, even though she had to sit there and take a few deep breaths. But she'd done it. She could do this. Except, damn, doing this meant working with Matt. Holy bajesus.

She brought her computer back to life and realized it was noon. Lunchtime.

Dulcie and Celina passed by her desk talking about where they were going for lunch. They didn't even look at her. The rest of the office was quiet, so everyone else must have gone out for lunch too. As they had yesterday.

From now on she would bring a bag lunch, which she could leave in the small fridge in the break room. She could eat at her desk while she was working. Assuming she had some actual work to do.

But today she had no lunch, so she picked up her purse and left the office. There were some restaurants in the area—there had to be somewhere she could quickly pick something up and bring it back to her desk.

As she left the Coliseum, she saw Matt Heller standing near an exit, looking down at his smart phone in his hand. She paused then started to walk past him, but he looked up and spotted her.

CHAPTER 4

Matt looked up from his phone and saw Honey walking toward him, her steps slowing. She carried her purse over her shoulder so was obviously leaving. "Honey," he said slowly. They stood and looked at each other for a long moment. Fuck, she made him hot. "Going out for lunch?"

"Um. Yeah."

He eyed her. "Alone?"

"Yes." She gave one of those big fake smiles she'd been throwing around yesterday and today.

"I'll come with you."

Christ. What was he saying?

She blinked. "What? Why?"

He made a face as he shoved his phone into his back pocket. "Eating alone sucks. And I'm hungry." Truth.

She stood there, clutching her purse. "That's not necessary. I was just going to grab something quick and take it back to my desk to eat... I have a lot of work to do."

"Oh come on. You can take an hour for lunch." He cupped her elbow and nudged her toward the door. "We'll just go to that Mexican place across the street."

"Matt…"

"C'mon, Honey. You've got me curious."

"What do you mean?"

He lifted one eyebrow. "I mean…here you are with a social welfare degree working for a non-profit organization and looking all…" His gaze raked up and down her. "Professional."

She lifted her chin and narrowed her eyes at him. "You don't have to sound like that's so impossible for me."

"Not impossible, no. Just…surprising. Which makes me curious. Let's go have lunch and…catch up."

Her lips tightened. "You make it sound like we're old friends," she muttered.

Things hadn't ended all that well between them eight years ago, but still. "We are," he clipped out. "Come on."

She planted her heels into the carpet then said, "Fine."

Curious. Yeah. Matt was curious about Honey. He knew the train wreck her life had become after the time they'd spent together that summer. He'd seen it happening, even then, and had worried about her. After he'd left, going back to play NCAA hockey at the University of North Dakota, he'd watched it all happen from a distance, watched it unfold in the media. He'd hated that, but the times he'd tried to call her to talk to her and find out what was going on with her, she'd been pissed off at him and basically told him to fuck off. In fact, those might have been her exact words.

So he'd left her alone, watching her self-destruct, feeling pissed off, guilty (although why, he wasn't sure) and worried. He'd forced himself to let go. Told himself it wasn't his business. Made himself not care. He'd had enough problems of his own, trying to get his career where he wanted it to go. Where he felt it *should* go, following along in the successful footsteps of his three older brothers.

Now he should be skating a big circle around Honey Holbrook, but here he was dragging her out for lunch.

Life shot some weird pucks at you sometimes.

Tamale, the Mexican restaurant across the street from the Coliseum, was basically fast food, but upscale fast food. They waited in a line to place their orders. Matt pulled out his wallet to pay even as Honey reached for her purse, but he shook his head and pulled out some bills. He carried the tray with their food and drinks to a small booth near the sunny front window and they spent a few minutes unwrapping and arranging their meals.

"You've probably never eaten at a Tamale restaurant."

She gave him a sideways, pursed-lip look as she pushed a straw into the plastic lid of her diet Coke. "Of course I have."

"I love this grilled steak burrito," he said. "It's huge."

"So's this salad," she said. "I can never eat it all."

"So." He eyed her across the table. Still so pretty, with her pale blonde hair, glowing fair skin and fine bone structure. Her face was a perfect oval with big eyes and full lips, her high cheekbones more prominent than they used to be. Her eyes held more shadows, and without all the makeup she used to wear, she looked delicate...almost fragile. He lifted his burrito. "Tell me how you come to be doing this job."

"I thought I told everyone in that meeting." She picked up a plastic fork. "I recently graduated and needed a job." She looked up at him again. "Did you finish college?"

"Yeah." He shrugged. His college degree was great, but he'd been impatient to play in the NHL rather than NCAA college hockey for three years. "I got a degree in business."

"I know you weren't happy that year...when you went back to school."

He nodded. "Yep. But it was the right thing to do." He'd been drafted by the Condors that year and wanted to turn pro and play in the NHL, but everyone had been telling him he needed more time to develop and grow—his parents, his older brothers, his college hockey coach and his unofficial agent Alvin (as per NCAA rules, he couldn't hire an agent, but his brothers' agent had given him off-the-record advice about his career). He'd been frustrated and pissed off, but had put his game face on and gone back to college.

"You were a great player. Everyone was talking about you and your future."

"They were talking about my brothers," he corrected her. It had bugged the fuck out of him at the time, how everyone expected him to be just like them, but that was now long gone. Like a game you lose ten-nothing, or a nearly career-ending injury, you had to put that shit behind you and move forward. "I wasn't ready. I had some skills, but they needed more work, and I needed to work at getting stronger. I'm tall like my brothers but I didn't have the muscle they had at my age. I'm not built quite like them. It takes work for me to keep weight on."

She smiled. "I remember you telling me that. So many people would kill to be able to say that."

He returned the smile. "I know. It is what it is, though. To play in the NHL I had to be strong enough to keep up and take the shit bigger guys are gonna dish out. I still have to work out a lot and drink a lot of protein shakes."

He caught the look she gave him, her gaze moving over his shoulders and upper body. Then she pointed with her fork to the giant burrito in front of him. "And eat like that."

He grinned. "Yeah." Then he frowned. Wait. How the hell had they ended up talking about him? "So you went to college, but not until you were…what? Twenty-three? Twenty-four?"

"Yeah." She hitched a shoulder. "Twenty-four. Finally got my shit together." She gave him a tight smile. "Like I said in the meeting yesterday, Dad pulled strings to get me this job.

But…" She sank those pretty white teeth into her bottom lip. "I'm wondering if it was a mistake."

"Bah." He waved a hand. "Haters are gonna hate. I've learned that. The people in that meeting yesterday were douchebags."

She blinked. "Ah…"

"Ignore them."

"I thought I was."

"Yeah. You did a good job." He hesitated. He'd been knocked into the boards when he'd seen her appear in that meeting, but he had to admit… "You impressed me, when you stood up to them. And when you didn't let them stop you. And you impressed me with how smart you sounded."

"You don't think I'm smart?"

He scowled. "That's not what meant. I mean, you sounded like you know what you're doing."

"You came to that conclusion from a one-hour meeting?"

He tipped his head to one side. "And from this morning's meeting. I'm a pretty good judge of people. And I know you're smart. I never thought you were stupid, Honey."

"Oh no? I got a different impression when you ratted me out to my dad."

He narrowed his eyes at her. "Ratted you out? What the fuck?"

"Hell yeah." She met his gaze head on. "That was what you did."

His forehead tightened. "Fuck, Honey…" He leaned forward. "You needed to smarten up."

Her eyes flashed at him. "Proving my point about what you thought of my intellectual abilities."

"Christ," he muttered. "Wrong word choice. You were doing stupid things. You were hanging around with stupid people. But I never thought *you* were stupid."

"Whatever." She didn't seem to want to accept his praise. "You were right."

"I just never got why."

Her eyebrows drew together. "Why what?"

"Why you were hanging around with stupid people, doing stupid things."

She sighed. "Long story. Took years of therapy to understand. It doesn't matter."

Weirdly, he felt like it did matter.

"Anyway, I'm not so sure I do know what I'm doing. Last night I was ready to quit this job."

"What?" He gaped at her. "Just because a few people were being dicks? You shouldn't let them chase you away. I mean, those are good people, I've met some of them before, but they'll get over whatever it was that was up their asses."

"It's not just that." She bent her head. Then she sighed and looked at him again. "They only gave me the job because of my dad. They don't really expect me to do anything. Except maybe sort paper clips." She gave a short laugh.

"I'm sure that's not true."

"I'm pretty sure it is. They think they know me," she said quietly. "They've formed opinions about me. They don't think I can do the job. They probably think I'll be more of a liability to the foundation than a help. And they might be right."

Shit. He stared at her. He got what she was saying. And there was some truth to it. "If you want to do this job, then do it. Show them."

Why was he encouraging her when it meant he was going to have to see more of her?

Fuck me. The truth was, he *wanted* to see more of her. He also found he didn't want to see her looking so doubtful of her own abilities.

She lifted her eyes again and met his briefly before her

gaze skittered away again. Then she asked in a low voice, "What if I can't?"

He studied her face, her pretty lips pressed together, her eyes lowered once again. He gave his head a small shake. "You said it yourself, Honey. You've got the education. You've got experience through your field work. You've got connections in L.A. You're smart. If you're willing to work at it, there's no reason in the world you can't do it."

He saw her throat move as she swallowed, using her fork to move lettuce and cheese and tomatoes around in her salad bowl, but not eating any of it. Then she lifted her eyes and met his.

"You don't even know me," she said quietly. "How can you be so sure of that?"

He wasn't sure how to answer that. It was true; he didn't really know her any more. But hell. He believed in her. He shrugged. "I don't know. But I am."

She nodded. "Well. Thank you."

Honey was kicking herself for confessing all that shit to Matt, putting her insecurities and vulnerabilities out there for him. She didn't do that with anyone, so why she was spilling her guts to Matt Heller she had no idea.

She'd just moved into an apartment that she needed to pay the next month's rent on. She'd met Farrah and Mia—not that they were best friends or anything, but Mia was cute and she liked hanging out with her. And if she didn't do well at this job, she'd just prove everyone right—she was nothing but a spoiled party girl. Those were all good reasons to stick it out.

But most of all, it was Matt's faith in her that cut right to her core.

Because in all her life, she didn't think anyone had ever believed in her like that.

It made her feel weird, all squishy and warm inside, a feeling that seemed to swell inside her. It made her want to leap across the table into his arms. Which was ridiculous. It also made her even more determined to go back to the office and prove herself. To prove Matt right about her.

She was going to do it, dammit.

She stabbed a piece of lettuce and lifted it to her mouth.

"Tell me about you," she said, when she'd swallowed. "Are you happy to be back with the Condors?"

"I'm happy to be healthy," he said. "And yeah, sure, happy to be back. Last year when I was an unrestricted free agent, I had a feeling St. Louis wasn't going to sign me again, or they weren't going to offer a good enough deal if they made an offer." He shrugged. "I'd had a few injuries but I felt like I had lot to contribute. My agent Alvin worked hard for me and the deal from the Condors sounded right. I was glad to sign with them and I felt like shit that I ended up out right at the start of this season."

She eyed him, her insides tightening. "You're okay? After…" Crap, she couldn't even say it. It had been a devastating injury.

"You knew about it."

"Who didn't?" She feigned casualness. "The whole hockey world was worried about you."

"Yeah. But I'm good. I feel really good."

You look really good. Whoops. She'd almost said that out loud. When he'd been talking about keeping weight on, she'd all but drooled when she'd studied his body. He was more muscular than he'd been at nineteen, but even then, he'd been totally ripped. She could only imagine how good he looked now with his clothes off.

She'd already noticed that his left hand had no ring on it,

although she was pretty sure she would've known if he'd gotten married. "No wife?" she asked casually. "No kids?"

"Nope."

"Girlfriend?"

He grinned and leaned forward. "Nope. I'm all yours."

She dropped her chin and looked at him from beneath her eyelashes. "Yeah, right." He hadn't wanted her eight years ago, so there was no way he'd want her, now, after the stupid shit she'd done. He was totally joking. But his words made her stomach do a slow, heady roll of lust.

Matt started talking more about the charities they'd discussed in the meeting earlier and some of her ideas for fundraising, and she was happy to move the conversation off personal stuff and back to business. Then she glanced at her watch. "I should get back."

He nodded, his burrito finished. "Okay."

They walked back to the Coliseum. Honey paused at the small side door they could only access with their security fobs. "Thanks for lunch," she said.

"I'll come in," he said. "Gotta get some things from my locker."

"Oh. Okay."

They passed through security then paused. The offices were upstairs and he needed to go down to the lower level to the dressing room. They faced each other and their eyes met. Something stretched between them, something warm and magnetic. Her body wanted to move toward him. She wanted to feel him, smell him…oh god, taste him.

This was not good.

"Okay!" she said brightly. "I'll get back to you by the end of the week on the things we talked about."

He lifted a hand and gave her a smile that crinkled up the skin around his eyes so attractively her knees went weak.

Then he turned and headed in the opposite direction to the lower level.

She bit her lip and walked back to her office. After dumping her purse in her drawer, she headed to Dulcie's desk. Dulcie was sitting there, looking at her computer, hand on her mouse.

"Hi," Honey said. "Do you have a few minutes?"

Dulcie glanced at her and Honey sensed her inner sigh. "Sure."

Honey rolled her lips in briefly then straightened her shoulders. "I know what the deal is here. I know I was just hired because my dad asked Trent to hire me. I know no one really expects me to do anything and you all have been trying to keep me busy. I've bugged you with questions because I want to learn and I want to contribute and I think I can."

Dulcie's eyes went wide and she sat back a little in her chair. "You heard us talking."

Honey didn't bother to acknowledge that. "I know everyone is thinking I'm a spoiled princess. I don't blame people for judging me on my past behavior. I did stupid things and I admit it, and I'm trying to move on from that. I busted my ass the last three and a half years at college to get my degree so I *could* move on from that. I busted my ass on my field placements, and the references I gave Trent when I started did not lie. I did a good job for them. I wanted this job to be a next step in my life."

Dulcie blinked.

"I *really* wanted this job to be a next step," Honey continued, emotion starting to swell in her chest and thicken her throat. She cleared her throat.

Dulcie sighed. "I'm sure we all wish we had your problems."

Honey's eyes bugged, then she closed them and nodded. "Yeah. I've heard that before. I'm not going to give you a big, long, poor little rich girl sob story. I know how lucky I am compared to a lot of kids I've worked with. I know I didn't appreciate what I had, compared to them. But there are things you don't know about me. And I want you to know that this job is important to me. I'm here. I'm ready to work hard. I just want a chance."

She met Dulcie's eyes, and the other woman's gaze slid away after a few seconds and her lips pursed. She nodded. "I'll talk to Trent," she finally said.

Honey nodded too. "Thank you, Dulcie."

The rest of her week passed much the same. She still felt like her co-workers didn't really expect her to do anything, but she began to make phone calls and set up meetings, consulting with Dulcie and Trent on various issues. She managed to solve a problem with one of the groups involving a scheduling mistake that had set an appearance by several of the players at a school when they were in the middle of a road trip.

Assistant Director Rick Tanner, and the other two Programming Coordinators, Aaron and Celina, did not go out of their way to help, but at least there was no overt hostility from them. And when Dulcie learned about the scheduling mistake and started cursing then found out Honey had already dealt with it, she'd been taken aback. She'd muttered, "Well, good, then." And moved on. It wasn't much, but it was better than nothing.

CHAPTER 5

Honey's last task of the day on Friday was to call Matt and let him know she'd set up an appearance for him the following week. The Condors were going to be on the road next week and she knew he'd have time since he wasn't travelling with the team yet.

She called his cell phone and he answered after two rings. "Hey," he said, his voice deep and a little rough. "Honey."

She melted a little inside at how he said her name. "Yes, it's Honey." She tried for a crisp tone. "I said I'd follow up with you by the end of the week."

"Yes, you did. And it's nearly five o'clock on Friday afternoon."

"Um. Yeah." Had she procrastinated on making the call? Maybe just a bit. But it wasn't as if he'd been sitting there waiting for her call, for shit's sake.

"Meet me for a drink," he said. "We can talk then."

She scrambled for an excuse. "Uh…"

"C'mon. It's happy hour."

She snorted. "For some people. People who work in corporate nine-to-five jobs. Not hockey players."

"Hey. I work hard at my job."

Her lips pursed and twisted to one side. "I know you do. That's not what I meant."

"We'll go somewhere close to the Coliseum," he suggested. Then after a pause, he said, "Or maybe not."

She smiled.

"Where do you live?" he asked. "Is there somewhere close to home we could meet?"

Once again she was silent as she struggled for a reply. She got tense thinking about some of the bars or clubs he might suggest they go to. "I live in Santa Monica. Sixth Street. But that doesn't matter..."

"Okay, somewhere downtown. How about Noir?"

Her muscles relaxed at the suggestion. A small, classy wine bar, Noir would probably not be full of the people she used to hang around with. She sighed. "Okay. I have a few more things to do and then I'm off."

"Meet around six?"

She agreed and hung up. Lunch. Drinks. She needed to be careful or she'd think Matt Heller was still interested in her. Or interested again. But that was just crazy.

She vaguely wished she had time to go home and change or redo her makeup. She'd had no meetings that day so she'd dressed in a pair of low-rise black pants with a white T-shirt tucked into them and a gauzy black and white scarf wound around her neck. But that was the old Honey, worried about things like clothes and makeup. It didn't matter what she looked like.

Parking for Noir was in a lot behind the building. She walked around the black-painted brick structure to the front entrance, a bright red double door, enjoying the late afternoon sunshine and the ocean-scented breeze. Inside, she blinked as she waited for eyes to adjust. Damn. Matt could be there but she couldn't see a thing. Then an arm slid around her waist and she jumped.

"Hey," Matt's voice said close to her ear. "Easy. Just me."

"Sorry. It's dark in here. I didn't see you." She focused on his smile. And on moving away from his very big, very warm body.

"I figured that. Come on. I got a table over here."

She followed him through the dimness to a small table for two in the corner. The place was full—happy hour indeed. People lined the bar and every table was occupied, that hum of voices mingling with shouts from bartenders and clinking glasses.

She hung her purse on the back of her chair, which Matt held for her with gentlemanly consideration. Even as a young guy, twenty years old when she'd last known him, he'd been like that. Different than most of the guys she'd hung around with, who'd been obnoxiously spoiled rich kids.

She ordered a glass of Cabernet Sauvignon from the large selection printed on the menu card on the table. A pretty black pottery bowl on the table held assorted olives. Nice.

"Thanks for meeting me," Matt said, picking up his own glass of red wine.

"You're welcome," she said. "But we could have handled this in a phone call. I'm sure you're a busy guy."

He shrugged. "Not busy enough. That's why I wanted to get involved with more things, to fill my time."

She nodded.

"I spent weeks in the hospital," he continued. "Then pretty much all my time on rehab, trying to get better. I'm ready to have a normal life again. Doing fun things. Doing things that matter."

She studied him, her heart going soft in her chest. Crap, he really got to her. Something about him just made her want to crawl across the table on her hands and knees and lick and kiss him everywhere.

"Was it hard?" she asked softly. She got a funny ache down low inside her thinking again about him being carried off the ice, thinking about him being in pain.

"Yeah." But he smiled. "Probably hardest thing I've ever done. But I don't like to dwell on it. Gotta put shit behind you."

She nodded. "That's a good attitude, I guess."

The server set her glass of wine in front of her, and Honey flashed a smile of thanks.

She found herself curious to know more than the bits of information she'd been able to get from newspapers and the internet, but if he didn't want to talk about it, she wasn't going to push him. She too had things she didn't want to talk about, so she totally got what that was like. Only she had a feeling Matt was better at actually putting things behind him than she was.

"So." He tilted his head in that way that made her breath hitch and her insides do a little flip. "Tell me what you've got planned for me."

Yeah, Matt knew what kinds of plans he wanted her to have for him. But somehow he doubted her plans involved whips, chains, handcuffs or even just a lap dance. He shifted in his chair.

"Well, after looking through the foundation's portfolio and doing some research, I have a few ideas."

Business. Sure. That was what he wanted.

Christ, getting dirty ideas about Honey Holbrook was not a good idea. The things his friends had said yesterday about her had pissed him off, but had also served as an eye-opening reminder of the reputation she still had.

Shit. That stunk worse than his hockey equipment after a game.

He watched her sitting there, looking sweet and clean, with glowy skin and pale, shiny lips, hair smooth to her shoulders, talking all earnestly about corporate donors and funding research into children's illnesses. She was trying so hard, it made his chest clench. How long were people going to judge her on her past?

Probably forever.

That fucking sucked donkey balls.

"Matt?"

He blinked at her. "What?"

She stared back at him. "Weren't you listening?"

"Nope," honesty compelled him to admit. No point in bullshitting. "I was distracted by your beauty."

Color washed up into her face, making her even prettier. But then her eyes took on an angry glint. "Don't bullshit me," she muttered.

His mouth fell open. He'd resorted to complete, unadulterated truth, and she accused him of lying. He frowned. "Uh. That *was* the truth."

Her lips thinned. "Come on, don't screw around with me. This is serious."

"I know, Honey. Give me a break. I'm a guy, and you're a gorgeous woman and I can't help but notice."

"Oh please. Men are perfectly capable of carrying on intelligent conversations with women. Your dick doesn't control your brain, despite popular opinion to the contrary. Men just use that as an excuse for bad behavior, like you're sex-crazed animals or something."

He laughed. He leaned forward, elbows on the table, fingers

loosely holding his wine glass. "Well. I wouldn't call myself sex-crazed, but…there is some truth to that theory about men being controlled by their dicks. When we see a hot chick, our brains produce dopamine and…and some other chemical that makes us feel good." Damned if he could remember the name of it, but whatever. "It affects how our brains process information. Sometimes we do stupid things because we're flooded with those feel-good hormones that we get when faced with…" He waved a hand toward her with an up-and-down motion.

Her lips twitched. "Uh-huh. Well, maybe you need to learn to use the big sex organ between your ears so you can control the smaller one between your legs."

He jerked his chin down with affront. "You did not just call my dick small."

It was her turn to laugh. "The ultimate male insult. I apologize. That wasn't what I meant. I know perfectly well how… big…" She stopped and blinked at him as if the words had started coming out before she'd thought that all through.

His mouth widened into a grin again. "Uh-huh," he said encouragingly. "You know perfectly well how big…what?"

Her cheeks got that rosy flush again. Her mouth twitched again too, and then she lifted her chin. "Fine. I'll say it. I know perfectly well how big the sex organ between your legs is."

Fuck, no, she didn't, because it was getting bigger by the second. Bigger and harder. He winced.

Their eyes met and he got the feeling maybe she *did* know what was going on with his dick. The air around them became hot and thick, making breathing difficult. Their eyes connected with a magnetic force that made it impossible to look away. Her tongue came out in a quick swipe over her bottom lip, and a sharp bolt of need shot straight to his balls. They continued to stare at each other as if they were both in a trance.

He felt like his entire body was pulsing.

Oh wow. This wasn't over between them. No way could he ignore the way the air buzzed, the way tension hummed around them, the need for her that surged through his body.

"So I was thinking the option that would do the most good and give us the most exposure for you and the team would be working with Franklin Middle School."

He tried to take in the words, heat still throbbing through his veins straight to his groin. The fact that he was proving his own point wasn't lost on him, the hormones racing through his bloodstream actually making it difficult to process her words. What? She was back on fucking business? And he was ready to grab her and throw her over his shoulder and carry her out of the bar.

"Need a minute," he muttered, setting down his glass and shoving his chair back. He rose and strode across the bar toward the bathrooms. He was probably walking funny, his dick so hard it hurt. He just needed to get away from her for a minute. She was making him fucking nuts.

In the bathroom, luckily alone, he paused with a hand flat on the wall, head bowed. Think of something else. Okay. Okay. The hospital. The neck brace. The pain.

Not that he liked to relive those days, but hell, it was working. Remembering the fear and agony was enough to deflate the most determined hard-on.

Honey. Goddamn her.

They'd been having a fun conversation, a little flirting, a lot of sexual tension. Fuck yeah, he knew it was a bad idea, but he had not been wrong when he'd said that hormones could mess with a dude's thinking process.

And…it was *Honey*.

Sure, people could cut her down and roll their eyes at her because of her reputation and the things she'd done, but sure as hell, ninety-eight percent of guys sitting across the table from her would be having the same problem he had. Because she was the shit. Smoking-hot body, gorgeous face and goddammit, a smart mouth. Which strangely turned him on most of all.

He sucked in a long breath and lifted his head to look at the ceiling.

Okay. What the hell was he supposed to do?

He wanted her. There was no getting around that. But there were probably a million reasons why that was a bad idea. Did he even have to go through them all? First, their history together. Second, her dad. Third, they were supposed to be working together. And then there was her reputation and what people already thought of her. He did not need that kind of attention in his life when he was trying so hard to come back from injury and prove he could still play. He also did not need the distraction of a hot chick when he needed to focus on his career. And then there was her dad…oh yeah, he'd already listed that one.

Fuck.

Okay. Just like she'd told him, he needed to use his big head here. He did not have to be driven by hormones. He could work with Honey and keep it all businesslike.

He returned to the table, watching her sitting there as he crossed the bar. Her silky blonde hair hung forward, her head bent as she scrolled through something on her phone.

"Sorry," he said as he dropped back into his seat. "So where were we?"

She turned those beautiful brown eyes on him and sweat popped out beneath his T-shirt. "Franklin Middle School," she said in her soft, husky voice that was like fingers stroking over his balls.

Christ, he was lost.

"I think we need another drink," he said hoarsely, tossing

back the last of his wine and looking around for the server. "Maybe tequila shots."

Her eyebrows lifted.

"Kidding," he muttered. "Sort of." He lifted a hand and the girl who'd served them earlier hustled over with a flirty smile. He ordered another glass of wine for Honey even though she protested, and a beer for himself.

"Okay, business," he said.

"This school has students who are of diverse ethnicity from economically challenged neighborhoods. Boys and girls can be involved. We use the game of hockey as a catalyst to attract youth to a program offering support for education, self-esteem building and life-skills training."

He forced himself to focus on what she was saying.

"I'm sorry, but you still seem distracted," she said a while later. "Do you want me to put this all in an email to you?"

"That's a great idea," he agreed. "Perfect."

"It's not that complicated."

"I know."

"Okay, then I should get going."

"No." The word somehow just popped out.

She paused and gave him the side eye.

"Let's get some dinner," he suggested. Fuck! What was he doing? All he knew was, he didn't want her to leave.

"Oh, I don't think…"

"I'm hungry," he said. "You probably are too. Unless… you have other plans." Christ, what if she had a date?

"Well, I…" Her hesitation told him what he needed to know.

"Great. I'll see if we can get a table in the restaurant." He shoved back his chair without giving her a chance to make up some excuse, and charged over to the hostess station. A few words with the hostess and they were on the list for the restaurant. "They said about ten minutes," he told Honey back at the table.

"Oh." She held her purse on her lap as if she was ready to bolt. "Matt…"

He sighed and put an elbow on the table then set his forehead to his fist. "I know. Believe me, I know every single reason we shouldn't do this." Without lifting his head, he met her eyes. "What would you be doing if we weren't having dinner? Going out with some friends? Hitting some Beverly Hills clubs?"

"I don't do the club scene anymore," she said quietly. "And I don't have many friends left in L.A. After being away at college for a few years, we haven't really stayed in touch. Well, the truth is, they were never that great of friends to begin with. So. To answer your question, I'd be doing what I do most Friday nights lately——eating dinner on my couch in front of my TV, possibly giving my eleven-year old neighbor a manicure, or knitting."

He lifted his head. "What the fuck? Knitting?"

"Yeah." The corners of her mouth lifted. "Knitting. I took it up as a hobby when I was in therapy. I really like it. It's very…soothing."

He gave his head a shake. "What do you knit?"

"Lots of things."

The waitress returned with their drinks and he gratefully reached for the cold beer and took a big gulp.

"When I started, I made a lot of scarves," she said, switching out her empty wine glass for the full one. "Some very crooked scarves. And afghans. Then I learned how to make mitts."

"Not much call for mitts in California," he muttered.

"True. I donate them all to charity, though, so they go where they're needed. I've knitted socks, and baby clothes, and I've actually made a few sweaters."

This was fucking with his mind—the image of Honey Holbrook, former wild child and half-naked *Mustang Magazine* model knitting baby booties.

"It's good to have a hobby," she said. "What about you? Don't you have some hobby you do in your spare time?"

He took another big swallow of beer. "Huh. Not for a while. My favorite activities are all pretty physical."

Their eyes locked again. And shit, he could tell that their minds had both gone the same direction.

"You know," he said quickly. "Swimming, water skiing, lifting weights. Beach volleyball."

"You used to like video games."

"Yeah. I still do, I guess. I got sick of that when I was in the hospital and there wasn't much else to do. I was anxious to get moving again."

"That must have been a hard time."

He nodded. "Knitting. Jesus."

She grinned. And fuck, the way it illuminated her whole face, brown eyes lighting up, white teeth flashing, made him feel like all the air had been sucked out of the room. "You're having a hard time with that, aren't you?"

He smiled too. "I guess. Just having a hard time picturing you back when you were nineteen sitting around knitting socks."

"Nineteen-year-old me wouldn't have done that," she admitted. "And back then I did a lot of things I wouldn't do now."

And once again, he was ninety-two per cent sure they were remembering the same things she'd done. The things they'd done together. Heat crawled up his chest, into his neck and his face. And once again they sat with their eyes fastened on each other.

"Heller party?"

He looked up at the hostess standing next to his chair holding menus and wearing a bright smile. "Yeah."

"Your table is ready, if you'd like to follow me."

He let Honey precede him into the restaurant, not so he could admire the rear view in the slim-fitting black pants she wore, but because he was a gentleman. Or at least he pretended to be a gentleman, because damn, he *was* looking. Her ass was fine.

Once seated, they opened their menus and conversation was limited to discussing menu items and debating choices.

"I'm starving," he said, eyeing the options. "I like all these small plates because you can try a bunch of different things." He looked at her over the top of his menu. "You up for sharing some things?"

"Sure."

They ended up ordering steak tartare, dumplings made with portabella mushrooms, meatballs, poutine and empanadas. "And some onion rings," Matt added, closing his menu.

"We're never going to eat all that," Honey said, handing over her menu to the server.

"Sure we will. Okay, so now that I've dealt with the whole knitting thing, back to what you'd usually be doing on a Friday night. What did you say about your neighbor?"

Honey smiled and the genuine fondness in her expression did something to his chest. "Mia. She's eleven. She and her mom live across the hall from me. Farrah's a single mom and works two jobs, so somehow I ended up looking after Mia a few days. We call it girls' nights, though, because she thinks she's too old for a babysitter."

He smiled. "That's nice."

"Well, before I started my job it was nice. Now I haven't been around during the day. But tomorrow I'm taking her to the aquarium."

"Cool. That sounds like fun."

"I hope."

"What are you knitting right now?"

She tipped her head. "Baby clothes."

He blinked.

"My sister-in-law is pregnant. James's wife."

"He's married?"

"Both my brothers are married. Jonathan has two kids, and this will be James and Kortney's second as well. So I've made a baby blanket and a few little things…a little hat and matching sweater and booties."

"Baby clothes. Huh."

"Don't laugh at my hobby."

"Was I laughing?" He held up his hands. "No, I was not."

"I get the feeling you want to. But that's okay." She tossed her hair back and sat up straight. "I enjoy it and that's what matters."

"I'm not…judging you. Christ. There's nothing wrong with knitting. I'm just surprised."

"I'm getting that. Maybe I should knit you a scarf."

"I dare you."

She tilted her head and the curve of her lips made his heart rate speed up. "I dare you to wear it."

"I totally will wear it."

And once more they both shifted into that state of awareness, a hot haze settling around them as they stared into each other's eyes. Then his gaze dropped to her mouth, that full lower lip and perfectly curved upper lip, and as he watched, her lips parted. So fucking sexy. And he couldn't stop from lifting his hand and reaching across the table to brush his fingertips beneath her chin and graze his thumb over her bottom lip.

Her eyelids lowered as he rubbed her mouth. His thumb pressed into the corner of her lips, then slid back to the center of her lip and the tip of her tongue touched the pad of his thumb.

His dick lengthened and thickened, once more back to a nearly painful erection. His entire body vibrated with sexual need. "Honey," he whispered.

Her long eyelashes drifted up again and she slowly drew back. He lowered his hand to the table. Once again they sat mesmerized with each other, saying nothing for long, heated moments.

"This is crazy," she said, a breathless quality to her voice.

"Fuck, yeah."

"I haven't felt this for a long time," she confessed.

He swallowed. "Me either."

She gave a wry smile. "As if you expect me to believe that. I know you've been with so many girls."

"You do, huh?" How did she know that? Sure, stuff had been in the news and blogs, but he wasn't that big a superstar. You'd have to be *looking* for that kind of news. He tipped his head to one side and studied her. "I'm not gonna deny I've dated. A lot. Even had a couple of relationships. But what I said is true, Honey. I haven't felt like this for a long time."

Her eyes darkened to nearly black.

"And I could say the same about you," he said quietly. "You've had a lot of guys in your life."

She slowly moved her head from side to side. "Not for a long time."

He stretched his hand out and found hers resting on the table. "What are we going to do about this?"

"I don't know. Honestly, Matt. I'm…confused. Conflicted."

"Yeah. I know. Christ, me too."

"I've made so many mistakes. With guys. I don't want to do that again."

"You think I'm a mistake?"

"Last time…I thought you were, yeah," she confessed.

Shit. He knew he'd screwed up then.

"At this point in my life, I think any guy is a mistake. There's so much I'm still working on, not the least of which is my new job."

"I get that." His fingers moved over hers. "I've got shit going on too. I need to get back playing. I want to prove I can do it. I was playing great before I got injured and I want to get back to that. So. Let's just…have some fun."

She regarded him cautiously. "I think I've made mistakes having fun too."

He nodded in acknowledgment of that astounding understatement. "But you have to have *some* fun."

"I do have fun."

Was she afraid to live now? He rubbed a hand across his mouth. "What time are you going to the aquarium?"

Her eyes widened. "Um. Mia's mom is dropping her off at one o'clock. Why?"

"That's such a coincidence," he said, releasing her hand and leaning back in his seat. "I was planning to go to the aquarium tomorrow at one o'clock."

CHAPTER 6

Honey and Mia approached the aquarium at the Santa Monica Pier Saturday afternoon. The day was lovely, bright but with a cool breeze that tugged at the big scarf Honey'd wound around her neck with a fitted black Lululemon jacket and T-shirt that she wore over jeans.

A man pushed away from the railing that edged the walk to the doors and moved toward them. Matt.

Was she really going to let this happen?

Judging from the way her heart bumped in her chest and her insides went all soft at seeing him, the answer was yes.

When he'd made that comment last night over dinner about planning to go to the aquarium, she'd known what he was doing. She hadn't protested or argued. Maybe she should have. Maybe she should have changed her plans with Mia, except she'd already promised the girl they were going and she couldn't bring herself to disappoint Mia.

After dinner last night, Matt had walked her to her car and said good night to her. They'd stood there for a pulsing moment in the dark, looking at each other, every nerve ending in her body screaming with the need for his touch. But neither of them made a move toward each other, not even a kiss or peck on the cheek.

It left her feeling…unsettled. Grateful. Relieved. Disappointed. A whole skein of tangled emotions that she had trouble picking apart and had thought a lot about, lying in her bed in the dark that night.

He hadn't asked her out on a date or anything. He hadn't given her a chance to say no. He hadn't put any moves on her other than touching her face and her hand. Sexual awareness had shimmered between them all evening though. They were both aware of it.

You have to have some fun.

She hadn't had fun for a long time. For her, having fun was synonymous with getting into trouble, getting unwanted media attention and getting in trouble with her parents. She'd been a serious student at college, rarely socializing. Most of the other students were younger than her anyway.

But there were definitely times she felt lonely. Could she go out with Matt (and Mia) and just have fun?

Now he stood in front of her wearing jeans, like her and Mia, and a thick Condors hoodie that made him look even more boyish. But the way the faded jeans clung to his hips and the bulge at his groin, and the shadow of stubble on his cheeks and jaw were all man. His smile was wide and engaging. "Hey, Honey. Imagine meeting you here."

She couldn't help the smile that tugged her lips. "Imagine that," she murmured.

"Who's your friend?" Matt looked down at Mia.

"This is Mia. Mia, this is Matt. He's a hockey player."

Mia gazed at him unimpressed. "Hi."

Matt lifted an eyebrow and returned his gaze to Honey.

She grinned. "Mia's not much into hockey."

"I'm famous," he told Mia, lips twitching, arms folded across his chest.

She just stared at him. "No, you're not. If you were, I would've heard of you."

Honey started to laugh. "That's very true, sweetie. Matt just thinks he's famous, apparently." She met his eyes and the way the corners of his eyes crinkled a little, she knew he was amused too.

"Are you going to the aquarium too?" he asked. And somehow they were all moving toward the entrance.

"Yes!" Mia answered with a skip. "We're going to see the sea urchins!"

"Somehow I felt I should do more educational things with her than mani/pedis," Honey told Matt in a low voice.

"Jeez," he said. "Are you her tutor or her babysitter?"

"Shh. She's too old for a babysitter."

"Right. Sorry."

And then he was paying their admission and they were all walking in together.

"You didn't need to do that," she said in a quiet tone to him, even though money was tight until she got her first paycheck.

He shrugged. "Whatever. I mean…it's my pleasure to have the company of two pretty ladies."

Mia gave him a suspicious look but was soon distracted by one of the exhibits.

"Did you make this scarf?" Matt asked, reaching out to touch the delicate, loose-stitched loops of blue and mauve around her neck.

"I did."

"Nice."

"Thanks."

They learned about sea horses and starfish and two-spotted octopi, then left the aquarium to go up to the pier.

"Remember the last time we were here together?" Matt asked her as they strolled across wooden planks.

She shot him a sideways glance. Of course she did. She'd been there since then, of course, but that night she and Matt had come and ridden the carousel, laughed and made out at the top of the Ferris wheel, had been a sweet memory that had always stayed with her.

By the end of the afternoon as they left the pier, having moved on to other attractions there including an early dinner, Honey was surprised to realize how good she felt. Relaxed. Happy. Just…good.

No large quantities of alcohol, illicit drugs or sex had been involved.

She still had a feeling this was dangerous in some way, but it was lovely to feel this way, and to see the big smile on Mia's face as they climbed the bridge toward Ocean Avenue.

Only one moment had blemished the afternoon. When someone had recognized Matt and asked for his autograph, Honey had immediately turned away, shepherding Mia a little aside. Probably nobody would recognize her, but she didn't want anyone to associate her and Matt together. You never knew where media, paparazzi or just eager fans with cameras in their smart phones could make an appearance and things could blow up.

"I guess he is famous," Mia cheerfully acknowledged as Matt took a few minutes to talk to the fans. "You're so pretty, you should be famous too, Honey."

Honey smiled at the girl, who had no idea about Honey's past, grateful that Mia accepted her for who she was right then.

When Matt joined them, he wore a faint crease between his brows. "Where'd you go?" he asked. "I thought I'd lost you for a minute."

"Just didn't want to be in the way of your moment there."

He gave her a searching look then nodded.

"Can we play on the beach?" Mia asked.

"I'm sorry, sweetie, your mom gets home from work about six thirty. I said we'd be home by then. And it's starting to get dark."

Mia gave a pout but accepted that. When they reached the sidewalk, they all paused. "Thanks for letting me barge in on your girls' afternoon," Matt said to them both.

"You're welcome," Mia said seriously. "It was fun! You're cool."

"Thank you," he replied equally gravely. "Honey's cool too."

"Yes!"

"Thank you," she said to him. "I had a really nice time."

"We could do it again," he said quietly. "Maybe just you and me."

"The aquarium? I don't think I need to go back there for a while."

"That's not what I meant, and you know it. We'll talk. There's a game tomorrow afternoon——maybe a late dinner tomorrow night?"

"Can't," she said. "Sunday dinner at my parents' place." She wrinkled her nose.

"Ah. Okay. I'll see you next week and we can talk."
She nodded.

Nothing bad had happened. She'd enjoyed herself. Matt was a great guy. Maybe she could do this. Maybe she could go out with a guy and just have simple, normal fun without all hell breaking loose. But the guy she should be trying that with probably wasn't Matt Heller.

Honey pulled up to the white gates of her parents' home and entered the code to open them. They swung open and she drove her BMW through them and up the driveway to the house. Luckily, her dad had let her keep her car. It was nearly eight years old but still ran great.

Traditional Sunday dinners at the Holbrook home continued, with her two older brothers both likely to be there with their families and often business colleagues of her dad's. The assortment of cars and SUVs parked out front indicated a sizeable crowd for this week's dinner.

She entered the house through the big, double front doors. A curving staircase wound up to the second floor, the ceiling above the foyer open to it with an enormous chandelier hanging above. She followed the faint sound of voices to the back of the house where French doors had been opened onto the patio.

Kids splashed in the pool and she grinned. She wasn't all that crazy about her family, but she had to admit she did like being an aunt. Oldest brother Jonathan and his wife Demi now had two kids, Kavita, four, and Sebastian, two. Her other brother James and his wife Kortney also had a two-year-old son, Burton, and, as she'd told Matt, Kortney was eight months pregnant.

James sat on the side of the pool wearing board shorts and watching the kids. The other adults sat on patio furniture sipping drinks. Jonathan spotted her and lifted a hand. "Hey, Honey."

Everyone else turned to watch her approach across the stone patio and she kept her smile in place. "Hi, everyone."

Her mom rose and moved toward her for a hug and some air kisses. "Honey! I'm so glad you could make it."

As usual, her mom was gorgeous, dressed in a floral print sleeveless dress that fit her tall, slender body perfectly. Her still-blonde hair and unlined face made her look much younger than her fifty years.

"Where on earth did you get that dress?" Mom asked, looking her up and down.

"You gave it to me," Honey reminded her.

Mom frowned. "I did?"

"About five years ago."

"Oh my god, and you're still wearing it?" She shook her head. "Come meet our guests. Your father's not home from the game yet, but he should be here soon."

Honey greeted some of her parents' friends she already knew, then her mother introduced her to some big entertainment lawyer named Hugo Cathmor and his wife Adelle.

"Your daughter certainly has good genes," Hugo said with a smile. "She's just as beautiful as you, Sela."

Mom laughed. "Oh, thank you. People often think we're sisters."

She loved it when people thought they were sisters, and if it didn't get mentioned, she'd bring it up. It made Honey grit her teeth.

"Are you a model, like your mom was, Honey?" Adelle asked.

Her jaw ached as she smiled. "No, I'm not. I work for the Condor Community Foundation as a Programming Coordinator." It felt good to say it, even though her insides clutched knowing that it wasn't a real job.

Adelle and Hugo nodded.

"Honey wasn't cut out for modeling," Mom added. "And of course it's really a tough field to get into. Not many aspiring models make it." In her mind, Honey tacked on, Like I did. Because that was what Mom was saying. Although the truth was, her mom had never been a top model. She'd done some catalogue work and a few advertising jobs. She'd continued to work a little after she'd snagged a rich hockey player husband, but the rich husband had been more of a goal than a successful modeling career that actually involved hard work.

And, not that Honey wanted to talk about herself, but the

mention of her new job had passed by without her mother even asking how her first week had gone. Ah well. She was used to it now.

"Want a drink, Honey?" Her brother Jonathan spoke up.

"I'll have a glass of white wine. Thanks." She smiled at him.

The oldest of the three Holbrook siblings, Jonathan had somehow managed to be the perfect son. James had as well, in their parents' eyes, although Honey well knew he was far from perfect. Their parents had focused all their attention on their two boys and what they wanted for them. Luckily, Jonathan and James had both been athletic, and although James had disappointed his parents by not pursuing hockey, he'd made them happy by becoming a pro golfer and doing well on the PGA tour, having just pocketed over a million bucks at Torrey Pines. Jonathan had played hockey in the NHL for twelve years before a career-ending injury, and now worked for the Condors as Coordinator of Player Development.

Jonathan handed her a glass of wine and she took a sip. Cold and crisp. She'd limit herself to one. The temptation to slide into old patterns, especially around her family, was always there.

Her mom as usual led the conversation where she wanted it to go, which meant it was about her, and she chatted about some big Beverly Hills party they'd been at last night and who had been there.

Then Honey's father arrived home, bringing a couple more people with him, the team's General Manager Rudy Thomas, and John Derwin, Director of Hockey Operations. Dad gave Honey a hug but the conversation turned to the game and the fact that the Condors had won. Matt had probably been at the game, no doubt happy that the team had won. It must be hard for him to watch and not play. Then she tried to push thoughts of Matt out of her head and took a seat on one of the padded lounge chairs, listening to the others talk, smiling and laughing as appropriate, trying as usual to be as inconspicuous as possible.

Her dad hadn't asked about her new job either, but that was probably because he knew it wasn't a real job. God, that was so embarrassing. Except she was going to make it a real job, dammit. She shot him a look, wondering if she should try to get him alone and give him hell for doing that, or if she should just keep her mouth shut.

As a child she'd wanted her parents' attention and approval. She'd learned that when she did what they wanted, she got that. When she didn't do what they wanted, that love was withdrawn. As she got older she started to resent the things they wanted her to do. Her brothers made them happy playing sports—hockey, baseball, golf—and doing it well. Honey wasn't into sports. In fact, as a child there hadn't been anything she'd been really good at. As she got older, a modeling scout had approached her and her family about doing some modeling. She'd been excited about it, thinking that maybe it was something she could be good at, something she could do that would please her parents. But her mom had shut that down right away. Her mom didn't want any female competition, even from her own daughter, and had done her best to make sure Honey knew she couldn't compete with her. That was when Honey had discovered that any attention was better than no attention. And that had led to a whole lot of trouble. Not that she'd seen it at the time.

But no more. She still wasn't entirely secure in her self-image, but she'd accomplished things she was proud of, even if nobody else noticed or cared. Maybe it hadn't been her choice to go to college, but when she'd hit bottom and realized she needed to make some serious changes in her life, she'd done it. Once there, she'd been the one who'd set goals for herself, put her head down and worked hard, and she had a college degree to show for it. And now she had a new job that she also wanted to be proud of.

But even though she was doing exactly what they'd wanted—staying out of trouble—they still weren't all that interested in her.

But that was okay, because now she knew that the only person's opinion she really needed to care about was her own.

A small, wet body landed against her, startling her out of her thoughts. "Auntie Honey!"

Honey screeched and laughingly set her little niece away from her. "Kavita! You're getting me all wet! Oh, who cares." And she pulled the little girl in for a damp hug. "You feel cold."

The sun was very low in the sky now and the air taking on a chill.

"I am cold," Kavita said, starting to shiver. She danced up on down on her little toes.

"Where's your towel, bunny?" Honey looked around. She set her wine glass down on a little table and reached over for a towel draped on a nearby chair. "Here."

She folded her niece up in the big beach towel and pulled her up onto her lap, wrapping her arms around her. "So, what's new, bunny? Got a job yet?"

Kavita giggled. "No."

"Well, that's no good! How are you going to support your parents?"

"I'm four, Auntie Honey!"

They were joined by Kavita's little brother Sebastian. Honey bent down to give him a smooch. "Hey, little dude," she said. "Have fun in the pool?"

He nodded, still not talking a whole lot, but since Kavita was only too willing to talk for her little brother, he didn't need to.

"Yes, he had fun," Kavita said. Honey grinned.

"Come on kids, let's go inside and get your clothes on for dinner." Their mom rose out of her chair and scooped up Sebastian. She held out a hand for Kavita who scrambled off Honey's lap.

"I'd better go check on dinner," Mom said, rising as well.

"Need any help, Mom?" Honey offered.

"No, I think Jess has things under control."

Her parents had a caterer they often used when they hosted dinner parties, who brought a small team into the kitchen and took over cooking and serving, after planning the menu with Mom.

Honey shifted her chair to face Kortney as James took their son into the house to get changed as well. "How are you feeling, Kortney?" she asked.

Kortney sighed. "Huge. Fat. Uncomfortable." And she launched into details about her last doctor appointment and how much weight she'd gained and a whole lot of other things pregnant women always seemed to want to talk about, including decorating the baby's room. Honey went with it.

Soon dinner was served at the big table in the formal dining room.

"We like family dinners," Mom told their guests. "So we keep things really informal."

That meant the kids ate with them, which meant a lot of noise and parental intervention and interjections of "Sebastian, stay in your seat" and "Burton, stop throwing peas at your cousin", which annoyed her mother who was trying to hold court, despite her claim that she liked things informal. It was all kind of fucked up.

Honey kept her thoughts to herself, ate her meal then volunteered to take the kids into the kitchen for dessert, partly so their parents and the other guests could enjoy their meal in peace, but mostly so she could escape.

In the kitchen, she got the kids seated at the big island on stools. Jess and her two girls were just about finished cleaning up and putting things away in the spacious kitchen. Honey pulled cartons of ice cream out of the freezer. She was going to scoop it into bowls, but on impulse peeked into the pantry and found what she'd hoped for—ice-cream cones. Ice cream was way more fun in a cone. Messier, but fun. Then she found some colored sprinkles, which was even more fun. Every kid loved sprinkles.

The three kids were thrilled by this and once she got them all sorted with ice cream in cones with their choice of colored sprinkles, she made one for herself, leaning on the counter across from the kids as they ate.

"You have so much ice cream on your face, we're going to have to throw you in the pool to clean you off," she told Burton.

His eyes went wide but the other kids giggled. "Do it!" Kavita cried.

"No! No pool!"

"Don't worry, I'm kidding," Honey assured him. "Maybe." But she winked at him. "Hey, guess where I went yesterday?"

"Where?"

"The aquarium. And we saw an octopus. Do you know how many arms an octopus has?"

Little heads shook.

"Eight! Eight arms. And he moved very fast in the water."

Three sets of eyes went round. "I want to go to the 'quarium," Kavita said. "Why don't you take us there, Auntie Honey?"

"Good question, bunny. Maybe I will someday. Now I'm living here we can do more stuff together."

"Yay! You can take us to Disneyland!"

Honey blinked. "Um…well. Maybe." That sounded like

fun, but she wasn't sure about taking three small children to Disneyland all by herself.

They all started chanting, "Disneyland!" at the top of their lungs, although the two boys were mostly just yelling wordlessly and Honey laughed. "Shhh," she said, making a shushing motion with her hands, but smiling.

Honey made her escape from the house not long after that. Driving the Ventura Freeway, she let out a sigh. She'd done her duty and showed up. Not a single person had asked about her new job. It was typical, but she no longer expected anything from them. Or from anyone.

CHAPTER 7

Matt was fucking sick of watching the games from the press box, dressed in a suit and tie. He wanted to *play*. He had an appointment with the team doctor tomorrow and he was gonna punch something or somebody if the doc didn't clear him for full contact play.

The post concussive symptoms had been gone for a while now. He knew they were just worried about the vertebra in his neck that had been fractured, wanting to make sure it was fully healed. And yeah, he wanted to make sure of that too — of course he did. Thinking about taking another hit like the one that knocked him out, possibly ending up with brain damage or spinal cord damage, paralyzed, made him want to vomit. Christ.

Every day he thanked God or his lucky stars or whatever or whoever he needed to be grateful to that his injury hadn't been worse than it was. It had certainly given him a whole different perspective on many things. He'd seen people in the hospital way worse off than him, and swore he was never going to whine or complain about petty shit again. He was going to appreciate everything he'd been given and make the most of it.

But he wanted to get back in the *game,* for fuck's sake.

He let out a long breath as he headed out of the Coliseum after the game, a nice win for the team. As he passed Steve Holbrook coming out of his private box up there, he greeted the team owner with a smile, but of course that immediately made him think of Honey.

Because Steve was on his way home, and Honey was there to have dinner with him. Would she tell her dad that they'd spent the afternoon together yesterday?

He had no clue.

Did he want her to tell him? He wasn't entirely sure of that either.

He remembered the guys' talk about how Holbrook had traded Heimdall just because he'd dated Honey. Was that true or just rumor? Would Holbrook trade any guy who dated his daughter?

Jesus, that was stupid. Holbrook was smarter than that. You couldn't run a hockey team that way.

He turned down an invitation to go out with some of the guys later and left the Coliseum to head home, thinking about the afternoon he'd spent with Honey the day before. The attraction between them was still there, sizzling hot, just as hot as it had been eight years ago when they'd gotten all tangled up in each other. Maybe hotter.

And it was weird, but being with her yesterday with her little friend Mia made his head all screwed up. Because not only was Honey gorgeous and sexy, she was…sweet.

Sweet like honey.

Jesus. He was getting fucking poetic.

Mia obviously was crazy about her, and Honey was great with Mia, genuine and affectionate, an openness in her eyes and her smile that he hadn't seen with other people, including him. Or maybe he'd caught a glimpse of it…but seeing her like that with Mia made him realize how guarded Honey was with most people.

He wanted to see more of her like that, relaxed and candid. He wanted to see what she looked like in bed, wanted to see her looking at him when he was fucking her into heaven. He wanted to see the expression in her eyes when she came apart underneath him.

Damn.

With all kinds of pent-up energy and frustration inside him — sexual, professional, whatever — as soon as he got home he changed into a pair of board shorts and headed to the pool. Nobody else was there, early Sunday evening, so he dove in and started doing laps to work all the frustration out of him. The cool water rushing over his body felt good. Using his muscles felt good.

He swam until his lungs burned and his arm and shoulder muscles screamed, then hauled himself up onto the side and sat there panting. Good. It was good for him. Distracted him from thinking about Honey.

Except there she was again, dammit.

"You can help me celebrate." Matt smiled at Honey across the front reception counter of Condor Community Foundation the following Thursday after their meeting. They'd met again to go over some of the details she'd arranged for a visit to Franklin Middle School.

She tipped her head to one side, totally being sucked in by his smile. God, what was it about him that just melted her inside? "Celebrate what?"

"I've been cleared for full contact," he said. "I can practice with the team and that means it won't be long before I can play again."

"Oh! That's great!" She couldn't help but smile at his obvious pleasure at this turn of events. "Will you be joining them on the road?"

His smile vanished. "No. I have to wait until they're back."

"Uh…when's that?" Crap, she didn't pay much attention to the team schedule. She was going to have to bookmark it in her web browser.

"They're back Sunday," he said. "Practice Monday morning. I guess we see how that goes and maybe I'll play next week."

She studied his face. It wasn't obvious, but she could read the anxiety and frustration in his eyes. "It's been a while since you played, though. They might not want you to jump right back into it."

He grimaced and shoved a hand into his thick hair. "Yeah. That's true. But fuck, I've been waiting for months now." Then he glanced around. "Shit."

Clearly he was trying to keep his frustration to himself.

"Well, it's still good news," she said. "Right? So you just have to wait a few more days while they're away and then you'll be practicing with them first thing next week."

"Right. Which brings me back to my invitation. To help me celebrate."

The glimpse of vulnerability she'd seen in his eyes a moment ago made it so hard to resist. But hell, she shouldn't be worried about him. She needed to be protecting herself, and going out with Matt Heller was the exact opposite of that.

"I don't think it's a good idea," she said slowly.

She remembered the Saturday excursion to the pier and

how much fun she'd had. Nothing bad had happened. But still...

"C'mon, Honey. The team and all my buds are away right now. Help me celebrate."

Irresistible. The word sprang to mind. When he smiled like that, the corners of his eyes crinkling up, all his attention on her, it was pretty damn compelling.

But there were good reasons to resist. What if the worst happened? What if someone in the media saw them together and went public with it? What kind of crazy shit storm could result from that? Her main goal these days, apart from trying to prove herself at the Foundation, was to keep *out* of the news.

"I'm all on my own," he said with an entreating look that made her nipples tingle. God! He could probably ask her to jump off the Santa Monica Freeway and she'd consider it.

She sighed. "Okay. But we have to go somewhere very low-key. Like, maybe Burger King."

He tipped his head back and considered that. "I like a good Whopper now and then."

She laughed. She couldn't help it.

He grinned too. "Okay. Low-key it is. I'll pick you up Saturday afternoon. One o'clock."

She blinked. "Oookay." An afternoon date somehow wasn't what she expected.

"Need your address, babe." He pulled out his cell phone and waited. She recited it and he entered it in then shoved his phone back into his pocket. "Great. See you Saturday."

Her second week on the job had gone much like the first, with people keeping information from her, going for lunch and coffee breaks without her and her generally feeling lost and useless—other than the work she'd been doing with Matt and the things she'd set up for him.

But she had some other things she'd been working on too.

Since nobody seemed to care if she was at her desk or not, she'd headed out to a few meetings with some contacts she'd made with some of her parents' friends. What the hell…she needed to use every advantage she had.

So she'd lined up some sponsorship money that nobody knew about yet. They'd been happy to help out, if a little amused at her earnest presentation, and overall interested in participating in the event she was beginning to plan. She'd also talked some people into donating awesome prizes for the silent auction at the upcoming ball that would have people's jaws dropping, and had convinced a couple of minor celebrities to attend the event.

Of course, she had no authorization at all from Trent or Aaron to do this, but if she had money and big names and things all planned out, there was no way they could say no. Right? Right.

She'd also identified some tasks that were going to need to be done, which Dulcie probably was trying to do before she left, and took care of them without saying anything, hoping she wasn't screwing up.

And now she had another date with Matt Heller. Well, not another date. You couldn't really call last weekend's meeting at the pier a date. As he'd said, they were just having some fun.

Her heart picked up its pace and breathing accelerated when she started thinking about seeing him again. It was bad, bad, bad, but she felt drawn to him, just the way she had when they'd met way back when she was a rebellious teenager out to do anything she could to piss off her parents, and he'd been one of the only people who'd ever given her the kind of attention she'd always craved.

Friday was Dulcie's last day before her mat leave, and everyone in the office took her out for lunch. They'd even actually invited Honey to go along, her first "social" event with her new coworkers. Everyone had contributed toward a baby gift which they gave Dulcie after lunch, back at the office.

"Thank you everyone," Dulcie said. "This stroller is the shit."

Honey laughed with the others.

"Guess you'll be taking the afternoon easy," Celine teased. "On your last day."

Dulcie frowned. "As if. I've still got a million things to do."

"Like what?"

"Like getting those check requisitions done so we can get money out to all the groups."

"I did that," Honey said.

Dulcie, Celine and everyone else in the office looked at her.

"I also followed up with the bank on that trust account error."

Dulcie blinked. "Thank you, Honey."

"No problem. I knew you were running out of time."

Dulcie lowered herself into her chair and laid her hands on her belly. "Okay. I feel better about leaving now."

The others drifted away back to their own desks but Honey remained and smiled at her. "You need to be worried about that baby, not work. Hopefully you get some time to yourself before she arrives."

Dulcie had mentioned once that she and her husband knew they were having a girl.

"I do want some time," Dulcie agreed. "But damn, I also want to get this over with. I'm tired of being pregnant."

"It's a long time, isn't it? My sister-in-law is pregnant too. She's due in about a month. I can't wait to have another niece or nephew."

Dulcie eyed her. "You like kids?"

"Yeah." Honey smiled. "My niece and nephews are a lot of fun. I'm glad to be back living closer to them."

After a short pause, Dulcie said, "Thanks for everything you've done, Honey. You've made it a lot easier for me to leave. I…" She hesitated again. "I didn't really think you were going to be much help. And I'm sorry if it hasn't been easy for you."

Honey's chest warmed. "That's okay," she said with a smile. "I'm glad I could help. I'd like it if you'd tell me what else I can do while you're away to keep things rolling."

Dulcie nodded. "Yeah. There are a few things you should know about."

They spent the rest of Dulcie's last afternoon going over things, and for the first time, Honey felt like she was being trusted and something was actually being expected of her. And she loved it.

Near the end of the day, she hurried back to her desk and lifted a gift bag out from the corner of her cubicle and returned to Dulcie's.

"Here," she said. "I know we all chipped in on your gift, but this is just from me."

Dulcie's gaze moved from the pink bag up to Honey's face, and back as she took it from her.

"It's really nothing," Honey added quickly.

Dulcie opened it and pulled out some pink tissue paper, and then unwrapped a square knit blanket in variegated shades of pink, along with a tiny cardigan, hat and booties.

"Oh my god," she said, touching her fingers to the wool. "So soft. And so pretty." She looked up at Honey. "These are beautiful. You didn't have to do that."

Honey smiled. "I know, but I wanted to."

"Where did you get these? They're absolutely gorgeous."

"I made them," Honey explained. "It's a hobby of mine.

I'm making some things for my brother and sister-in-law right now too."

Dulcie's mouth opened. And closed. She blinked. "You made these?"

"Yeah." Honey grimaced. "I know knitting is a lame hobby, but I enjoy it."

"Knitting."

Honey smiled and nodded. Her insides twisted a little. God. Why had she done this?

Dulcie looked down at the tiny garments and blanket sitting on her lap. She stared at them for a long moment.

"All the best, Dulcie," Honey said, pushing away from the cubicle wall where she leaned. "I can't wait until you bring the baby in to visit."

Dulcie nodded, still not looking up. Honey returned to her desk.

Whatever. It didn't matter. She didn't expect anything from anyone. She'd done it because she liked doing it and she had learned a lot from Dulcie the last two weeks, despite the rough start. And babies were pretty special.

Okay! It was the end of the week. And for something different, she was looking forward to the weekend because she had a date with a hot hockey player.

CHAPTER 8

Matt arrived at her apartment a few minutes before one on Saturday. She buzzed him in and waited for him to come up, her insides fluttery. She somehow didn't think they were going to Burger King, which meant she did not know where they were going, which therefore meant she had no idea what to wear. She'd dressed in jeans rolled up at the ankle and a sheer flowery top. She answered the door still in bare feet, unsure whether heels or flip flops were more appropriate.

"Hey," he said, stepping into her apartment with his wide, white smile.

His broad shoulders and muscled frame filled her small space and she could even smell him, a clean spicy scent of shampoo or shower gel, or maybe both. She waited for him to look around her tiny apartment and make some comment, but instead his gaze travelled over her, from bare feet up to her face, and his eyes showed warm approval.

"Am I dressed okay?"

"Jeans are great," he said. "But you might want to change to a different top. There's a cool breeze today and we're going to be outside."

"We are?"

"We're going to rent bikes at the beach," he said with a grin.

She paused then shook her head. "Well, that answers my question about footwear. I'll be right back. Have a seat if you like."

That would give him lots of time to realize what a little dump she lived in.

She was ready to defend her little dump, though. Even though she'd only lived there a few weeks, she was making it her own. She hurried into the bedroom and closed the door behind her, then whipped off the blouse. She hung it in the closet then yanked open a drawer and pulled out a Berkeley T-shirt. She pushed her head and arms through it and tugged it down, then reached for a black hoodie hanging on the hook on the inside of her closet door. Once she had that on, she grabbed her Nikes on the floor of the closet and returned to her living room.

Matt stood at the window looking down onto the street. He turned when she entered the room. "There," she said. "So seriously, we're going bike riding?"

"Sure, why not? It's a nice day for a ride along the beach. We can stop somewhere along the way and get something to eat."

Well, she'd asked for low-key. "I haven't ridden a bike in years."

"I hear it's something you never forget," he said solemnly.

Her lips twitched. "I've heard that too. I just hope I can keep up with a professional athlete."

"I'll go slow," he promised, eyes gleaming.

"I wouldn't want to hold you back." She sat to put on her shoes and lace them up.

"Don't worry about that."

"You should know I haven't even worked out in a long

time. I had no time for that when I was in school. I've been meaning to get back into it."

She didn't have cash for expensive gym memberships, but she had her Nikes and an iPod and she could run along the beach. She just hadn't actually done it yet.

"This'll be good for you then," he said, approaching her, hands in the back pockets of his jeans.

Jeans that fit him perfectly, despite his size. Jeans that were softly worn and rode low on his hips. He wore a black T-shirt that hugged his shoulders and biceps but hung loosely over his flat abs.

"Do *you* have a jacket?" she asked.

"In the car. Ready?"

"No."

He grinned again.

"I won't bring my purse," she said. "Since we're going bike riding. But I need something. Hang on." She made another trip to her bedroom to retrieve the small black messenger bag she could wear across her chest. It didn't hold a lot, but what did she need—a little money, a credit card, sunglasses, her phone, a lip gloss…and she called it good.

"Low maintenance," he murmured, watching her adjust the bag over her shoulder.

She set her hands on her hips. "Are you being sarcastic?"

"No!" He held up his hands. "I'm serious. Girls usually carry a big bag of shit around with them."

She laughed. "Yeah. It's called a purse. Why do you sound surprised I'm not?"

He gave her a look, chin down.

"Okay, maybe I used to be high maintenance."

"Uh…*yeah*."

Her eyebrows lowered.

"I just find it…interesting."

"Ooookay."

"You interest me, Honey. Not gonna deny that. Let's go."

She interested him. She didn't know what to do with that comment so she followed him out, locking the door behind her and adding her keys to her small bag.

"Oh hell no," she said when he paused beside the little black Porsche. "This is your car?"

"Yeah. Sweet ride, isn't she?"

He opened the passenger door and she slid down into the luxurious interior. "She? Please don't tell me you've named her."

He laughed as he closed her door. Moments later he was inside, and the top of the convertible was lowering as they pulled away from the curb. "Nah. But I do think of her as a 'her'."

She stroked a hand over the dash. "Very pretty."

"Bought this when I moved here," he said. "It seemed appropriate for California."

"Do you like living here?"

"It's crazy," he said. "It's a long way from where I grew up."

"Winnipeg."

He glanced at her, the corners of his mouth lifting. "You remember."

"Sure."

They'd talked about that way back when they'd first met. Although Honey'd been born in the United States, her father was Canadian, born and raised on the Canadian prairies, and had never forgotten his roots. He'd made sure all his kids had travelled through Canada. Winnipeg wasn't that far from Moose Jaw, Saskatchewan, where Grandma and Grandpa Holbrook still lived, and where Honey'd visited many times. Mom and Dad may live in a gated acreage in Thousand Oaks, but Grandma and Grandpa's two-story house in Moose Jaw was good for keeping your feet firmly planted on the ground.

"It's definitely different," she agreed. "When's the last time you went home?"

"I try to go back every Christmas if I can, and for sure every summer. My brothers and I all do hockey camps there in the summer and we organize a charity golf tournament."

She nodded. Matt was another guy who'd apparently kept his feet fixed to the ground. "Your dad still owns the sporting goods store?"

"Two stores," he corrected her with a smile. "And he's still waiting for one of us to step up to take over running them."

"He must be ready to retire."

"He's sixty-eight. Past retirement age, but he loves what he does. I don't know what else he'd do. He even still coaches minor hockey in the winter."

"God! Kids must love having him for a coach! Four sons in the NHL."

"There are only actually two of us now," he said. "Logan and me."

"Right. I watch Jason on TV sometimes. When I watch hockey. Which isn't very often."

He eyed her. "You don't like hockey?"

"Not really."

"Shuddup," he said mildly. "How can that be?"

She grinned. "Sorry. The hockey gene missed me."

"Maybe you could learn to like it."

"Maybe I could. But why?"

He shook his head, smiling. "I just don't get it."

"You love hockey."

"Uh…*yeah*. But you work for the team."

"Not the team exactly. For the foundation."

"Whatever. How can you do that if you don't like hockey?"

"It's not that I hate it. I can watch a game. I can promote the sport. It's just…oh hell. Probably the only reason I don't like it is because it was a small form of rebellion against my parents."

He shot her a sideways glance as he slowed for a red light. "Ah yes. Rebellion."

For a moment they both fell silent. He was probably thinking about the same things she was—namely all her stupid rebellious stunts. "I'm not proud of some of the things I did," she finally said in a quiet voice.

"What's done is done," he said with a shrug.

She blinked at him from behind her big sunglasses. Yeah. She'd been working on that kind of attitude for years now. It was easy to beat herself up over and over again for the mistakes she'd made. Therapy had helped somewhat, but she sometimes fell back into that hole. She nodded. "Yeah."

Matt parked in a lot near the beach and they walked to a shop that rented bikes.

"They rent skates too," Matt said with a wicked little smile at her. "Maybe we should roller blade."

She gave him a look, raised eyebrows, pursed lips, and he laughed.

With helmets on, they soon set off along the paved path that crossed the expanse of pale sand. Lots of others were out walking, running, cycling, and they steered around them. They passed tall skinny palm trees and farther on short, stubbier ones. The sun shone brightly, but a brisk wind kept the air cooler, especially nearer the ocean. Honey cycled along behind Matt, who was no doubt keeping a slower pace for her, admiring not only the view of the man in front of her and his ass on the bike seat, but the ocean on their right, sparkling in the sun. The bright light and scenery and using her muscles created a lovely feeling of being at peace. Happy. She couldn't help but smile as they cycled farther, Matt occasionally dropping back to ride beside her and point out sights.

The path was so smooth and Matt was moving faster, so

she put some weight into her pedals to keep up with him, her thigh muscles developing a pleasant burn. And she laughed out loud.

They slowed their pace to watch a couple of guys in wetsuits surfing. Sandpipers ran back and forth in front of the waves as they rolled onto the flat, wet sand.

They continued on to Venice Beach, with more palm trees, more surfers and lots of people. They passed buskers and mimes and a woman skated past them from the other direction who looked exactly like Dolly Parton, in a pair of short pink shorts and tiny tank top that showed off ginormous hooters, blonde hair out to there. Matt paused to look at Honey and they both burst out laughing.

Then they continued on to Marina del Rey with all the gleaming yachts in the harbor, circling around them, then stopping at a little restaurant right on the water. They sat out on the patio eating clubhouse sandwiches and curly fries. When Honey couldn't finish the second half of her sandwich, Matt enthusiastically took it from her and devoured it.

"God, the way you eat," she said, smiling.

He eyed her. "You don't look like you need to watch what you eat."

His appreciative gaze made her feel warm. It was true that she'd inherited a good metabolism from both her mother and her father. "I should eat healthier," she confessed. "More veggies. Living alone means I often don't feel like cooking a big meal."

"Yeah, know the feeling," he agreed. "One of my buddies —he plays for the team too, Chris Dobie—is health nut, so he's always giving me nutritional advice. Gotta eat healthy."

Honey dipped a curly fry into ketchup and popped it into her mouth. "Okay. Starting Monday."

They shared a smile.

"Doing okay on the bike?" he asked.

"Yeah, fine."

"Want to ride farther, or turn around and go back?"

She lifted a shoulder. "I'm good to keep going. I might not be able to walk tomorrow…"

"I have a hot tub at my apartment," he said. "We should hit it after this. That'll help your sore muscles."

"I didn't bring a bathing suit."

He grinned.

"Don't even say it. And don't remind me that I've done it before."

Yes, there were photographs to prove it —she and three guys in a pool at the house of famous actor who would remain nameless, in the water, but clearly she'd been topless. Those images had been all over the internet back a few years.

His smile disappeared and his eyebrows drew together above his nose. He made a small noise like a grunt.

She looked down at her plate. "Sorry, Matt. I can't change the past."

"Christ," he muttered. "You think I don't know that? Fuck, if I could change the past I wouldn't have spent weeks in the hospital and months in rehab."

She lifted her gaze. "That wasn't your fault."

"Doesn't matter," he said. "We don't get do overs, no matter whose fault it is. People make mistakes. Shit happens. It's how you deal with it that matters."

She nodded slowly. Once again, his lack of judgment baffled her. She wasn't used to that. She'd grown up constantly not living up to expectations and being punished for that.

"And I'd say from the looks of things that you're dealing with it pretty well," he added.

She experienced a funny ache in her chest and pressed her lips together. "Thanks. I'm trying."

"And it's not like I haven't done crazy shit in the past too," he added.

"Yeah," she said slowly. "But when the media got hold of your crazy shit, they made you out to be a stud, whereas I was made out to be a slut."

He stared at her. "Fuck. You are so right. That is not fucking fair."

She looked at him, all big and gorgeous with his boyish smile and tousled hair, not judging her and saying things like "what's done is done" and "that is not fucking fair" and making her feel so good about herself. Something inside her melted and cracked, like a hard shell breaking open and warm softness spreading through her body. And she found herself experiencing an overwhelming urge to hurl herself into his arms and kiss him all over his face and hang on to him with everything she had.

She inhaled a long, shaky breath.

"We'll stop and buy you a swimsuit," he said, setting his empty drink up on the table. "Let's go."

She gaped at him as she followed him off the patio. Was he serious?

Once more mounted on the bicycles, they pedaled on. Manhattan Beach and Hermosa Beach had a cozy feel despite the pricey ocean-side homes. People played volleyball on the beach and they took another break to stop and sit on a bench to look out at the ocean.

"Is this fun for you?" she asked Matt, leaning back on the bench. The sun warmed her face deliciously.

"Yeah." He turned to look at her, his eyes hidden behind sunglasses as were hers. Their helmets sat on the bench beside them. "Not you?"

"No! I mean, yeah, it is fun. Strangely. I feel really… relaxed. Tired, but good."

Also intensely aware of him sitting beside her, one of his

arms along the back of the bench behind her, his long muscular legs in faded blue jeans stretched out in front of him, crossed at the ankles.

She'd asked for low-key, and this was perfect. Scenarios of him being mobbed by paparazzi or eager fans had formed in her head, and she'd envisioned how unpleasant things could get if people recognized her, with him.

"I guess this isn't like going to a big party at some Beverly Hills mansion, or a Hollywood club," he said.

"No," she agreed. "And that's just fine with me. I'm not sure why I even found that fun, back when I used to do those things." The meaningless frantic pace of one party after another, all of them blurring together into a fog of alcohol and drugs and music and faces that she could barely remember. She'd laughed and danced and now she couldn't even remember what was so funny or who she'd been with some nights. "I was wondering if that's the kind of fun you like to have these days. Rich, famous, handsome young hockey player."

He snorted. "I've done it," he said. "Won't deny that. I like going out and having fun as much as the next guy. But since my injury, that kinda lost its appeal."

"When do you think you'll get to play again?" she asked.

His lips pursed. "I'm hoping Tuesday night's game. I guess we'll see how Monday's practice goes."

She nodded. "That would be great."

"Fuck yeah." He sighed. "I feel like I'm ready."

"Then you probably are. You're the best judge, right?"

He grimaced. "I don't know. They keep telling me not to push it too fast. It's possible I'm a little impatient."

"No!"

He slanted her a crooked smile.

"Hockey players are crazy," she said. "You think you're so tough. Didn't you play with a broken finger once?"

"Yeah." He shrugged. "It was taped up. It was the playoffs."

"And I seem to remember once you were playing with a cut on your head that was gushing blood and needed stitches."

"They put a butterfly tape on it and it was fine until the game was over."

She eyed the small scar just above his right eyebrow. "My brother played with a broken bone in his foot," she shared. "Idiot."

He laughed.

They sat a while longer, chatting about nothing much, admiring the vast blue view in front of them, sunlight glinting off waves, foamy whitecaps crawling onto shore. Eventually, Honey said, "We should probably get moving or I might never be able to get up off this bench."

"You got it."

When she stood it wasn't as bad as she'd expected. They climbed back onto their bikes and fastened their helmets and cycled back toward Santa Monica, experiencing the earlier ride in reverse. The sun was lower now as they approached the sphere of the Ferris wheel at the pier.

When they'd returned the bikes, Matt started guiding her in the opposite direction of the parking lot. "Where are we going?" she asked.

"To buy you a swimsuit."

"Oh my god. Really?"

"Yeah. Really. It'll be good for you after all the riding. I'm also really good at massage."

The idea of his big hands on her naked body massaging her made her belly swoop. "I don't know, Matt…I should go home…"

Her protest was half-hearted and he knew it.

"We'll go back to my place and order in some dinner," he

said. "Keep it low-key, right? A little time in the hot tub, a glass of wine, maybe some seafood…sounds pretty good to me."

It sounded frackin' awesome.

But also frackin' dangerous.

CHAPTER 9

Matt was ninety-nine percent sure there was a little shop across the street that sold souvenirs and beach crap, hopefully including miniscule bikinis. Now he had that idea in his head —Honey in the hot tub mostly naked, all mellow and warm— he was determined to make it happen. But as they passed by a liquor store, he stopped and made a sharp turn. "Wine," he muttered to her. "Unless you want to drink beer."

"I hate beer."

"I know."

He did know. It was weird, that he knew things about her. Despite all the years that had passed. He knew she hated beer and cucumbers and the smell of bananas. She loved shrimp and Kahlua and any kind of cake but especially chocolate. Her favorite color was pink and she hated plastic purses and wedge shoes.

She chose a bottle of wine and he paid for it over her protests. Christ. He had more money than he knew what to do with, he could afford a fucking twenty-dollar bottle of wine. Then he led the way to the next shop where they found a selection of bikinis. Since he knew she liked pink, his eyes went right away to a pink suit on a hanger. *Please let it be her size.* Except he had no clue what size she was. His gaze moved back to her as he held it up, then he squinted at it.

She laughed and grabbed it from him. "I am not size eighteen."

"I thought it looked a little big," he mumbled.

"I do like the color, though." She shook her head, muttering, "I can't believe we're doing this," as she rifled through the rack. Finally she pulled out another one, a pink and yellow print. "I suppose I should try it on."

They moved to the back of the store where there were a couple of small change rooms and she disappeared behind a curtain. Matt leaned against the wall, holding the bottle of wine in the paper bag, imagining her getting naked only a few feet away.

Finally the curtain drew back and he straightened, ready to see her in the bikini. But she was dressed. He frowned. "Didn't it fit?"

"It fit fine."

"You didn't show me."

"No, I didn't."

"I wanted to see it."

She lowered her chin again and gave him that look, that Honey look that was sweet and sexy and a little snarky. "Apparently you'll get to see it soon enough."

She turned and headed to the front counter and he stalked after her so he could pay for the suit too. Also against her protests.

"Jesus," he said. "I can afford it. It's not like back when we were kids."

Eight years ago, he'd been a poor college student, living off his parents and a hockey scholarship, and she'd been the spoiled daughter of a Los Angeles billionaire hockey player-slash-businessman. She'd thrown money around like it reproduced overnight in her wallet and he'd been uncomfortable with it.

After the tussle over who was paying for the bikini, they left that store and returned to his car in the parking lot, then drove to his apartment building. He entered the underground parking with his swipe card and found a spot near the elevator.

"Nice building," she said inside the elevator, which *was* pretty nice, he supposed, all granite, stainless steel and glass.

"It's okay. Feels too much like a hotel for me, but it's something."

They rode to the fifteenth floor and he led the way to his apartment.

Again, funny how things had changed. Earlier when he'd picked her up, he'd been taken aback by where she lived. A small four-story building that was basic and that was putting it nicely. A small one-bedroom apartment, attractive and comfortable but a far cry from the luxury she'd grown up with. He'd been invited to her parents' place where she lived back then only once, but at the age of twenty his exposure to that kind of wealth had been limited. Even though his brothers had all had lucrative contracts at that time, none of them lived like that.

Now here he was in a pricey high-rise apartment while she lived modestly. He got the feeling she didn't have a lot of cash and that too made him curious.

He watched her look around then stroll over to the big windows that looked out toward the ocean and the sunset.

"This is one of my favorite times of day," he said, dumping the bottle of wine and the bag with the bikini onto the bar that separated kitchen from living room. "Sunset."

"It's amazing."

The sun was low to the horizon, a bright golden ball, tinting the clouds and sky peach and purple and pink.

Usually he loved to look at it, but tonight he looked at Honey, watching her profile as she gazed out the windows. Her nose was small and straight, and long eyelashes fluttered when she blinked. She had her sunglasses on top of her head, holding back her long straight hair, which was tousled into messy strands from their bike ride.

His gaze wandered down over her throat and chest, lingering on her breasts outlined by the snug black hoodie she wore half-zipped, the T-shirt beneath looking well-washed and soft. He wanted to touch it. He wanted to feel the soft curves beneath it. He wanted her underneath him.

Fuck. He closed his hands into brief fists. "I should order dinner. What would you like? We have a concierge service here and they'll get meals delivered from a bunch of places. We can get pretty much anything you like. Except sushi."

"Why not sushi?"

"Because I hate sushi." He grinned.

"Ah. Okay." She smiled. "It doesn't matter to me."

"Shrimp?"

Her smile went crooked. "Yeah. I like shrimp."

"I know."

Her eyes shifted away from his and he pulled out his cell phone and moved away from her to place the order. When he finished, he said, "I'll open the wine. Have a seat."

He dug around in a drawer for a rarely used corkscrew, opened the wine and poured some into a glass for Honey, then found a beer in his fridge for himself. He returned to the living room to find her sitting on his brown leather couch, still gazing out the windows. The colors of the sky had deepened even in that short a time, lights flickering out on the ocean in the lowering dusk.

"Dinner will be about an hour." He sat beside her.

"This apartment is awesome." She took the wine he handed her. "And huge."

"Yeah. Three bedrooms, which I don't really need." He shrugged. "I'd like to have a house eventually. You're just never sure how long you're going to be in one place."

"How long did you sign for?"

"Three years. One year no-trade clause. It wasn't the greatest, but I was happy with the money and the chance to play here. I just haven't had a chance to prove myself yet."

"You will."

"I sure the fuck hope so." He changed the subject and they chatted easily about the things they'd seen on the bike ride until their food arrived.

She rose too and helped him unpack the containers from the bag and set them on his dining table, a sleek modern style in dark wood. He retrieved cutlery and plates from the kitchen, and they spent a few minutes transferring their dinners to plates and sitting down. Just before he sat, Matt moved across to the living room to start some music on his sound system. The first song queued up was Calvin Harris's "Feel So Close".

Honey looked down at her plate. Big shrimps, scallops and chunks of either lobster or crab—maybe both— nestled in the creamy sauce and linguine. "What did you get?"

"Prime rib. Here, have a piece of garlic bread."

The food was hot and fresh and really good despite having been delivered, his beef tender and juicy.

"Once again, I'll never eat all this," she said. "Especially after that huge sandwich for lunch."

"There's dessert too," he said. "Save room."

"Oh my god."

But she was digging in and eating and making sexy little pleasure noises as she did so, which made him think, of course, of sex, and sex with Honey, and the noises she'd make with him inside her...Jesus. He was getting hard. He gave his head a shake.

When they finished, he leaned back in his chair. "Dessert now? Or the hot tub?"

She too, leaned back and laid her hands on her belly as if she was fat, which she was far from. "I don't think I want to put that bikini on after eating all that."

He snorted. "Oh please. Come on. We'll have dessert afterward."

She nodded and set down her glass. "Where's your bathroom?"

He handed her the bag with the new suit in it and directed her to the main bathroom while he went into his bedroom to put on a pair of board shorts. He pulled a couple of big beach towels from the closet in the hall and was ready with one for her when she emerged.

She'd pulled her hair up with an elastic band and fastened it on top of her head in a messy knot, pieces sticking out from it and hanging around her face. He took in the halter-necked top of the suit, the cleavage of her sweet tits revealed in the V shape, then his gaze moved down over the smooth curves of her waist and hips to the tiny bows at the sides of the bikini bottom.

His dick immediately hardened. Again. Fuck. This was not good. He cleared his throat and handed her a towel. "Here," he said. "The suit, uh, fits, uh good."

She wrapped the towel around her body and tucked the end between her breasts, saying nothing.

"We can take our drinks down," he said. "Let me get a koozie for my can. And we can put your wine in a travel mug."

"Classy."

"That's me."

They lucked out and nobody else was at the pool, which was located on a terrace on the third floor. The hot tub sat silent in the corner and he headed over there to the switch that would activate the jets. They left their towels on two nearby chairs.

"This is nice here too," she said, looking around.

Palm trees and pots of flowers gave an exotic feel to the pool deck, and the furniture wasn't cheap plastic, it was nice wicker with padded seats. Small lights shone up into the palms and provided ambient lighting around the hot tub.

They stepped into the bubbling hot water and he tried not to stare at her half-naked body, he really did. Okay, he didn't try very hard, but he knew he should. Whatever. The little bottom barely covered her ass, and her legs were long and slender. He knew this. He'd had those legs wrapped around him. A long time ago.

She took her time submerging herself into the water, taking one step down into the pool, then another, then standing there with her hands clasped in front of her chest. He dropped down onto the seat that ran around the tub.

"How do your legs feel?" he asked.

"Um. Fine, at the moment. I probably won't feel it until tomorrow. I think my ass is going to be sore."

He almost groaned at her driving his attention back to her sweet little ass. The bottoms of her cheeks made his hands itch to reach out and touch. Christ.

Then she bent her legs and lowered herself slowly until the water was at her chin. She floated over to the side of the pool to sit. The side far away from him. Damn.

They talked a little as the water bubbled around them, warming and relaxing their muscles, and drank their beverages. Honey leaned back, closed her eyes, and stretched her legs to float out in front of her, which pushed her tits out of the water and made his dick even harder. He stared at her, his entire body burning hot, and not from the water. He took a big gulp of his beer.

Did she know what she was doing to him? Fuck!

"Honey," he rasped.

Her eyes fluttered open. "What?"

"If you stay like that with your tits shoved up in the air, I'm not going to be responsible for what happens next. Just sayin'."

She blinked and lowered herself back into the water with a splash. "Um. Sorry."

"Fuck." This time he muttered it aloud. "You know how hot you are."

Her lips parted and she stared at him. "Not really."

"Oh for fuck's sake. You can't be fucking serious."

"You don't need to swear that much."

"Yeah I do. I'm a hockey player."

That earned a laugh from her and he shot her a rueful grin. "Seriously, Honey. You know you're gorgeous. Give me a break. In that little bikini, you're making me feel like I've got a hockey stick in my shorts."

She choked on a laugh. "A hockey stick! Come on, dude, even you aren't that big."

He had to smile. Dammit.

Then she swiped her tongue over her bottom lip, and if she didn't look so confused he would have been certain she was being deliberately seductive. Most girls he knew would be. But he had a feeling she was genuinely puzzled.

"Honey. You're not an innocent girl," he reminded her. "You know what you do to guys."

Her head gave a little jerk. "Maybe once, a long time ago. Not anymore."

"Oh Christ. You can't be that dumb."

Her eyebrows jerked together. "Well, thanks a lot."

This was another thing girls did —pretended they didn't know how fucking hot and sexy they were. They tried to get guys to notice them and make them all hot for them, then pretended innocence and modesty.

She sighed. "It's true, Matt. I know I used to run around in skimpy clothes—"

"Or no clothes," he reminded her, which then made him want to punch himself, because that was uncalled for.

She swallowed. "Or no clothes. I did the hair and makeup thing, got breast implants, all trying to be as sexy and attractive as I could."

His head jerked back at the mention of implants. Holy shit. When had that happened?

"Because it drove my parents nuts," she continued. "And yeah, I attracted attention from guys. But when I went away to college, I stopped getting hair extensions, stopped with all the makeup and the mani/pedis, started wearing jeans and sweatshirts. And guys stopped looking at me."

"Bullshit." That was whacked.

"Well, they might've looked, but nobody ever asked me out." Her voice took on a slight edge.

"Are you telling me you haven't dated...at all...or anything, for...how long?"

"Let's just say it's been a while." She gave him a faint scowl.

"Well hell." He sat there and stared at her across the steamy pool.

"It's fine," she said. "Not a big deal. I've been too busy for hooking up or dating. And if anything, it made me realize how shallow and stupid most guys are, if they're only interested in half-dressed girls with big boobs and bleached hair."

"Not all guys are like that. Most guys aren't like that." He paused. Actually he wasn't a hundred per cent sure of that. Some of his team mates definitely fit that description. "Ninety percent of guys aren't like that." Also, her boobs weren't big. They were nice. Really nice. But considering she'd had implants, they weren't huge.

She laughed and lifted a hand let water trickle through it. "If you say so. I guess I've met the other ten percent."

"Honey. Come here."

She met his eyes and went still. "No."

"Yes."

"No."

"*I'm* not like that," he said softly. "Because I fucking wanted you since the minute you walked into that boardroom, dressed in your little suit with your hair pulled back. Even though I was pissed as hell to see you again."

Her eyes widened. "You were pissed?"

"Hell yeah. Weren't you?"

"Um. Well, not pissed exactly. I was surprised. Embarrassed."

"Why embarrassed?"

"Because...you know why," she whispered. "Because...oh never mind."

"No. Why? And get your ass over here. I'm tired of shouting this conversation across the hot tub."

For a moment she held his gaze then slowly she eased her way through the water toward him. He dropped his nearly empty beer onto the cement deck next to him and reached for her. His hand slid on her skin, finding her waist as she got closer and he pulled her more forcefully toward him, onto his lap. He shifted her legs to the side and one of her arms made its way around his neck.

"Matt..."

"Why were you embarrassed?"

She bent her head. "I don't want to talk about it."

He lifted her chin. "Tell me."

Once again, their eyes met and held and once again, something hot expanded inside him.

"Because of the things I've done," she whispered. "You and I...we were together...I know it was a long time ago, and

I know I was pissed at you when you went to my dad behind my back, but I wanted…I didn't want…" She exhaled sharply in apparent frustration. "At the time I was acting like that, I wanted attention. From anyone. Even negative attention was better than no attention. I was pissed at you and that made me act out even more. At the time, I wanted you to see that. I wanted you to know how much fun I was having without you."

"Fuck *me*," he whispered. His heart constricted and his hands tightened on her hips.

"But now…it's just embarrassing."She paused. "Why were *you* pissed?"

Damn. He had to think about that. "Because I wanted you. But I didn't want to want you. Does that make any fucking sense at all?"

She sucked briefly on her bottom lip. "Yeah. I think I feel the same."

"Great." Okay, she wanted him too. Good. That was good. Neither of them was happy about that. But what the hell. They'd gone this far…might as well keep going.

"I think I need to get out," she said, her voice a tiny bit slurred.

"Enough heat?"

"Yeah. I think so."

"Okay. We can go back up and have dessert now."

She started to shift off his lap.

"But first I want your mouth."

She stilled again. "What?"

"Your mouth. I want your mouth, Honey." He slid a wet hand into her pulled-up, damp hair and brought her face to his. He tipped his head right, she did the same, and their mouths met in a long, clinging kiss.

Fuck yeah.

He moved his mouth on hers, opening wider, and she

responded. He slid his tongue inside, found hers, warm and wet. She made a soft little sound in her throat that went straight to his dick. He kissed her again, and again, hot, wet kisses, until the fire burning in his groin had spread all the way through his body and his control started to fray.

"I'm surprised the water in this pool isn't boiling," he muttered, setting his forehead against hers, still holding her head.

She panted against him, her body soft and lax. "It's hot enough," she said. "I'm cooked."

He gave a low laugh. "Yeah. Time to get out."

He eased her off his lap and stood, then climbed out first and held out a hand for her. "Come on. Let's go eat…dessert."

CHAPTER 10

Honey wasn't sure if she could walk. Luckily Matt was there to guide her into the elevator and back up to his apartment.

She had a feeling that it was mostly Matt's kisses that had her head whirling. And the things he'd said. The things they'd shared. This was freaky deaky. He made a whole bunch of weird feelings twist up inside her. Attraction. Affection. Lust. Gratitude.

In his living room, she collapsed onto the couch, the towel wrapped around her. "Good thing it's leather," she mumbled.

"Yeah. You okay, Honey?"

"Oh yeah. Just nice and relaxed."

"You want to change before we eat?"

"I don't think I can move." She was sitting there in a wet bathing suit and damp towel, but she was so warm and lethargic she really didn't care.

"Fine by me," he said. "I like that suit a lot."

She smiled, head resting on the cushioned back of the couch.

Matt disappeared and returned wearing a T-shirt over his board shorts. He brought her another glass of wine, this time in a real glass, and another beer for himself, along with a container and two forks.

The music was still playing, now Eminem. Huh. She lifted her head to peer at the dessert. "What is it?"

"Chocolate Kahlua cake with chocolate mousse icing."

"Oh holy mother of cake," she breathed. She loved Kahlua and she loved chocolate cake. Together…yum. He grinned and handed her a fork. Sitting beside her on the couch, he held the container as they both forked up mouthfuls.

"So good," she moaned.

"Fuck," he muttered, sounding as if he was in pain. She realized how she might have sounded.

Matt was right. She wasn't innocent. On the other hand, she hadn't been with a guy on a date or even flirted with a guy for a long time.

"I should go change," she murmured when they'd finished. The towel had fallen down around her waist.

"Cold?"

"Mmm…no…but I'm wet…"

"Wanna make you wetter," he murmured, his face moving closer. His hand slid around her neck.

And her stomach did a slow, happy roll.

His mouth brushed over hers. Her breasts swelled and her nipples tingled while heat curled low in her belly. What he did to her…it could be because, as she'd said earlier, it had euphemistically "been a while". Probably that was why she was so turned on by him.

Right.

She was so attracted to him it almost hurt. It wasn't just because she hadn't had sex in over a year. It was just…him. Matt.

She opened her mouth for him and kissed him back. Her head spun a little again, and sure enough, heat flooded through her veins as his tongue licked into her mouth. A moan climbed up her throat.

"Maybe the bedroom would be better for this," he whispered against her lips. "Come on."

He rose and drew her up and then to her shock he bent and slid an arm under her knees and picked her up. She grabbed onto him and emitted a little gasp but he was already striding down the hall toward the bedrooms.

Somewhere in the back of her mind she questioned her sanity at doing this. But it was only a whisper, a vague thought that spun away when he set her on the floor. "Get on the bed, babe."

She'd lost the towel, somewhere. She climbed on and sat there, butt on her calves, hands on her thighs, watching as he reached behind and pulled his T-shirt forward and off over his head. Her lips parted as she once again took in his nearly naked body. Earlier, in the hot tub, she'd been struck dumb by how gorgeous he was. He was big. She knew that. He'd talked about his struggles to keep weight on, but wow, he'd been pretty damn successful. His shoulders were bigger and more muscled than they'd been at nineteen. The muscles in his arms bulged as he pulled his shirt off, revealing a powerful chest and abs that were totally ripped.

Holy crapping crap.

Then he climbed onto the bed, surprising her by moving behind her, also kneeling. His fingers at the ties of the halter top loosened it, but he didn't remove it. All the while he was kissing the side of her neck and the top of her shoulder with hot, open-mouthed kisses. Her eyes drifted closed and still she floated. She lifted her hands from where they rested on her knees and held the triangles of fabric to her aching breasts as he kissed her shoulder, then nuzzled her ear. Her body tingled everywhere, especially between her legs.

His hands curved around her upper arms, then stroked up

and down. More sensation shimmered over her, more heat built low down inside her. Then one of his hands released her arm, slipping between it and her body, skimming over her stomach and down to her bikini bottom.

Her neck became too weak to support her heavy head and she let it fall back against him. And his fingers slipped lower still, inside the fabric, over the small patch of curls there. He brushed the curls with his fingertips and, so sensitive there, a hard shudder worked through her. Then his fingers pressed in, right on her public bone where she was even more sensitive, and her back arched as a gasp left her lips.

Her breathing became a series of gasps and pants as his hand slid lower, right down into the heat of her.

"Oh god," she whispered. "Oh my god."

"Sweet Honey." He kissed her shoulder. "So wet and hot. Just like I wanted you."

She made an inarticulate sound of agreement. His fingers slid through liquid, back and forth, then found her clit and circled it, over and over and over until her body was buzzing and her hips moving. Then he withdrew his hand.

She gave a soft cry. "Wha—?"

Matt shifted and pushed her down onto her back in the pillows then moved over her. He bent his head and again kissed and sucked gently on the side of her neck. His hand slid up over her ribs to her breast and gently cupped it, then squeezed it, through the fabric of her bathing suit top. God that felt good, her breasts aching to be touched.

"Nice," he murmured. "You feel so good, Honey. Such sweet tits. Lemme see them."

And he drew down the undone ties and lowered the top, revealing her bare breasts to him.

The room was semi-dark. The sun had long since set, but enough light came down the hall from them to see each other in shadow. She watched him look at her breasts, his expression burning hot.

"Beautiful," he whispered.

She resisted the impulse to tell him they weren't real. Because why did she keep doing that, putting herself down? As a teenager, all her friends had been getting implants. Her mom had implants. It was the thing to do. He'd never even realized she had implants back when they'd first been together. He liked what he saw, he saw *her*, and that made her happy.

She rolled her bent knees to the side, the side away from him, still flat on her back, and he continued to kiss her collarbone, her shoulder, her ear, while fondling her breasts. He caressed one, then the other, then shifted his head lower to — oh god! — take one nipple into his mouth. She cried out again at the pleasure that streamed through her, all the way to her aching pussy. He drew a nipple into his mouth and suckled gently, moved to the other and did the same.

Honey's mind began to whirl away again.

Matt lifted her top leg and tossed it aside, moving between her now spread thighs. He grabbed her hands and pressed them to the mattress up near her shoulders, holding her down. For a moment, she went still, gazing up at him, her blood rushing hotly through her veins, but when their eyes met, fear was replaced by excitement. He lowered his head and kissed her again, and again, long, slow and deep.

Another moan climbed her throat, her entire body burning with need. Her pussy clenched and she could feel the wetness there between her legs as he devoured her mouth, rubbed her tongue with his and gently nipped at her bottom lip.

He released one of her hands so he could touch her breast again, plumping it, shifting down to suck on the nipple. She cried out as he pulled the tender tip between his lips, and heat rushed through her body. "Feels good," she whispered, head tossing on the pillow. "So good."

He moved from that nipple to the other, supporting himself on his knees and one arm, suckling and nibbling on sensitive flesh until she was dazed and delirious. Then he paused above her to trail the backs of his fingers lightly across one nipple, watching it. Her breasts tightened and ached. Her head went back, mouth open, panting, watching his face as he watched his fingertips trace over her nipples, back and forth, the pads of fingers then the backs of fingers. His eyes were dark and heavy-lidded, his mouth wet and beautiful, his expression searingly erotic.

He did the same to the other breast. Shivers cascaded over her entire body, tingles running up and down her spine, liquid heat building between her thighs. Her clit pulsed with an insistent ache. Moving helplessly on the bed, she licked her lips and her eyes drifted closed. Then his fingertips slid up over her chest, her throat, to her mouth. One fingertip touched her bottom lip and she opened her eyes to look at him. Their eyes met in a collision of sparks. Watching her with hot focus, he placed his hand over her mouth, palm flat, holding it there so gently, and she groaned. Slowly he brushed the pads of fingers over her bottom lip.

Holy hell and shit fire, this was unbelievably hot and sexy. She was dying with need for him, her entire body throbbing.

"Matt…"

"Yeah, baby?"

"You're making me crazy."

"Yeah?"

"Um…yeah."

"Good."

Still he watched his fingers play with her mouth, his index finger touching her bottom lip then slipping into her mouth. She lifted her head seekingly then dropped it back to the pillow as he brushed his fingertips up and down over her lips. He once more bent his head to take a nipple into his mouth, drawing hard on it, and sensation shot through her, her body shivering with tortured need. Her hips moved restlessly, knees bent, Matt kneeling between them. His finger touched her bottom lip, pulling it down gently, again and again, and then his thumb slid into her mouth. She closed her lips around it and sucked, and he lifted his head. Their eyes met with blistering heat. Sucking him, even his finger, felt so good, but made her want so much more. She whimpered.

He slid his thumb out of her mouth, trailed his index finger down over her lip, her chin, her throat, then down the middle of her chest. He reached for the bikini bottom and she lifted her hips to help, pushing her feet into the bed. His hand rubbed up over her abdomen, between her breasts, over each breast, squeezing briefly, then played with her nipples.

Noises were coming from deep inside her, soft noises—gasps, pants, cries. She couldn't stop them as he played with her pussy with tormenting slowness, rubbing his fingertips over her folds, dipping inside, rubbing slick moisture around. One hand circled around her hip to brush her clit from above while he slowly pushed the long finger of his other hand into her vagina.

"God," she whispered. "More, Matt, please. More…"

His fingers circled her clit as he pumped two fingers in and out of her with the other hand. Once more she lifted her head to study his face, the intent, heated expression making her heart contract. With her arms above her head on the pillow, she gasped, "Yeah, oh yeah…*yeah*."

"So pretty," he murmured. Her hips lifted into his touch. "Sweet, Honey."

She closed her eyes, tingling starting to radiate from a spot deep inside her, warm and lovely. God, she was going to come.

"Wanna taste you," he muttered, and then his touch was gone as he shifted lower on the bed. Damn! Her body protested losing the sensation when she'd been sliding toward climax. But then his mouth was on her and, holy flying fuck, it was even better, warm and wet, his tongue licking her, his lips pulling her flesh into his mouth and gently sucking, his beard stubble abrading her with delicious friction.

She managed to move her heavy arms and thread her fingers into his thick hair. He again slid one arm around her hip and rested his hand flat on her lower belly where she ached. His other hand held the back of her thigh while he ate deeply at her. The onslaught of pleasure was almost unendurable and her fingers tightened in his hair. Every nerve ending in her body jumped, and that tingling started to circle again, low down inside her, ripples beginning in her pelvis, spreading through her body, making her arms and legs even weaker.

"God, Matt!" Her chin went up, her eyes squeezed shut and exquisite pleasure tore through her as sensation built to a sharp peak. And she made more unintelligible sounds, orgasmic sounds that she couldn't stop.

His mouth kept at her, drawing her orgasm out almost unbearably, until she was limp and quivering, her hands falling to the bed beside her. He gave her one last long, slow lick, a closed-mouth kiss to her pulsing clit and then he moved up over her to kiss her mouth.

She tasted herself, and that was hot. When his tongue slid into her mouth, she licked it back, and moaned.

"You taste amazing, Honey," he said. "Love licking you. Love making you come in my mouth like that."

She couldn't speak, could barely move her head in agreement. She wanted him inside her, wanted to make him feel as good as she did. Matt moved beside her, stretching out and pulling her to his side, arms around her. She snuggled into his warmth, vaguely noticing he still wore his board shorts, the tech fabric long since dry. So good. So very, very good…

Honey struggled to open her eyes, emerging from sleep. She spent a few minutes figuring out where she was, so comfortable and warm in a big bed…with a big warm body pressed up against her back…

Her eyes flew wide. Holy crapping crap!

Once again she searched through her memories…Matt. She was in bed with Matt.

Holy bajesus!

She'd fucking slept with Matt!

She sorted through more memories and came up empty. Other than him going down on her and a spectacular orgasm.

But actual sex? Um…she had nothing.

"You awake, babe?" Matt murmured behind her.

She blinked. She could fake being asleep. She could get up and run. Maybe to Canada… "Yeah," she whispered.

"Me too." His arm around her tightened across her abdomen.

Her mind zoomed around for what to say, what to do.

Last night…she tried to go back in time…remembered dinner…the hot tub…the unbelievable foreplay and oral sex on the bed, and then…nothing.

"I fell asleep," she whispered.

His arm tightened. "Yeah, babe. It's okay."

She closed her eyes. God! She'd freakin' passed out!

What made that knife twist deeper into her was the fact that it wasn't the first time that had happened. "I didn't drink that much."

He nuzzled her hair and caressed her belly. "I know. I was

pouring the drinks. Although…who knows how much Kahlua was in that cake."

He was trying to joke around, but this was horrifying.

"Relax, Hon," he murmured in her ear. "You only had a few glasses of wine. I think everything else snuck up on you…all that exercise…"

Yeah…

"The fresh air. The dinner. The wine. The hot tub."

Yes, yes, yes.

"The orgasm."

Her eyes popped wide open again.

Oh yeah. That.

"I'm sorry," she managed to say through tight lips. "I…I mean, thank you, but…"

His body shook behind her. He was laughing! He kissed her neck then sucked gently on her ear lobe. She gave a full-body shiver. "It's okay," he said. "We'll talk about what you owe me later." She stiffened and he gave a low laugh, this time audible. "Kidding, babe."

She twisted in his arms to face him. "No you're not."

"Well. Sort of." His eyes searched hers. "You okay?"

"Yeah. No. I mean, I'm a little, um…freaked out."

His eyes warmed. "Yeah?"

She closed her own eyes briefly. "I need to brush my teeth."

His lips twitched. "Okay. I think I have an extra toothbrush somewhere."

She rolled away from him and he followed her out of bed. They were both completely naked. Awareness of that made her skin tingle. He walked over to an attached bathroom and flicked on a light.

She stared at his body from behind. Holy hell and shit fire, he was built. He had the muscular ass of a hockey player all right, and truly massive thighs. And she knew the front view was just as…er…massive. Her pussy quivered.

"Here you go," he said, handing her a cellophane package. She fought to keep her gaze averted from his big naked body as she took it. He gave his own teeth a quick brush as she unwrapped the new package, focusing carefully on it. Then he left her alone to use the bathroom and she had to pause to get her breath. Whoa.

When she was done cleaning her teeth and dragging a brush she'd found through her atrocious hair, she paused with her hands gripping the vanity counter. Now she had to walk back out there and…and… She licked her lips.

Running to Canada again seemed like a good idea. On the other hand she did kind of owe him. But the real truth was… regardless of any perceived debt, she wanted to go out there and jump him and lick him all over. All righty then.

CHAPTER 11

Matt returned to the bed, hoping he wasn't being overly optimistic that Honey was going to come back and join him there. Yeah, he was horny as a three-peckered tom cat, painfully hard, and yeah, he wanted to fuck, but he also wasn't ready for Honey to leave.

He'd been disappointed when she'd fallen asleep on him last night, but also amused. He'd done that to himself after he'd worn her out biking then got her so relaxed and mellow with food and wine and the hot tub, all it had taken was one good orgasm and she was out.

He wanted to give her more orgasms. Lots more.

He gave his throbbing dick a few strokes while he waited for her to come out of the bathroom.

When he'd realized she was out for the night, he'd ruefully climbed out of bed, returned to the living room and watched his boys play against the Caribou. When he'd gone back to bed, she hadn't even budged.

She emerged from the bathroom, beautifully naked. She had an amazing body, with long legs, slender graceful limbs, and sleek curves. He watched as she crossed the carpeted floor to the bed, picking up on her uncertainty in her measured steps. He lifted the covers in invitation.

She hesitated only a fraction of a second then slid into bed beside him. "What time is it?"

He glanced at the digital alarm clock on the nightstand on his side of the bed. "Nine-thirty."

"Ah."

"Still early. Unless you have somewhere to be on Sunday morning."

"I do need to get to church."

His chin jerked down. "Really?"

"No."

He huffed a laugh. "Okay then. We have all day."

"I'm invited to my parents for Sunday dinner. As usual." And she rolled her eyes.

"Okay. Almost all day."

He reached for her and pulled her against him, almost on top of him. "Now. Where were we again when you fell asleep…?"

She smiled. "I said I'm sorry."

He grinned back at her. "Yes you did. I'm teasing you." His hand smoothed down her spine, stopping just short of her sweet little ass, then back up all the way into her hair. He pulled her head down to his and caught her mouth. Mmm. Minty fresh. He slid his tongue into her mouth and she opened to let him in.

Blood rushed through his veins, straight to his dick. His arms banded around her and his hands moved on her skin. Smooth. Warm. Silky. Oh yeah. This was what he wanted. He shifted her so she was lying on top of him, pulled one of her thighs so she straddled him. They kissed again, lazy wet kisses that went on and on. She sighed into his mouth.

He pushed her hair back and their mouths separated but only by a breath. They stared at each other, breathing the same air, and then she moved to suck his bottom lip softly into her mouth. Flames licked over his body and a groan rumbled in his chest.

They rubbed together, skin to skin, hands touching each other everywhere they could, mouths joined, tongues sliding. Her breasts pressed against his chest felt so damn good. The kisses grew harder, faster. He nipped at her lip and the heat between them intensified, becoming scorching. His heart thudded and he felt like he was going to burst out of his skin.

"Need a condom," he mumbled and stretched his arm out to slap it around and find the package he'd left on the bedside table. Honey took it from him, ripped it open, then sank her teeth into her bottom lip as she moved off him.

His lungs seized as he watched her focus on the task, taking his cock into her soft little hands, rolling the latex down over his aching shaft. Lust pulsed in his balls. Then she moved back over him. With her eyes on his, she reached for his cock again and slowly lowered herself onto it.

He lowered his gaze to where they joined, watched his dick enter her sweet pussy with gritted teeth. "Fuck that's good," he groaned. "So hot. Tight little pussy. Christ, Honey."

He reached for her waist and held her as she moved on him, down and down until he was fully seated inside her, pulsing. His jaw ached as he tried not to come. Not yet. Dammit.

She bent over to kiss him again, stretching out on his chest. He circled one arm around her back and their mouths joined again in a hot, hungry kiss. She slid an arm beneath his neck and buried her face in the pillow beside his head as she moved on him, hips lifting up and down.

Sensation shot through him, exquisite pleasure at the slick pull of her body on him.

He slid a hand up into her hair and held her head, his other hand going down to the swell of one firm ass cheek, cupping it as it lifted and dropped again. She whimpered soft little noises near his ear.

"Okay, baby?"

"Mmmm."

Electricity sizzled through his body, tightening every muscle. He lifted his hips to meet her body, pushing up deeper inside her, making her gasp. His fingers tightened in her hair and tugged, and she gave a low moan. "Oh yeah."

"Like that?" he whispered.

"Uh-huh…"

Good to know. He liked it too, and he gave another pull. Her breath hitched and her pussy squeezed him. *Fuck.*

Then he released her hair and gripped both her ass cheeks to help her move on him, pulling on the resilient flesh as she lifted, quickening the pace. He slipped one hand between her cheeks, his middle finger brushing over her anus, and she gave another sharp inhalation. Her face turned into his neck, her lips finding his skin.

"Okay?" he murmured. She nodded against him then pushed up onto one arm. Making eye contact, he buried his hand deeper in her crease, rubbing over her anus with more deliberation. Her eyes blazed and her lips parted as she stared down at him. "That's fucking hot."

She gave a slow nod, still moving on him, his fingers still playing with her ass. "God yes."

"Christ, you feel good," he muttered. "Riding me like that. Fuck me, Honey."

Her tongue touched his skin with what felt like a sizzle.

The hand she had beneath his neck found his shoulder and her fingers dug in. He reached down lower and pulled his dick out of her pussy, tapped her ass with it, then slid it wetly up and down the crease of her ass, over her anus. He guided himself back inside her then used that slickness on her cheeks to play more there, circling and teasing.

She pushed up to sitting and his hands moved over her waist, her rib cage, both breasts. Their eyes locked on each other. He filled his palms with pliant flesh, her nipples hard. She covered his hands with hers, helping him massage her breasts, still lifting and lowering on his cock. Then her hands slid over his wrists and stroked up and down his arms, making his skin prickle all over his body.

"So beautiful," he whispered. Her hair was a golden tangle around her head, her cheeks and jaw pink from rubbing against his stubble, and her mouth swollen and pouty. He'd never seen anything so sexy in his life.

His hands moved from her breasts to her waist then back again, unable to resist gently squeezing those sweet tits. Then he contracted his abs to roll himself up to sitting. His slid his arms around her waist and bent his head to taste one of those nipples.

Fuck yeah. He closed his lips around the nub and drew it into his mouth, eyes falling closed. One of her hands landed on his shoulder, the other slid up his back as she made more soft, sexy noises of pleasure. Her back arched. One hand on her back, holding her, the other back in the crease of her ass, he spent long, delicious moments sucking her nipples, moving back and forth between them.

"That's so good, Matt," she whispered, her hands stroking over his shoulders, his back, his hair.

"Yeah. Fuck yeah." He rubbed his face against one soft curve, kissed her between her breasts then rolled down to his back. His cock slid out of her and he eased her to her side next to him, lifting her thigh over his hip then entering her again. Once again, he slid his fingers through the crease of her ass over her anus. Her face against his shoulder, her arms around him, her knee bent and up at his waist, she petted his back as he caressed her ass, all while sliding in and out of her tight wet pussy.

This time, he let his middle finger penetrate her opening there.

Her body spasmed in his arms and she gave a soft cry.

"Okay?"

She gave a jerky nod. The sexy noises she made conveyed her high excitement as they fucked each other, harder, faster. Flames burned in his balls and the base of his spine ached. He kissed her shoulder and then her breath came faster, her body tightened against him and with a long, hard shudder, her pussy rippled around him and she gave a soft wail.

"Oh yeah," he groaned. "Love that. Fuck yeah, Honey."

And then it overcame him, rolled over him, slamming him with unbearable pleasure. His vision darkened, his arms convulsed around Honey as wave after wave of ecstasy rocked through him.

"Holy fuck," he croaked, moments later. "Holy effing fuck."

He felt her smile and he gathered his energy to roll her to her back. He kissed her mouth, hard.

"That was outstanding," he pronounced.

She gave a soft laugh. "I agree."

"Be right back."

He quickly got rid of the condom and washed his hands then slid back into bed, tucked her in against him, both of them arranging themselves to fit together. He pulled the comforter up over them. The room was still dim, the blinds on the window keeping out most of the morning sunshine.

"Need more sleep," he mumbled into her hair.

"Mmm. Maybe me too."

He awoke a while later and had to glance at the alarm clock to see they'd slept a few more hours and it was now past noon. Sweet.

She stirred in his arms, waking too. "Wow," she murmured. "I did go back to sleep."

"Nice, huh?"

She gave him a shy little smile that tickled him inside. He stroked her shoulder. "Tell me more, Honey," he murmured.

"More about what?" Her brow creased.

"About how you ended going to Berkeley. How you ended up going into social welfare. Back when we met, I never would have thought that's what you'd end up doing."

"Ha. Me neither. I didn't have much choice."

"You didn't want to go to college?"

She buried her face against him. "I did and I didn't. Basically, my parents gave me two choices. Either, they were kicking me out of the house and cutting off my allowance, and I could find a job and an apartment and support myself—or they'd pay for me to go to college."

"I guess I can figure out why they did that. I know your dad wasn't too happy about the things you were doing, and that was before…"

"Go ahead. Say it. Before I really went crazy."

His jaw tightened. "That wasn't what I was going to say." But the truth was, he wasn't sure what he was going to say, what words he was going to choose to describe the way she'd lived her life years after they'd been together. He didn't want to imply that she'd been mentally unstable, although he'd wondered about that a few times. He didn't want to judge her, though, without knowing more. One thing he'd learned was that there was always more to things than was on the surface. And Honey was complicated. Last night she'd said that even negative attention was better than no attention…he wanted to know what she'd mean by that.

"Whatever. I was out of control and it was only getting worse. They figured they needed to put a stop to it, and they tried the tough-love approach."

"Ugh. So you chose college."

"No. Actually at first I didn't." She still kept her face

hidden. "Of course I didn't have any intention of getting a job, either. I figured I had friends who'd let me live with them and I'd just keep partying. And they did let me live with them. For a while. But I had no money and they got tired of me mooching off them all the time. In fact, they got tired of it pretty quick. Turned out a lot of them liked the fact that I had lots of money. When I couldn't pick up the tab at clubs or pay for limos to drive us around, or…supply them…other things… they weren't that interested in me. I moved from one friend's house to another, and then another. And then…" She moved her face against him. "I didn't have anywhere left to go."

Fuck. His chest ached. "Honey."

"I spent one night partying all night—I went home with a stranger because I had nowhere else to go."

Now his guts twisted.

"He was a little…off. I was scared. In the morning, I hated myself," she whispered. "I sat in my car on Sunset Boulevard sorting through options. I was terrified. Lost. Alone."

His arms tightened around her and he closed his eyes, hurting inside.

"I'd been pissed at my parents for months for putting me in that position, for not caring enough about me. And I was super extremely pissed that I felt so trapped and backed into a corner that I had to do what they wanted and go to college. But I just couldn't see myself living in my car, getting guys to buy me drinks every night and going home with them because I had nowhere else to go. I saw a hooker on Sunset, looking so defeated and worn out and sad and I started crying because I felt like that was me. That was where I was going next. And that wasn't how I wanted my life to be."

Matt's eyes stung and he squeezed them tighter closed. "Honey."

"Do you hate me now?" she asked.

"Fuck no!" He jerked back, and with his hands on her shoulders he moved her away from him and stared into her eyes. "Jesus Christ, no, I don't hate you." He slowly shook his head. "Look at you, Honey. Look at what you accomplished. Hearing that, knowing what you've done, just impresses the hell out of me."

She stared at him with those beautiful brown eyes, close enough that he could see the flecks of gold in them. "Really?" she whispered. "'Cause if you did, I'd understand." She lifted one bare shoulder.

"Christ." He pulled her against him again, tipping his head back, closing his eyes. "No." He swallowed. "So you went to college."

"Yeah. They paid for it. Got me a little apartment. I was still angry about it, so I was determined that I wasn't going to take much from them. Just what I absolutely had to. So my apartment was just off campus and it was tiny. I was so scared of what my life was turning into, I buried myself in my school work. I didn't make a lot of friends, or socialize much. I took extra classes, went to school through the summers so I could finish as fast as possible and be done with owing my parents. Then when I graduated Dad got me this job. At first I was going to tell him to shove it, but then I decided that was stupid. I was scared again, thinking back to that morning in my car, thinking about my choices of either sleeping in my car at the beach or going home with strangers, and I figured taking the job was one last thing I would let him do for me and that was it. Too bad the job didn't turn out to be what I'd hoped."

"What does that mean?" He shifted again and tipped her face up to look at him. "What's wrong with the job? I thought it was going well."

"It's going okay, but it was clear when I started they only hired me because they had to."

"Yeah, I got that from the comments in that meeting that day."

"It was true. I knew it. Everyone knew it. But I naively thought I'd just get past that once I got into the work. But they didn't really expect me to do anything. They were coming up with make-work projects just to keep me out of their hair. I was so disappointed. I really wanted to contribute."

"You are contributing. We've been working on stuff…"

"Yeah. But I'm basically doing it on my own. Dulcie did help me learn some things, but now she's gone." Then she gave him one of her smiles, a bright, beaming smile that showed perfect straight white teeth, the smile just like her model mother's, but it didn't reach her eyes. "So I'm winging it, but it'll all be good."

He stared at her. He felt like he'd been whacked in the chest. He wasn't sure what to do with everything he'd just heard. Something big and almost painful rose up inside him, some emotion he wasn't even sure he could name. All he did know was, he wanted to punch something or someone on her behalf, he wanted to protect her from the world and all the stupid fucking people in it. He wanted her.

"What's your relationship with your folks like now?" he asked. "Are they proud of you for what you did?"

She laughed. "No. I don't know what they are. They don't really pay much attention to me, as long as I'm staying out of trouble and out of the limelight. At one time in my life that would have been enough to make me go skinny dipping in a pool with a bunch of guys knowing there were cameras there and my picture was going to be all over the internet the next day, so my parents would be all pissed off and yelling at me… but now…" She shrugged. "It is what it is. I'm doing what they wanted, but I'm not doing it for them. I'm doing it for me."

Fucking amazing. He didn't even know what to say. Had no words.

All he could do was show her. So he rolled her to her back, moved over her and kissed her.

CHAPTER 12

Honey was only too glad to switch from talking about her fucked-up past to, well, fucking. Because sex with Matt was off the charts hot, steamy enough to take both their minds off the stupid shit she'd shared when she was all softened up by Matt and his focused attention and damn sweet charm.

So they spent the afternoon mostly in bed, Matt heading to his kitchen at one point to make them fried egg sandwiches and orange juice, which they ate and drank in bed. But eventually all good things had to come to an end, and she was expected to show up at her parents' home for Sunday dinner as usual.

For a moment, when she was dressed in her jeans and T-shirt and hoodie from yesterday, and they were leaving his apartment so he could drive her home, she had the wacko idea of inviting him to come with her. She felt a really weird reluctance to leave him. But that was a truly fucked-up idea, so she kept her mouth shut as he drove her home, walked her to her apartment door and paused there.

Like he was waiting for something.

Still she kept her mouth shut, other than to smile and go

up on her toes to give him a quick kiss on his mouth. "Thanks," she said, with determined cheer. "For the bike ride and the new bathing suit and all the food and…" She winked. "All the orgasms."

The corners of his mouth lifted into what looked like a half-hearted smile. "You're welcome. Any time."

Was he expecting more? She had no idea what. But she did know better than to expect anything from anyone, including Matt after a hot and sexy weekend together. They had physical chemistry, no doubt about that, and exploring it had been fun, but that was all it was and she had no illusions or expectations of anything more.

"I'll talk to you next week," she said. "We're going to visit the kids at Franklin Middle School."

"Yeah. Great." He still didn't move for a moment, studying her face. She kept her smile in place until finally he nodded. "Okay. See you later."

Then he was gone and she was alone in her little apartment.

Even though she'd spent a good part of the last twenty-four hours in bed, she wanted to climb into her own bed, pull the covers over her head and relive every moment she'd just spent with Matt. But that wasn't an option and she only had an hour to make herself look presentable for her parents.

Her hair had been damp from the hot tub and she'd slept on it, so it was wild and wacky. She'd washed her makeup off her face, after she'd slept in it, which was never a good look, and there were still remnants of mascara smudged beneath her eyes. She had pinkish beard burn on her face that she was going to have to disguise somehow. Holy crapsickle. She had serious work to do.

She wasn't going to beat herself up for sleeping with Matt. It had been fantastic. She liked him. They were both adults, both free, and obviously with some attraction between them. It might not have been the smartest thing to do, but no one else knew about it. The idea of sleazy news reporters finding out and splashing that all over the internet and TV made her eye twitch—she did not want that to happen to Matt. He deserved better than to get linked up with someone with her past.

So she just tried not to think about him.

But much as she tried not to, she *had* thought of him, remembering that he'd been cleared for full contact practice with the team, and Monday morning he was there in the Coliseum somewhere, doing that, and she wondered how it was going. He so badly wanted to play again and weirdly, she found herself anxious about that. Not that she cared. It didn't matter to her. But she wanted that for him. Since it was so important to him.

He didn't call or text her. She emailed him to confirm the time of their visit and arrangements to meet there.

She kept busy, though. Without Dulcie there to ask questions of, she felt even more on her own. But she was figuring things out and moving forward with her own plans, which she knew she was going to have to share with Trent at some point and hope he didn't freak out.

There were some last minute details to be worked out for the annual Sweet Affair gala, a major fundraiser that the Foundation had been organizing for the last few years, which also kept her busy. Luckily Dulcie had allowed her to help with this project, so Honey knew what was going on with it.

She spent two evenings that week with Mia when Farrah got called in to work a couple of unexpected evening shifts. Mia wanted to learn how to knit, so she started teaching her and got her working on—what else—a scarf. And when

Farrah invited her to come over for a glass of wine when she got Mia put to bed, she found herself accepting, even though she knew it wasn't a good idea to get too close to her neighbor. But it was nice to have a little company over a glass of wine.

Farrah was another person who didn't judge her—she knew who she was, but basically didn't care. She trusted Honey to look after her kid, and that meant a lot to Honey. And Honey respected Farrah for raising a good kid on her own, never complaining, just working her ass off doing her best.

Then on Friday she had to see Matt again, and when she came face to face with him at Franklin Middle School on Friday afternoon, the small explosion of heat she felt inside her was…disconcerting.

Crap, he was good-looking. There was just something about his smile, the way his eyes crinkled up, the way the corners of his mouth lifted, the way his eyes gleamed…his smile made her feel like he was giving her something special. Probably everyone felt like that when he smiled at them, though.

The kids definitely liked him, super excited and bouncing off the walls to have him there. It was enough to make her feel all warm and fuzzy. She leaned on a classroom wall, watching him interact with them, smiling.

Then somehow she got drawn into the conversation when one of the kids said something about girls not liking hockey.

She blinked. "You mean girls don't like to watch it? Or girls don't like to play it?"

The kids hooted at the idea of girls playing hockey. She straightened from the wall. "Of course girls play hockey."

Matt grinned. "Not you."

"Not me," she agreed. "But there are some great female hockey players. It's an Olympic sport, guys."

"My mom played hockey," Matt shared. "Not in the Olympics, though. Also my sister-in-law played hockey. And I've met some of those female Olympic hockey players when I played in the Olympics. So he—ahem, heck yeah, girls can play hockey."

Honey made a mental note to see if she could track down a female Olympic hockey player in the Los Angeles area who might want to visit the school. Just an idea.

"Girls can do anything," she affirmed, sending smiles toward the girls in the room.

When they were done, the principal and the Phys. Ed. teacher walked them out and they paused inside the front entrance of the school to chat, the principal expressing her thanks for the visit. Honey shared some of the work they'd be doing to fundraise and their gratitude was heartwarming.

Then she and Matt walked out and headed to the parking lot where they'd left their vehicles.

"Done for the day?" Matt asked her. "Or are you going back to the office?"

"I was going to see how we did for time." She glanced at her watch. By the time she got back, everyone else would have left. "I guess I'm done."

"Dinner?"

He stood in front of her, hands in the pockets of his expensive-looking dark jeans, a zippered black Condors sweatshirt open over a black T-shirt. Their eyes met.

"How did your practices go this week?"

He smiled. "Good. I'm playing tomorrow night."

A rush of happiness soared through her. "Oh that's fantastic! Congratulations! You must be so happy." She had to restrain herself from running to hug him.

"Yeah. Come celebrate with me."

"That was your reason for us going out last weekend," she reminded him.

"I'm doing a lot of celebrating lately."

How could she say no? Her heart felt warm and full. She smiled. "Okay." Then she added, "But low-key again, right?"

He pursed his lips. "Huh. Really? I was thinking we should go somewhere really nice...Lux. Or maybe Coco's."

She bit her lip. Those were popular L.A. restaurants. It was *his* celebration after all. But taking a chance on them being seen together... "I don't know, Matt..."

"Why?" He stepped closer.

"You don't want to be seen with me," she said quietly. "If the media are there, they can turn it into a big deal, and—"

"What the fuck?" He stepped closer still, now nearly touching her. "I don't care who sees me with you."

Her mouth fell open. Once again, he floored her. "Well, you should," she said quietly. "I come with a lot of crap. I don't want to bring that onto you."

"Oh for fuck's sake. I don't give a shit about your past. Didn't I make that clear?"

Yeah, actually he had. "Yes, but...you should."

His thick eyebrows pulled together. He gave her a long look. A muscle in his jaw twitched. Then he said, "When I was in sixth grade, there was this kid in our school who had Asperger's. He was...different. He came across as a little odd. He didn't have very good social skills. Other kids made fun of him."

She gazed at him wide-eyed. What the hell was he talking about?

"But he was really smart and he and I both liked science. We were all supposed to pair up to do a science project and of course nobody wanted to be his partner, so I volunteered. We hung out a bit, working on our project after school. My friends told me I shouldn't hang around with him. People were starting to say that we were *both* freaks."

"Matt—"

"That pissed me off," he said quietly. "It pissed me off that people were mean to the kid. It pissed me off that my friends told me not to hang around with him. It pissed me off that people would say things like that about me, just because I associated with him. You know what?"

"Um, what?"

"I did it anyway. I didn't give a shit."

Her throat closed up and the corners of her eyes got wet. She felt her bottom lip trembling. And in her chest, her heart was doing that weird cracking, melting thing again.

"I am who I am," he continued in a low voice, his face moving toward hers. "Stuff like that is bullshit."

As he brushed his mouth over hers, she breathed in his scent, and had a weird sensation of falling, falling through space, falling hard.

"Fine," she whispered. "We'll go wherever you want."

If he'd wanted them to have dinner at Spago naked, at that moment she would have agreed to it.

"I'll make a reservation," he murmured. "I'll text you."

She nodded and he kissed her again then moved away.

She stared at him walking to his car. Holy effing crap.

She was in her apartment when he texted her to tell her he'd gotten a reservation at Lux for eight o'clock. How he'd done that, she had no idea, but then again, rich, famous, handsome hockey players could often get whatever they wanted.

Even from her, apparently.

She stared into her closet, which was sadly lacking in elegant dressy outfits. It had been a few years since she'd needed anything fancy, but she did still have a couple of dresses from way back. The ones she'd kept had been more classic styles—a sleeveless sheath style dress in black sequins and a strapless one in gold lace. Doubtfully, she eyed them both. Were they too much for dinner at Lux? Crappity crap, she had no frickin' clue. Lux had only been open a few years and she'd never been there.

Hell, it was Hollywood—you could wear anything, right?

The gold lace one was the less flashy of the two, but she didn't have great shoes to wear with it. At least she had nice black pumps, which she wore almost every day to work, which would go with the black sequined dress. So the black it was.

She showered, shaved her legs, rubbed lotion into her skin and spritzed with some of the expensive perfume she'd gotten for Christmas from her brother and his wife. It had been so long since she'd done this pre-date primping ritual, it felt weird. She decided to try something with her hair, teasing the top and pulling the front back to pin it at the back of her head, leaving most of it down. She turned back and forth in the mirror, unsure if it looked chic or stupid.

Whatever.

How the hell had she gotten herself into this?

She paused to take a breath. Okay. She had to get back into some kind of social life at some point in her life. She had to go to the Sweet Affair fundraiser in a couple of weeks. There would be other social events she had to attend for her job. She was going to have to appear in public and people would know who she was. She hadn't planned on having a relationship, but on the other hand she didn't really like the idea of spending the rest of her life alone. She hadn't made a decision to never date again. So this had to happen sometime.

And when Matt arrived at her apartment and walked in looking so freaking fantastic, she remembered exactly how she'd gotten herself into this.

Matt.

She wanted to sigh with pleasure at seeing him. And it wasn't just the way he looked, which was awesome, dressed in a suit—a dark suit, with a subtly patterned dark shirt open at the neck. It was the way he looked at her when she opened her door, a look of wonder and awe and appreciation. It was the way he smiled at her. It was the way he drew her into his arms, whispering, "Holy fuck, Honey," and then kissed her, stealing her breath and turning her legs to pudding.

Holy fuck indeed.

The restaurant was lovely. The big, arched windows were dark, and wall sconces on ochre-colored walls created a golden glow. White cloths covered each table, topped with silver and sparkling glasses and candles flickering in small votive holders. Dark leather chairs sat at each table. They were seated at a table for two, the service attentive but discreet. Honey did a double take when she saw Bradley Cooper a couple of tables away. Well. If there were paparazzi there, they'd be more focused on him than on her and Matt, for sure. Hockey still wasn't that popular in Los Angeles that the players were instantly recognized walking down the street. Not like movie stars.

When the server approached them for drink orders, Matt surprised her by ordering champagne. The sommelier came and they had a brief discussion about which kind. Matt looked at Honey for input. She did know her champagne, but even though she knew Matt had money, she hesitated at ordering the bottle of Veuve Clicquot. But he just gave a nod of approval and they were soon sipping the bubbly wine from elegant flutes as they studied the menu.

"Oh my god, this is so good," she murmured after her first sip.

"They have crazy food here," Matt muttered.

She shot him an amused look over her menu. "Why did you want to come here? We could have gone to Taco Bell."

He grinned. "You know, I would've been good with somewhere like that."

"Or Burger King for your Whopper."

"Yeah. But I wanted to take you out somewhere nice. Because we're celebrating. Right? And you can't get Veuve Clicquot at Taco Bell."

"True." She bent her head to the menu, afraid for a moment, because he was being so sweet and this was a date and she was getting in way too deep. She needed to be really, really careful here.

They made their meal selection, starting with trendy kale chips with smoked sea salt, and toasted baguette with bacon jam. Matt selected the New York steak with espresso-cocoa butter and Honey ordered tuna tartar tostados.

When the server had withdrawn and removed the menus, Honey leaned on the table and lifted her flute toward him. "To your first game back tomorrow." Their eyes met across the small table. "Good luck, Matt."

His eyes warmed. "Thank you." They touched their glasses together and then sipped the wine.

Honey's attention was drawn to a group of people being seated nearby and she choked on her champagne. "Fuck," she breathed.

Matt's eyebrows lifted and he turned his head. "Oh."

Her parents were taking seats at a table for six, along with Rudy Thomas and his wife, Marta, and the Commissioner of the NHL and presumably his wife.

CHAPTER 13

Matt turned his gaze back to Honey, who stared over at her parents with her mouth open. Then she blinked and snapped her lips together.

"I don't suppose we could make it through the entire evening without them noticing me," she muttered.

"Want to go say hi?"

"Not really."

He got that her relationship with her parents wasn't that great. For sure, different from his own with his folks. He could understand there might be some strain after the grief she'd given them as a teenager and then a young adult, and after they'd played the "tough love" card and threatened to cut her off.

But that was a few years ago, and she'd been the good girl they wanted her to be ever since, so one would think the relationship might have recovered by now.

Steve Holbrook was a good guy, a revered hockey player and respected businessman, and an influential team owner in the NHL. His wife Sela was a former model, beautiful — in fact Honey looked a lot like her — and gracious, always smiling. Matt wasn't a parent, but he could imagine how hard it might be to see your child's life spiraling out of control and how fucking hard it would be to actually carry through on cutting her off, if it meant she was practically living on the street. Even if you thought that was for the best, it would be hard to do.

He wasn't sure if he could ever be that tough, but he assumed they'd tried everything they could to get Honey to get her shit together before they'd gone that far.

"Well, *I* have to say hi," he said quietly. "Those are my bosses over there."

She stared at him and the fear and apprehension in her pretty eyes made him reach across the table to squeeze one of her hands.

"This is really awkward," she whispered. "I'm sorry."

"You don't have to apologize." He'd pushed away his own apprehension about Steve Holbrook finding out he was seeing his daughter and tried not to think about it. Really, they'd gone out once, although that had turned into a good part of the weekend in bed. You couldn't count that first lunch they'd had together. So this was only a second date. Who knew where things were going with them?

That was bullshit of course, because he was finding himself more or less obsessed with Honey Holbrook, thinking about her all the fucking time, fascinated with her, worried about her and protective of her and...hell. But no one else needed to know that right now.

"Come on," he said, pushing his chair back. "Let's just do it."

He caught the tension in her mouth as he moved to pull her chair out for her and then together they zigzagged around a couple of tables to approach the group of six.

Steve looked up and saw them first, his eyes alighting on his daughter with surprise and a smile. Then he saw Matt behind her and his eyebrows flew up. "Honey," he said, and Sela Holbrook's head turned as well.

"Honey!" she said, immediately rising from her chair. "Darling! Hello!"

Mother and daughter embraced in a barely touching hug with air kisses. Steve rose too and gave his daughter a more substantial hug.

"Imagine running into you here!" Sela said. "But what on earth are you wearing?" She gave Honey an up-and-down look. "Sweetheart, sequins are a little much for dinner here, don't you think?"

Color flooded into Honey's cheeks.

Matt's insides went cold.

"Matt," Steve said, extending a hand. "How are you?"

"Great, thanks."

"I hear you're playing tomorrow."

"I am." Matt flashed a smile. "We're celebrating tonight." He glanced at Honey.

He could see the questions on the other man's face, and in Sela's eyes as well.

Matt greeted the others at the table and they made some small talk, but he overheard Sela murmuring to Honey, "What are you doing with him, Honey?"

"Having dinner, Mom."

"But…have you two…?" Her question trailed off. Clearly neither of her parents knew what to make of this.

They'd known about him and Honey seeing each other eight years ago. He'd never really known what they thought about it. When he'd been leaving to go back to college, he'd been worried about Honey and the friends she hung out with and he'd talked to Steve about it. Steve hadn't said much to him, but he'd gotten the furious phone call from Honey afterward, so clearly Steve had told her about the conversation.

It had all been a long time ago. But yeah. Honey was right. This was awkward.

Matt kept his smile firmly in place until they returned to their table with an invitation to join the group for drinks after dinner if they liked.

"I'd rather eat my hair," Honey muttered, taking her seat.

Matt repressed his smile.

Honey picked up her champagne flute and drained it. The server immediately appeared to refill it and she picked it up again. When the server went to pour more for Matt, he shook his head.

"Game tomorrow," he said to Honey. "Also I'm driving."

"That encounter put a damper on the evening."

"It's okay, Honey," he said quietly. "It's fine."

She took a big breath and let it out. "Right." Clearly she didn't agree.

Honey's sequined dress probably was a little flashy for this place, but he couldn't believe her mom had said that to her. It made his blood run hot. He didn't even know what to say to her about that, to make her feel better. "You look beautiful," he said finally.

She shook her head and looked down. "I didn't have much else to wear," she said. "I gave away most of my fancy clothes years ago, and I haven't needed anything else lately."

He wanted to tell her he'd take her shopping and buy her whatever she wanted, but something kept his mouth shut. He had a feeling that would only make her more uncomfortable. "The dress is hot," he said, picking up his champagne. "And you're beautiful, and it doesn't matter. You could've worn jeans and it wouldn't matter."

Now he felt guilty for bringing her out to a place like this, dammit. They *could* have gone to Taco Bell—he didn't give a shit where he had dinner.

Her smile went crooked as their eyes met. "You have to stop being such a nice guy."

He widened his eyes. "You want me to be a dick?"

She lowered her gaze, shaking her head, smiling. "It'd be easier to resist you if you were."

That sounded good.

"I've had dick moments," he said. "Don't worry, I'll screw up at some point and piss you off."

That made her laugh. And that made him happy.

"Or maybe you've forgotten my dick move from eight years ago," he said.

"I haven't forgotten it," she said. "But now it doesn't seem quite as dickish as it did back then."

"I was worried about you."

Their eyes met again.

"I know. And you had reason to be."

"Tell me why things are so tense between you and your parents."

"I'd really rather not, when they're sitting right over there."

"Yeah. I get that. Okay, you can tell me later."

Her lips curved. "Maybe. So. You were good with those kids this afternoon."

"Changing the subject," he murmured. "That about gave me whiplash."

Her smile broadened. "It's good that you like kids."

"I guess. I have fun with my nieces and nephews, when I get to see them."

"Your brothers all have kids?"

"Tag and Kyla's kids are seven and five. Josh and Amy. Jase and Remi's are five and three and she's pregnant again, due in a couple months. Brandon's five, Kevin is three. They're hoping for a girl. Logan and Nicole have only one so far, Chris is three."

"Chris is a boy?"

"Yeah. Christian."

"Wow." Like hers, his siblings were way ahead of him in the reproduction game. "Any hockey players?"

He rolled his eyes. "Uh…*yeah*. All of 'em. They've even got Amy on skates already."

"Could be a whole Heller team."

He chuckled. She seemed a little more relaxed now, even though she kept casting glances toward her parents' table.

Their appetizers arrived and they shared the kale chips and the baguette with bacon jam.

"Bacon jam," Matt said, spreading some onto a slice of bread. "This better be good." He took a bite, and his eyes went wide. "Hey. It is good. Sweet and bacony."

"So who are you playing against tomorrow?" Honey asked.

"Ha. Yeah. Game tomorrow." His insides gave a leap of excitement. "Boston."

"How are they doing?"

"They're on a five-game winning streak right now." He made a face. "Time to put an end to that."

She smiled.

"They haven't been consistent this year, though," he continued. "Their power play sucks. They've got a few guys out with injuries, and Fedotenko—their goalie—is showing signs of fatigue. He's played…Christ, I don't know how many games in a row. But if they put in Chazona, that's great for me." He sat back for a moment and grinned.

"Why?"

"We played together in St. Louis. I know him. He has a weak five-hole when he loses focus. Most bad goals go five-hole for him. Plus he can't cope with guys setting up behind the net. He's terrible with wraparounds."

"So that's your strategy…circle around behind the net until you find an opening."

"Yeah, I—" He paused. "Hey. I thought you didn't know anything about hockey."

"Pay attention, dude. I said I don't like it. I never said I don't know anything about it."

A slow grin took over his mouth. "Babe."

They sat and smiled at each other, only looking away when the server came to clear their appetizer plates and refill water glasses.

He talked more about the next day's game while they ate their meals. Honey was by no means an expert but she got what he was talking about, and hell, he liked that. Not the typical puck bunny giggling away and not having a clue.

"Are you nervous?" she asked at one point.

"Bah! Of course not." Then he grimaced. "Well. You know. A little keyed-up." He lifted one eyebrow. "I know what would help with that…"

She burst out laughing.

They were done with their meals before Honey's parents, which made sense since there were more of them. "Dessert?" he asked.

"No thanks. Let's just go."

"Am I keeping you from something?" he joked.

She gave him a look and a head jerk toward her parents. "I don't want to have drinks with them after. We can stop by and tell them we're going somewhere else."

He leaned forward. "Yeah. My place."

She gave a few rapid blinks at that, then waved a hand. "Whatever."

Having drinks with the team owner and GM and Commissioner of the NHL might have been cool, but obviously still awkward for Honey, so he handed over his credit card to pay their check.

"I'm sorry," she said once they were out on the sidewalk. "I didn't mean to rush you through dinner."

"You can make it up to me later," he murmured, circling her wrist with his fingers.

"Yeah, um…I don't know…"

"Want to go somewhere for a drink? Or just my place?"

Her lips pressed together then she said, "Your place."

"Perfect."

But once they were in the car, she said, "Maybe you should just take me home."

He gave her a frowning glance. "Why?"

She didn't answer, just sat there clutching her little purse on her lap. Finally she said, "This might not be such a good idea. You know. You and me…"

"Is this because we ran into your parents?"

"No. Well, not really. I mean…" She turned her face away from him and looked out the window as they drove down Wilshire Boulevard.

"How about we go back to my place and we can sit and talk about this face-to-face and you can explain to me what the fuck ever it is you mean."

She bent her head in what he took to be a brief nod. Holy mother of fuck, she was complicated. Sweet and sexy, but complicated as fuck.

They were soon in his apartment. He turned on the gas fireplace and shrugged out of his suit jacket, then draped it over a chair. Honey set her purse on the coffee table and sat on the couch.

"Drink?" he asked.

"Mmm. I'm okay. I drank most of the champagne."

He sat beside her and stretched one arm along the back of the couch behind her. "Okay. Dial me in, babe."

Her lips twitched. She shifted a little so she was facing him.

"You can talk about your parents now. They aren't here."

"Thank god." She sighed. "Sorry. Okay. It's not so much my dad, it's more my mom. My dad…well, he just didn't know what to do with a daughter. He was all focused on his sons. I guess he figured my mom was taking care of me, but she…this is complicated."

"I'm getting that."

"She doesn't like me."

His eyebrows flew up. "Yeah?"

"I know that sounds stupid. What mother doesn't like her own daughter, right? She'd totally deny it. In fact she has. We tried to get some counseling together at one point. I can't explain it because I'm not in her head, and my therapist has told me over and over again I can't control her, I can only control myself. I can only tell you my experience and how it affected me, but I can't tell you why she is the way she is, other than I think she has some kind of narcissistic personality disorder."

He blinked. Then he reached for her. He needed to touch her. And he had a feeling she needed it too. He pulled her up against him, tucked her into his side. Her sparkly dress rode up on smooth thighs.

"When I was a kid, my parents wanted my brothers to play hockey. Obviously. The entire focus of our family, especially my dad, was their hockey. And golf in the summer. Turned out James was better at golf and that was what he wanted to do, and that was acceptable to them. Both my brothers were both great athletes. Me…well, there wasn't anything I was really good at, and I just…faded into the background. When I got to be a teenager, I thought about doing some modeling. I thought my mom would approve of that, since she'd been a model, and maybe she'd like it if I was following in her footsteps like Jonathan was with Dad. But right away she told me I'd never be successful modeling. I didn't have what it took. She said she didn't want me to be disappointed or hurt."

"Fuck me," he muttered.

"That's how it was. Every conversation with her made me feel like a loser. When she bothered to talk to me. People only saw the outside, what a beautiful family we were, but on the inside, I was miserable." She pulled back to look at him. "I don't want you to feel sorry for me. I just want you to understand that I'm never going to have a normal, loving relationship with her."

His chest ached a little. "Yeah."

"So you can imagine what happens to a girl who doesn't feel loved. A girl who's a little insecure. Okay a lot insecure. I wanted to belong somewhere. I wanted attention."

He found he had to clear his throat.

"But I had no idea how to get it, and I did all the wrong things. I started partying. Drinking. Experimenting with drugs. And sex."

Yeah, there it was. The ache behind his breastbone turned to a hard burn.

"My parents hated it," she continued, her voice a whisper. "But the more pissed off I made them, the more attention they paid to me. I liked that. So I just kept getting wilder and wilder."

Now his throat started to hurt. "Then they did the tough-love thing."

"Yeah. But I don't hold that against them! Really, I know that was for the best. I had to sink all the way down before I was ready to get back up. It's sad, but true. I mean, I'm pretty sure my mom had just had enough and didn't care that it was the right thing to do. I think it was harder for my dad. They spoiled me, with material things, so for Dad to cut me off was a pretty big thing. And honestly, I'm grateful for that. It was hard at first, I was pissed off and resentful, but years later when I got my head screwed on straight, I realized it was for the best. So I talk to my parents and go there for Sunday dinners and I do family things like birthdays and Christmas. It's all okay. But it's just better for me to not spend too much time with them. I'm good with it. I know who I am now. I'm working on being a better me."

"Fuck." He swallowed.

She extricated herself from his grip and pushed away. She met his eyes, smiling, but it was a sad smile. "Anyway. I should go."

Hell no.

"Why?" he asked. "You told me all that, but I don't get what that has to do with us."

"Matt. It has everything to do with us. You don't need all my crappy baggage. You're a good guy."

He snorted. "Oh please. You want to dump me because I'm too nice? For fuck's sake."

"Well...yeah."

He scowled. "You want me to be a dick," he said, like he had earlier. "Like the fucktards you hung out with back when we met. Like the assholes you associated with after that. The ones who used you for your money and left you holding the bag, literally, when the cops busted you for drugs."

She stared at him, her lips parted. "You knew about that?"

"Hell yeah, who didn't? That's what you want, Honey?"

CHAPTER 14

How could she tell him the truth?

She was trembling inside, her mouth dry, her palms sweaty. Confessing all that stuff to Matt had not been easy. She did not want his pity. She did not want him to know what a screw up she was. Or rather, used to be. Because she was proud of what she'd accomplished so far, and she had more she wanted to do. But even so, making herself that vulnerable was terrifying, especially when it was him, and he'd broken her heart once before when she'd let him in. How could she risk that again?

She closed her eyes at the stab she felt in her heart. She'd known it earlier, when they'd been standing outside the school and he'd told her the story about the kid with Asperger's. She was falling. She cared about him. And that was something she couldn't let happen. At dinner when he'd been so sweet about her parents and her mom's stupid comment about her dress, she could have burst into tears. She needed to get away from this guy before things got way too involved and messy.

Because yeah, he was a good guy, damn him.

"No," she finally whispered. "That's not what I want."

"Do you think you're still doing that? Still trying to get attention and affection?"

Her eyes sprang open wide with genuine shock. "No!" She laid her fingertips on her throat. "No, that's not it at all. But the reality is, crap is going to hit the fan if it gets out you and I are together. Because of my past. And you deserve better than that."

"Bullshit." The harsh expletive startled Honey. "That is the most fucked up bullshit I have ever heard. Not letting you go," he muttered and he reached for her again. He hauled her onto his lap, shoved a hand into her hair and held her head while he slammed his mouth down on hers.

She moaned a protest, put her hands on his shoulders. Physically, he was bigger and stronger. But he wasn't using brute force to convince her. He was using that chemistry they had, that sexual attraction. His kiss took over her body, warming her and softening her, seducing her.

"Fuckin' complicated," he muttered against her mouth. "But you're fuckin' worth it."

Oh my god.

She loved it that he thought so. She wasn't sure if anyone else ever had. And that softened her even more. She opened her mouth and kissed him back, her fingers digging into his shoulders.

Honey's security pass for the Foundation offices granted her access to the entire Coliseum. On top of that, security personnel all knew who she was. She got a couple of surprised looks as she entered the building Saturday afternoon shortly before the two o'clock start time, since she rarely attended games, but nobody stopped her from taking the elevator up to the press box level. She walked down the hall, the heels of her boots clicking on the hardwood floor, until she came to the open area where the press all sat lined up along the counter overlooking the ice. Sports reporters filled every chair, laptops open in front of them. She passed by them and entered another hall where the private areas were separated from the print media—the NHL video review judges, the local radio station that broadcast games, NBC, and then, right above center ice, the door of her father's private box. She lifted her chin, sucked in a breath, and opened the door.

Her dad was alone up there. Sometimes he watched the games with friends or other stakeholders or her brothers, but this afternoon he was sitting at the narrow counter overlooking the ice by himself. He turned at the sound of the door opening. "Honey."

He pushed back his chair and stood. She crossed over to him for a quick hug, though she'd just seen him last night at Lux. "Hi, Dad."

"What are you doing here?" he asked.

"Came to watch the game." Their eyes met.

His eyes warmed and he smiled. "Uh-huh. Have a seat."

They sat side by side. She dropped her purse to the carpeted floor at her feet. The arena below them was dark at the moment, "Sandstorm" by Darude blasting from the sound system.

"Did you enjoy your dinner last night?" Dad asked.

"Mmm. It was amazing. You?"

"Yeah. Great place." Silence. Other than pulsing electronic music. Then he spoke again. "You and Matt...what's up with that?"

She hitched a shoulder without looking at him. "I'm not sure."

The announcer's voice boomed out the introduction of the

Condors. "And nooooooow…your California Coooon-doooors!"

The players raced onto the ice one after the other with spotlights and flashing strobe lights and pumping music, all full of energy and enthusiasm.

She sensed that Dad wanted more from her but wasn't going to ask. And she wasn't sure what to say.

"This afternoon's starting lineup for your California Condors," the announcer boomed. "Today's center…Eric Zuhler." The crowd roared. "On left wing…number eight, Joe Barzetti." The crowd cheered again. "Aaaaand….starting at right wing…nuuuuumber foooorty-twoooo, Matt Heller!" And the crowd went nuts, standing and clapping and whistling.

Apparently the fans were happy to have him back, judging from the ovation. Honey smiled, her heart expanding. She picked out Matt on the ice as they lined up for the national anthem. Although he was pretty tiny from up this high, she could clearly tell it was him.

"He's pretty popular," Dad said.

"He's been off for months."

"Yeah. Still. Everyone was concerned about him. And he's been involved with community stuff. As I guess you know."

"Yeah."

"How's the job going?"

She turned to give him a long look. "Dad. That's the first time you've asked me in the three weeks I've been there."

He gazed back at her. "Uh…"

"Did you know they never intended for me to actually do any work?"

He frowned. "What? No."

"Really? Trent didn't want me there. He told me himself. He only hired me as a favor to you."

"Well…yeah. But I thought they needed someone. He was

complaining about Dulcie leaving to have her baby. Has she had it, by the way?"

"Not that I've heard. But we weren't exactly BFFs, and nobody else in the office talks to me much either."

He frowned again. "I'll talk to Trent—"

"No. That's not necessary. It's my job and I'm dealing with it."

He cleared his throat. "All right."

They both stood for the Star Spangled Banner. Honey's gaze went back to Matt. He was shifting back and forth from one foot to the other, almost bouncing, and rolling his shoulders. The adrenaline must have been roaring through his system, his first game back.

He hadn't talked much about his injury. Which, now that she thought about it, after everything she'd shared with him, wasn't fair. But he'd seemed so healthy and fit and confident about his ability to play, she hadn't given a thought to his safety out there. Hockey could be a dangerous sport. She bit her lip. Hopefully everyone was right in making the assessment that he was ready to return to the lineup.

The crowd cheered as the anthem ended, and she and her dad both took their seats again. His booth wasn't a luxury booth like the ones below them, with leather couches and food and beverage service. Up here, it was basic, just a small room with the counter and a few chairs. The view was spectacular, though.

The players lined up for the opening face-off, Matt on right wing bent over, poised and waiting to snap up the puck if Zuhler won the faceoff. Which he did. And the game started.

"Who's in net for Boston?" she asked her dad, having failed to pay attention the Boston starting lineup.

"Chazona."

She smiled.

The action was fast paced right from the opening faceoff. Honey kept her eyes on number forty-two, watching him handle the puck. He headed toward the Boston end, circled back toward his own end to avoid being hit, passed the puck then received it back again as he and Barzetti toyed with the Boston offense. Then he deked around a Boston player in a smooth move that made the crowd shout and cheer. He hesitated a fraction of a second at the blue line, waiting for Barzetti to catch up to him to prevent an offside call, then they both went in, two on one. Matt passed the puck to Barzetti. Honey rose up out of her seat, fingers gripping the counter. Barzetti started to shoot, drawing his stick back, then at the last minute passed the puck back to Matt, who took a one-timer and slapped the puck toward the net.

The crowd went wild as the goal light came on and the horn blasted, and Honey stared in disbelief. She looked at her dad who was grinning widely.

"Holy shit!" he yelled. "First play of the game and he scores! Holy shit!"

She laughed out loud, clapping along with everyone else in the Coliseum.

"Unbelievable," Dad said, shaking his head, standing and clapping, still smiling.

Everyone was standing, giving Matt another ovation.

Wow.

Happiness swelled in her chest like a balloon, and she couldn't keep from smiling too, her hands starting to hurt from clapping so much. "Five hole," she murmured, watching the replay on the screen on the score clock.

When the noise eventually subsided and play had resumed, and they were both sitting again, Dad said, "He's got a lot of talent."

She nodded with a sidelong glance at him.

"I always felt like he wasn't living up to his potential,"

Dad continued. "We could see glimpses of it, but he was inconsistent. Seemed like he was coasting along."

"You mean before you signed him."

"Yeah. I listened to Rudy and Kevin." One of his top scouts. "They like him too. He's a great team player. Everyone loves him. Great skills, when he used them. They thought he could fit in with our team. We hoped he would live up to his potential."

"Then he got hurt."

"Yeah."

"For what it's worth, I think his injury really affected him. He hasn't said much about it, but he seems pretty determined to come back and show you did the right thing signing him."

"Honey."

"Yeah?" She glanced at him again.

"I haven't seen you look this happy in…Jesus, I can't even remember. Might've been the Christmas when you were ten years old."

She realized she was still smiling.

She *felt* happy. Happy for Matt. But she didn't know what to say, so she just nodded.

"I want you to be happy," Dad said in quiet voice. "I never knew exactly how to get that for you. Other than to give you everything you wanted."

She turned to face her father, the game for the moment forgotten. "But you *didn't* give me everything I wanted," she said. "You gave me everything money could buy—toys and designer clothes and luxury cars, expensive vacations—but what I really wanted was…" Oh god, this sounded so needy and pathetic, but her therapist had encouraged her be honest about it. She'd told Matt about it, and somehow his acceptance made it easier for her to share it again. "I wanted you. Your time. Your attention. Your love."

Dad was six foot three inches, over two hundred pounds,

big alpha male former hockey player. Not unlike Matt. Except unlike Matt, he had no clue what to do with that information. Discomfort tightened his features.

"Of course I love you," he said gruffly, turning back to the game.

That might be as good as she was going to get from him. Or maybe he'd think about what she'd said.

"Thanks, Dad, I love you too."

And they watched the game.

By the end of the first period, Matt had an assist and the Condors were up two-nothing.

Following a long stretch of play with no whistle that included several hard hits into the boards and some words exchanged between a couple of opposing players, Matt went to the bench. The camera zoomed in on his face as Joe Satriana's "Crowd Chant" blasted through the arena.

The intensity on his face took her breath away.

It was almost hard to realize this was the same man as off the ice—often laughing, easygoing, with a boyish smile. Now, even through his visor, she could see the fierce expression on his face, the burning in his eyes and the grim line of his mouth. Wow.

By the end of the game, Matt had another goal and three —count 'em, three!—assists, and the Condors won five-one.

Honey picked up her purse and tossed her empty Diet Coke cup into the trash. "Thanks for letting me watch with you, Dad," she said.

"Any time." He gave her a considering look. "Maybe you'll come more often now."

"Maybe." She smiled at him.

"Coming for dinner tomorrow?"

"Yep."

He hesitated. "Want to bring Matt?"

Her fingers curled tightly around her purse strap. "No!"

"He's welcome to join us."

"No. It's not like that with us. We've only gone out a couple of times."

Last night she'd been determined that things had to end between them. He was making her care about things that she shouldn't. It could only lead to disappointment and hurt, if she cared. But somehow he'd gotten her past that and she'd spent the night with him again. And here she was watching his game, goddammit. Taking him home for Sunday dinner with the family was way out of her comfort zone.

She wasn't even sure if she was going to see him again.

Until eight o'clock that night when he showed up at her apartment. She was sitting in front of the television, weirdly watching the Philadelphia-Vancouver game, which she cared less than nothing about, knitting on the little sweater she was making for James and Kortney when her phone buzzed to announce a visitor.

"It's me," he said. "Matt."

She leaned her head against the wall. Frack. "Come on up."

"Hey," he said, walking into her apartment, all big and gorgeous in an expensive suit and tie. Holy bajesus. "Wasn't sure if you'd be home."

"Congratulations."

"Did you hear? We won."

"I watched the game."

He lifted an eyebrow. "Yeah?"

"Yeah. With my dad. Up in his box."

"Huh. I never saw you up there all the nights *I* was watching from up there."

"That's because this was the first game I've gone to since I've been back."

He gave her a slow, sexy smile. "Oh yeah?"

She nodded.

"Because of me." He reached for her and pulled her up against him.

She lowered her chin and looked at him through her eyelashes. "Oh please. Maybe I just wanted to see a game."

He laughed. "Admit it. You wanted to see me play."

"I did not."

"Did so." He found her mouth with his and it was amazing, a long, hard, jubilant kiss. "You have no idea how much that turns me on."

"Are you kidding?" Her arms went up around his neck. "That turns you on?"

"Everything about you turns me on."

"Breathing turns you on."

"I have a healthy sex drive."

She snorted out a laugh and leaned her forehead against his shoulder. "Oh my god."

His hands squeezed her ass.

"Admit it," he murmured. "I turn you on too."

She shook her head, rolling her forehead against his shoulder, but she was smiling. "Okay, okay, I admit it. I wanted to watch you, and yeah, I was turned on."

"I knew it." Satisfaction edged his voice.

"Seriously." She tipped her head back to look up at him. "Congratulations. You played great. You scored or assisted on every single goal."

"I know. It felt great." His grin was infectious.

"What are you doing here though? Shouldn't you be out celebrating with your team mates?"

"We did go out for dinner. They were going to some club. I…didn't feel like going. But I didn't feel like going home either."

Her heart went soft. "Oh." And then there was that scary feeling again, a feeling of falling, a feeling that she was going to fall so fast and so hard it was going to hurt like hell when she landed. Maybe even more than last time.

But he was right. The sexual attraction between them was narcotic. Irresistible. So, as long as they kept it to sex and she stopped spilling her guts to him, stopped letting him see all her soft spots, maybe it would all be okay.

She went up on her toes and threaded her fingers through his hair and planted a big kiss right on his lips. Then she whispered, "I *was* turned on watching you. It made me want to do…this…" And she slid her hands down his body as she went to her knees in front of him.

CHAPTER 15

Matt thought he'd been keyed up before the game yesterday, but now…fucking hell. He rang the doorbell then rubbed his palms over his thighs, standing outside the Holbrook mansion.

The door opened and a little girl dressed in a pink bathing suit looked up at him. "Hi," she said, studying him.

He grinned. "Hi."

"Kavita, what are you doing answering the door by yourself?" A woman on high heels tapped up behind the girl.

"Grandpa told me to answer the door," Kavita said.

The woman moved into view — Honey's mom Sela.

"Oh, hi, Matt," she said, giving him a flirty look. "Steve told me he'd invited you for dinner. Please come in."

He entered the house and handed Mrs. Holbrook the expensive bottle of wine he'd brought. "For you," he said. "Thanks so much for having me today."

"Oh, you didn't need to bring anything! But thank you. Come in, the others are all out back on the patio."

The others. He had no clue who all was going to be there. He followed Mrs. Holbrook as she again tapped her way down the hardwood floor of a wide hall, past vast rooms including a formal dining room with a long table all set with flowers and table cloth and sparkling dishes, through a kitchen/great room where two women worked at the stove and counter preparing food, and out through French doors onto the patio.

Yeah, there were a lot of people there. More kids splashing and yelling in the pool. A lot of adults sitting around on patio furniture. Matt spotted Steve Holbrook standing beside an outdoor bar talking to Rudy Thomas and a younger man that Matt recognized at Honey's brother James. He'd never met him, but had seem him on TV when he'd watched PGA golf.

"Come say hi to Steve," Mrs. Holbrook said, leading the way across the stone patio.

There was Jonathan Holbrook. Matt had played against him many times and now knew him from his management role with the Condors. He didn't see Honey.

Steve spotted him, smiled, lifted his glass. "Matt. Glad you made it. Can I get you something to drink?"

"Beer if you have it."

"Absolutely." Steve moved around behind the bar and removed a bottle from a small fridge. Jesus. "A glass?"

"The bottle's fine."

"There you go. You know James?"

"We've never met in person, but I've watched you golf." Matt smiled and shook the other man's hand. "You're a great golfer."

"Thanks." James smiled. He looked nothing like Honey, taking more after his dad. Thank Christ Honey didn't look like her dad. No offense to Steve, but his large nose and chin would not look good on her. Instead, she'd gotten her mother's genes—her height, her slender grace, her blonde hair, perfect skin and glamorous smile. "This is my wife Kortney."

He shook hands with a very pretty, very pregnant woman.

Kavita had done a running jump into the pool as they'd walked outside, and was now with the other kids. Matt turned to survey them with a smile then realized that one of the kids in the pool was…Honey.

Their eyes met across the distance.

She was apparently treading water in the deep end, her hair wet and slicked back from her face. She didn't smile.

He held up his bottle to her with a grin, then lifted it to his lips and took several healthy swallows.

She wasn't exactly running over to greet him.

"Great pool," he said. "I love swimming."

"Steve!" Mrs. Holbrook said. "You should have told him we have a pool! He could have brought a swimsuit."

"Sorry," Steve said. "Never thought of it."

"No worries. I have a pool at my apartment building, so I get to swim a lot. It was great rehab after my injury."

That led to a conversation about his recovery and how he was doing and how great he'd played yesterday, which, thank fuck, was true. He tried to focus on the people he was talking to, resisting the urge to keep turning and looking at Honey in the pool, playing with the kids as if she was one of them.

Eventually she did get out, water running down over her sleek body in the pink and yellow flowered bikini he'd bought her as she grabbed a towel from a chair. She gave him a look that could have shriveled his nuts, except he was turned on by seeing her all wet and half naked. Like that night in the hot tub.

"Honey, come say hi to Matt," Mrs. Holbrook called.

What the fuck were her parents thinking? He had no fucking clue. He stood there holding his beer, smiling, as Honey approached, a towel now wrapped around her.

"Hi," she said cautiously, her eyes darting around from him to her mom, her dad, back to him.

"I invited Matt for dinner," Steve said. "Thought it would be great to talk about his first game back yesterday, since he played so well."

"Uh-huh," Honey said. She was too polite to make a scene in front of bunch of other people, so she pasted on that wide, white smile that didn't reach her eyes. "I better go change before dinner."

"Still about an hour," Mrs. Holbrook said. "But yes, you do need to clean up."

Matt's chin dipped and his mouth tightened.

"Grandma, I'm hungry!" Kavita wailed below them.

Matt looked down at her.

"Come on," Honey said, taking the little girl's hand. "I think we can find a cookie."

"Don't ruin their appetite for dinner!" Mrs. Holbrook called after them as they walked away.

"Don't worry, Mom," James said. "They'll never sit and eat that fancy food you serve anyway."

He said it with a teasing smile and soft tone, and Mrs. Holbrook smiled, apparently taking the comment as a compliment to her food, but Matt sensed the subtext.

Ooookay. So Honey had vanished and here he was with her dysfunctional family. Great.

He'd wondered about the dysfunction after she'd spilled all that shit the other night. To the rest of the world, they seemed like a golden family, even more so than his. The media made a big thing about his family—four brothers playing in the NHL. But her family was more high profile than his. His parents were regular, middle-class types, living in a small city that nobody in the States had ever heard of. Honey's parents were rich and famous and living a Hollywood lifestyle in the entertainment capital of the world, with two successful athlete sons and…Honey. Who'd attracted as much media attention from her antics as her dad had as one of the top NHL players.

No, wait—*more* media attention, given that Los Angeles was not a hockey town, whereas half-dressed gorgeous girls doing crazy things in bars and clubs and parties was the lifeblood of Tinseltown.

Anyfuckinghoo. He'd wondered if she'd exaggerated just a little how bad things had been for her growing up. He hadn't been sure if accepting Steve's invitation last night after the game was the right thing to do. He was ninety percent less sure that accepting it and showing up without telling Honey was the right thing to do. But his curiosity about that won out and here he was.

The group chatted on for a while, and since the talk was mostly about hockey, he noticed Mrs. Holbrook's smile fade and, after a failed attempt to change the subject, she excused herself to go into the house to check on dinner.

Where the fuck was Honey? Matt wanted to go hunt her down. Eventually he excused himself to go into the house on the pretext of using the bathroom. He walked inside and immediately saw Honey at the big kitchen island with three little kids around her laughing as they tossed something… candies?…into the air and she attempted to catch them in her mouth. The kids giggled every time she missed.

Then she caught sight of him. He smiled and moved toward her. "What are you doing?" he asked with amusement.

"Auntie Honey's being like Shamu," Kavita explained. "He catches fish."

"Shamu? The killer whale?" One of his eyebrows rose.

Honey grinned. "No comments about my weight please."

Matt held both hands up in front of him. "Hey. Not going there." Then he rolled his eyes. "As if."

She was all relaxed and happy looking. "I better clean up the floor. " She made a face at the kids.

"Yes, please, Honey," Mrs. Holbrook spoke up. "Look at the mess you've made."

Honey bugged her eyes out at the kids, a look that said, "See, told you" and they snickered.

"It's just a few gummy candies, Mom."

"I'll do it, Honey," said a woman Matt didn't know, wearing a uniform. She'd been one of the two he'd noticed earlier working in the kitchen. She grabbed a broom from a tall closet and began to sweep the floor. "I had to sweep anyway."

"Can you catch a gummy fish in your mouth?" Kavita asked Matt.

He pursed his lips and slowly nodded. "I'm ninety-eight percent sure I can."

The kids giggled. "Honey will throw one to you," Kavita said, handing Honey a candy.

Their eyes met. "I'm good with my mouth," he murmured.

Honey's cheeks went pink, and she gave him a little eye roll that amused him. He lifted his chin and opened up. She tossed the candy to him and he only had to move a little to catch it neatly in his mouth.

"Yay!" The kids cheered.

Matt grinned as he chewed on the candy. "I love gummy fish."

"Me too," Kavita said.

"I like the blue ones best." He winked at her.

"Me too!" Her eyes widened.

"You play hockey?" Matt asked her.

She laughed. "Noooo. Hockey is for boys!"

Matt widened his eyes into a horrified expression and turned them on Honey.

She grimaced. "She's not *my* kid."

"How about you little dudes?" Matt asked the two boys. "Play hockey?"

They shook their heads.

"Not yet," Mrs. Holbrook said with a smile. "They will."

Honey pursed her lips and did another bug-eyed look at Matt.

"Honey, you need to go get cleaned up for dinner," Mrs. Holbrook said.

"I am, Mom."

She'd changed out of her bikini into a short-sleeved baby-doll-style dress and flip flops. Her hair was still damp. She didn't have much makeup on, but she had some. She looked sweet. And hot.

"You need to fix your hair," her mom said with a disapproving glance at the half-dry strands.

"I did," Honey said again. "It'll dry."

Mrs. Holbrook sighed then sent an apologetic glance at Matt. "Sorry, Matt."

"For what?" He gazed back at her, perplexed.

"Honey just doesn't like to listen to me," she said with a smile. "When we have guests we try to show them some respect by looking nice."

"You're disrespecting me?" he asked Honey, trying not to laugh.

"I didn't even know you were going to be here." And she sent him a meaningful look. "You'd think that might have come up in conversation…"

"Oh, did you two go out again last night?" Mrs. Holbrook interjected. "Where did you go?"

Honey's eyes hit his. "Uh…no. We didn't go out last night. Okay, kids, enough snacks for now. What do you want to do until dinner time?"

Kortney and Demi, the two mothers, appeared. "They're going upstairs to get cleaned up," Demi said, grabbing one of the boys off a stool. The kids were all still wearing swimsuits. "Thank you, Honey, for entertaining them all afternoon."

Honey smiled as the two women led their kids out of the

room, the boys jumping up and down and flapping their hands for some reason with mind-boggling energy.

"You look gorgeous, Honey," he said in a voice loud enough for her mom to hear. "I don't feel disrespected at all."

She rolled her eyes and gave him a crooked smile. "Thanks. Come on back outside."

He followed her out, but instead of letting her lead him back to the conversation the others were having, he said, "Let's look at the pool," and nudged her toward it.

"It's a pool," she muttered, but went with him. They stood beside it.

"Your dad invited me yesterday after the game," he said. He searched her face. "I wasn't sure if I was going to come. So I didn't tell you."

"Why did you come?" Her forehead creased.

"I wanted to see you." His answer came without hesitation.

Last night he'd acknowledged it, to himself at least. When the other guys had been going out to some nightclub, talking about hookups with puck bunnies, he'd had no interest. He'd wanted to see Honey. He'd wanted to share his happiness and relief at how well the game had gone with her. Yeah, he'd wanted to fuck her brains out, but that wasn't the only thing he wanted.

After spending another night with her, he'd decided on a plan of action. He wanted her. She was going to be his. There was undeniable attraction between them, explosive sexual chemistry and she seemed willing to explore that. He got that she had some walls up. She had some baggage. He could see how she tried not to care, how she tried not to expect anything from people, including him.

He wanted to show her that she could expect things from him. That he was there for her. No matter what. He wasn't sure exactly how to go about that, but one thing he did know was he had to see her to do it, so he'd called Steve to accept the invitation to dinner.

Her gaze slid away. "Matt…"

"Honey." He set his hands on her hips and turned her to face him. "I'm here. Deal with it."

She made a series of faces so bizarre—scrunching her face up, then grimacing, then biting her lip— he burst out laughing.

"What was that?" he said. "I can't even guess."

"I'm frustrated!"

"Relax, babe." His hands slid around her hips a little farther, nearly onto her ass. He had to remember her dad was standing not far away. "Let's just enjoy this."

Sucking briefly on her bottom lip, she held his gaze then nodded. "Fine."

"Glad you're so enthusiastic," he muttered, releasing her.

"I don't know what Dad was thinking," she grumbled. "Oh wait. I do."

"What?"

"Daddy's trying to give his little girl everything she wants," she said on a sigh. "As always. He just doesn't think. I'm sorry."

"Fuck, don't be sorry! I said I wanted to see you. I was kinda freaked out when he invited me, but it's all good."

She shook her head. "Okay. Sure. I just wouldn't want you to think you had to, um, date me because he's…you know…your boss."

He stared at her, his jaw going slack. "What in the holy mother of fuckers are you talking about?"

Her lips twitched. "I mean—"

"I know what the fuck you meant."

"You know, that swearing is really excessive."

"Like you've never dropped an F-bomb."

"Once in a while, maybe," she said primly. "Not every other word!"

He slashed a hand through the air. "Off topic," he snapped. "You grew up with men, men who are hockey players, so I know language doesn't bother you. Let's put that whole fucking nonsense to bed, and no, I'm not apologizing for swearing again. I like swearing." He leaned closer to her, almost nose to nose, staring into her gold-flecked brown eyes. "I'm not here because I'm sucking up to your dad, and I'm not dating you because I'm sucking up to your dad. I'm dating you because you're sweet and strong and funny and sexy as fucking hell. Okay?"

"We're dating?" she whispered.

"Yeah." He held her gaze.

"Oh." She blinked. "I don't—"

"I said, deal with it." He took her hand. "Now let's get you a glass of wine or something."

They were about half way through dinner when Matt arrived at the conclusion that Honey had not been exaggerating. Her mom was a whack job.

It was subtle. You might not even notice it unless you were sensitive to Honey's feelings. Honey handled it all with apparent unconcern, but he could definitely see how the constant put downs, the comments that sounded helpful, or sounded like compliments, but...weren't, could erode a person's self-confidence. And if she wasn't putting Honey down, she was ignoring her and praising her sons.

Matt had discovered that complimenting Mrs. Holbrook made things good. He fucking hated sucking up, always had, so he didn't go overboard because it made him uncomfortable, but if he got a chance for a genuine nice comment, such as how great the dinner had been, he took it.

But it was so different than the easy, relaxed atmosphere in his own family. Unless he or his brothers swore too much, then his mom got testy. But that was nothing compared to the feeling of walking on eggshells he had around this family.

Honey's brothers were okay dudes. They seemed to get it too, careful to praise their mom and never criticize. Their wives didn't have it so easy, and Matt was definitely getting a vibe from them that was strained.

Christ. If he wanted Honey in his life, her nut job family came with her. The idea made him want to give up hockey and take Honey away to a South Pacific Island for the rest of their lives.

Heh. He had to play for a few more years, but maybe one day that could happen.

Fantasy.

Fantasies could be fun though.

He looked at Honey sitting across from him. Oh yeah. He had some fantasies… She looked up at him as if sensing his stare. Then, as if reading where his dirty mind was going, her eyes widened.

He smiled.

She shook her head and looked down at her plate.

Now he was wishing he'd had the guts to phone her and suggest he pick her up and bring her to this shindig. Because they both had cars there, he had no reason to drive her home. Or abduct her back to his place.

And fuck, the team was leaving on a road trip Tuesday, not back until the weekend again. Hell. He was glad to be playing again, but just when he'd made up his mind that he was going after her, he was leaving town. Shit.

Steve had asked him a question and he turned his attention to the man who was, ultimately, his boss, as well as the father of the woman he'd just been remembering on her knees in front of him. Sweat broke out beneath his shirt. Yeah, just a little awkward.

CHAPTER 16

Dulcie's baby arrived the next week, a little girl as had been expected. Honey was happy to hear the news when Celine announced it to everyone, glad mother and baby were healthy and doing well. Dulcie promised to bring the baby in soon.

Honey was busy at work preparing for the gala fundraiser to be held the following week, along with other projects. She still felt like she was flailing around blindly in the dark most of the time, and everything probably took her twice as long to do as anyone else because she had to figure so much stuff out. She didn't like to bother the others with a lot of questions given the cool reception she usually got, so she only did it when she absolutely had to. But she'd learned a lot already and she was going to make the best of this. By the time Dulcie came back in a few months, she'd have some experience in a real job (sort of) on her resume that would help her find another job.

Matt was away on the road trip and Thursday night she left the office earlier than she sometimes did so she'd be home in time to watch the six o'clock game on TV. Suddenly she'd developed an interest in hockey. This made her smile.

She made herself a grilled cheese sandwich for dinner, then got out her knitting and arranged herself on the couch in front of the TV.

After Matt telling her they were "dating", she hadn't even seen him. He'd been busy with a practice and some kind of promo work his agent got him, and then the team had flown to Philadelphia for a Tuesday night game. He had, however, texted her numerous times, little update texts that made her smile, or texts asking how her day went, and some giggle-inducing messages about why it was good to date a hockey player. "I have great hands," he texted. "Also I know how to find the opening and get it in."

She grinned remembering that one.

The puck had barely been dropped on the opening faceoff when someone knocked on her door. She frowned, setting aside her wool and needles. It had to be Farrah, otherwise people had to buzz to enter the building. Still she checked before she opened the door. Yep, Farrah.

"Hey," she said with a smile.

"Is Mia here?" Farrah demanded.

Honey's smile faded and her forehead creased. "No. Why?"

Farrah closed her eyes and Honey noted the tension in her mouth. "Shit. I don't know where she is."

"What?"

Farrah opened her eyes. "I let her come home alone from school today. It was only going to be a couple of hours because I was off at six. I got off a little early, so I just got home and she's not there."

"Oh my god." Honey gripped the edge of her door, leaning against it. "Where could she be?"

"I don't know. God, I don't know." Farrah covered her face with her hands. "I never should have let her come home alone, but she keeps telling me she's old enough not to have to go to a babysitter's. Shit, shit, shit. I thought maybe she came over here."

"No. Come in. Let's think. It'll be okay, Farrah."

But Honey's stomach had seized into a mass of knots. She tried to clear the clutter of worry in her brain. "Have you called any of her friends?"

"No." Farrah looked a little dazed. "I could do that. Um… I'll go home and…"

"I'll come with you." Honey grabbed her keys and they both headed across the hall to Farrah's apartment.

Farrah grabbed her cell phone and began swiping through her contacts. "Okay," she muttered. "Jennifer is her best friend…I'll try there first."

But there was no answer at Jennifer's home.

Farrah kept phoning the numbers she had, but none of Mia's other friends knew where she was.

"Fuck," Farrah said. "Fuck. If something happened to her…oh my god, Honey, what will I do?"

"It'll be okay," Honey repeated, firmly hoping that was true. She squeezed Farrah's arm. "Should we go out and look? Maybe go to her school and retrace the way?" She didn't know what else to suggest. God. God. Mia was the sweetest little girl, what if…fuck, the what-ifs were terrifying. The world was a scary place.

"Yeah," Farrah agreed. "I guess. I could phone the police… How long does someone have to be missing?"

"I'm not sure. But if it's a child, I don't think it's the same. Wouldn't they start looking for her right away?"

"Yeah. Okay. Police." Farrah bit her lip as she found the number to call. "I should have bought her that cell phone she keeps asking for. Dammit. I can't afford it, but it'd be totally worth it to be able to call her, or know that she could call me…"

The apartment door opened and they both jerked around to stare at Mia.

Mia's eyes went wide. "Mom. Uh…hi."

Farrah tossed her phone aside and rushed at Mia. She grabbed her up into a big hug, bursting into tears. Honey sank down onto Farrah's couch, her legs weak with relief.

"Oh my god, you're all right," Farrah sobbed, squeezing Mia. "Oh thank god." Then she pushed Mia away and glared at her. "Where were you?"

Mia's eyes shifted away and her little mouth pouted. "Um…Jen and I went to Starbuck's after school."

Farrah's eyes widened. "What? Why? You were supposed to come straight home!"

"I know, but the older girls from middle school go there, and we wanted to see what it's like… I knew you had to work until six, so I figured I had lots of time to get home before you got here, only we were having fun and…you're home early."

"Yeah." Farrah's mouth thinned. "I'm home early. And you are busted."

Farrah had gone from terrified and worried, to angry in a flash and Honey didn't blame her. She knew exactly how she felt. She shook her head at Mia, understanding her desire for independence, but holy shit, this could have been so bad.

"Grounded," Farrah snapped. "Forever."

"Mo-om!"

"Go to your room. Right now. I need to think about this."

Mia met Honey's eyes with an appealing look. Honey gave her a small smile, but shook her head. "Your mom and I were worried sick," she said quietly.

Mia rolled her eyes, sighed dramatically and stomped into her bedroom with her backpack.

Farrah's shoulders slumped and she walked over to drop onto the couch beside Honey. Honey put a hand on her shoulder and rubbed. "It's okay. She's fine. It's fine."

"Oh, Honey. I was so scared. What if I lost her? She's all I have."

"You didn't." Honey's eyes stung a little too. "You're going to get her a cell phone. We'll find a super cheap plan. You're going to talk to her about being safe. Because she *is* almost old enough to be out on her own."

"I can't handle it."

"You can. What choice do you have?" Honey smiled, even though it was heart-wrenching. "Keep her locked up until she's an adult?"

"Until she's thirty."

They both smiled.

"I need a drink," Farrah said. "Have a glass of wine with me while I calm down."

"Sure." Honey wondered how the hockey game was going, but for the moment this was more important. Also, she needed that drink too.

"Oh my *god*!" Honey's back arched, her head fell back, and she reached behind her for Matt's thighs. Flat on his back in the bed beneath her, Matt powered his hips up into her and his thumb circled over her clit. She cried out again as sensation whipped through her, his enormous cock thrusting up into her, so deep, igniting every nerve ending inside her. Fire spread through her body and her womb tightened.

"Fuck yeah," Matt growled. "Ride me, babe."

Her breasts bounced with each impact of their bodies and he lifted one hand and covered one soft globe. She looked at him, his face taut, his eyes narrowed and intense as he watched her.

"Feels so good," she whimpered. "So...so...good..."

"Yeah."

The tightening inside her wound up higher and she let out a long groan as she reached for it, wanting that ultimate peak…and there it was, oh *yeah*… She cried out as she came in long ripples of exquisite pleasure, one of Matt's hands between her legs, the other cupping her breast. She gave a few more small whimpers.

"Pussy squeezing me," he muttered. "Fuck, that's good."

Then he rolled up to sitting, grabbed her hips, and in a fast movement swung her onto her back and beneath him. God, he was so strong. She loved it.

He entered her again, on his knees between her thighs, driving into her still quivering pussy with hard strokes. Hands at her knees, he lifted her legs and again stared down at her with hot intensity as he fucked her, hard. She stared back at him, her body jerking with every lunge. She hadn't finished coming and the continued pressure inside her prolonged the ecstasy, a burning sensation moving over her clit, her limbs weak.

"This is called…taking the body hard," he said through a tight jaw.

A bubble of laughter rose in her despite her enervation from an amazing orgasm."I'll say," she gasped. Their eyes met and held and then he groaned himself, his head tipping back, and he held himself deep inside her, all throbbing heat and pressure. His fingers might be leaving bruises on her legs where he held her, but she loved how into it he was, how she made him lose his mind like that.

"Christ, Honey." He fell over her, taking most of his weight on his elbows, but still his big body was a delicious pressure on her. He buried his face in the side of her neck, his breathing rough. "Sweetest pussy I've ever had, honest to fuck."

She wrapped her arms around him, hands smoothing up and down his damp flesh, and kissed the big shoulder that was right at her mouth, a long, slow, open-mouthed kiss. She closed her eyes as emotions churned up inside her.

"Missed you, Honey," he murmured into the side of her neck.

She pressed her lips to his shoulder again then whispered, "Missed you too."

They stayed like that for a long time, their bodies slowly recovering, heart rate slowing, respiration evening, and then he rolled off her, withdrawing from her body in a long slide. "Be right back."

He disappeared to her bathroom for a few moments. While he was gone, she slipped beneath the comforter on her bed, and when he returned he joined her there, reaching for her, tucking her up against him. As she lifted her leg to his hip, he flinched and made a rough noise.

"What?"

Their eyes met in the dim room. "Took a hard check into the boards last night," he said. "Little sore."

"Oh no. Where?" She ran her palm over his hip.

"Yeah. There."

"Are you okay?"

"Yeah, trainers checked me out after. I'm fine."

"Did you ice it?"

"Yeah."

"Ibuprofen?"

"Don't like drugs."

"Uh-huh." She was used to the tough guy act from her dad and brothers. "I didn't see it." Maybe that was just as well. "I missed most of the game. I started watching it and then we had a little crisis."

"Who did? What happened?"

She told him about Mia's brief disappearance and the moments of panic.

"Babe," he murmured, running his hand down her shoulder and arm. "You love that kid, don't you."

"No! Don't be silly. I've only known her, like, a month."

He smiled. "Yeah."

"I was worried about her, like anyone would be."

"It's okay to care, Hon."

She was silent for a moment then said, "Whatever."

His body shook a little and she realized he was laughing. "So you were watching the game, huh? You seem to be watching a lot of hockey lately."

"Um. Yeah."

"Did you watch Tuesday's game?"

She didn't answer immediately. "Um…let me think…"

"Babe." He squeezed her.

"I can't remember what I did Tuesday night."

"Right."

"Okay, okay, I watched."

"See my goals?"

"Yes." Once again he'd led the team in points, with two goals and two assists. "You're pretty good."

His arms banded around her again. "Pretty good, huh."

She hitched a shoulder. "You know. For an NHL guy."

She felt his laughter again. "At least I won't get a big head around you."

Her mind went straight to the gutter. And apparently met his there.

"I mean, the other head," he qualified. He nudged her with his hips. "Always got a big head for you."

She couldn't help it. She started giggling. She tried to push away from him, but he wouldn't let her go. He lifted her chin so he could get her mouth. And he kissed her, even though they were both smiling.

After a while they got out of bed and ordered pizza. Matt had come to her place right after work on Friday and had barely walked in the door before he had her naked in her bed. Not that she minded.

After pizza, they snuggled on her couch and watched another hockey game. This was getting ridiculous. But again…she didn't really mind. They *had* to watch, because it was Winnipeg versus Pittsburgh, and Matt's brother Jason was doing the color commentary.

"You're cheering for the Jets, right?" she asked.

"Right." He slid his fingers through her hair. Mmm. That felt so good. "And so are you."

She grinned. "I don't know…I kinda like Pittsburgh."

"Bullshit."

She smiled against his chest. Of course she was cheering for Winnipeg, his home town.

The Jets soon had a two-nothing lead, so they were both happy.

"Look at that poke check," Jason said on the television, followed moments later by, "They are getting banged *hard* against the boards."

"He does that shit on purpose," Matt muttered.

She blinked. "What shit?"

"Making everything sound dirty. Banged against the boards. Poke check."

"Um… a poke check is pretty common. I don't think he made that up."

He grunted. "It sounds dirty. Especially when I've got a hot chick pressed up against me."

They continued to watch, Matt drinking a beer, her sipping a glass of wine. Then Jason said on TV, "Look at him get his stick in there," and Honey dissolved into giggles.

"Okay, I see what you mean," she said.

"He really does do it on purpose. He told me that."

She laughed even harder. "He can't do it on purpose."

Matt grinned. "Well, he looks for every opportunity he

has to say something that sounds dirty."

"Lots of chirping between the benches tonight," Jason said. The camera showed him talking for a moment. He stood between the two players' benches at ice level to do his commentary, another guy up in the press box calling the play by play. God, he looked like Matt, a little more mature but with the same boyish grin and charm. He wore a dark suit that fitted his big body perfectly, with a pale blue shirt and elegant silk tie. "Things are heating up down here." And he was proven right soon when a fight broke out between two players.

Honey turned her face into Matt's chest. "I hate fighting."

He laughed. "Seriously?"

"Of course."

"So did my mom. Even more so when it was me and one of my brothers fighting."

"You fought each other?" She lifted her head to stare at him in horror.

He shook his head. "No. Well, yeah, but they were a lot older than me, so we never really played against each other, other than at the community center. I do remember Jase and Tag going at it once. Holy fuck, thought my mom was gonna have a stroke."

"I cannot imagine having four boys and watching them play hockey, let alone watching them beat the crap out of each other."

He grinned. "Eh. It was fine. She's tough." Then he tipped his head to one side. "I want you to meet them."

Her forehead wrinkled. "Meet who?"

"My family. My parents."

Her insides squeezed painfully. Holy crapping ducks. "Uh…"

"My family's great," he said quietly. "No offense, but you were right…your family's fucked up. Saw that last weekend."

Her brain went into spin cycle. She didn't know what to say. Why did he keep doing this to her, throwing her way off balance?

"My family's awesome," he continued, oblivious to her emotional instability. "Although there were probably lots of times I didn't fully appreciate that."

"Well. Maybe I'll get to meet them some time."

"Count on it."

A strange wistful longing rose inside her. Damn. She wanted to meet his family. She wanted to see him with his parents and his brothers. She wanted to be a part of something like that. She always had. As a kid she'd dreamed about warmth and laughter and hugs and happiness. Unconditional love.

One of the Jets got a breakaway, racing to the Pittsburgh net, took the shot, and the puck went right into the pads of the goalie, who made a great save. "*Look* at that," Jason cried. "Daneck was wide open up top. Marchant just couldn't get it up."

And she and Matt both burst out laughing.

"Don't know about Marchant," Matt said, leaning forward to set his beer on the coffee table. "But *I* can get it up."

Honey smiled at him. "Oh, I know you can."

"Maybe you need a poke check."

"Maybe I do."

As the second period came to an end, Jason on TV asked the question, "Can the Colts come from behind and win this game?"

"Intermission," Matt said, lifting her away from him and standing. He pulled her with him. "*I'm* gonna come from behind."

"He shoots," Honey said, smiling, as she let him lead her into the bedroom. "He scores."

CHAPTER 17

As the Condors had a stretch of home games, Matt was around quite a bit the next week, and they spent most evenings together when there weren't games. The first night he came to pick her up to take her out for dinner, he handed her a small box. She looked down at it and frowned, then looked back up at him. "A cell phone?"

"Yeah. For Mia."

Her heart swelled alarmingly as she gazed up at him, and then her eyes stung in the corners.

"I paid for a two-year contract," he said. "Nothing extravagant, but it should be what they need. Uh…did she already get a phone?" he asked.

She blinked rapidly and shook her head. "I don't think so." She swallowed through a throat gone suddenly tight. "I'll give this to her later. I think Farrah's working tonight."

Mia was ecstatic. Farrah protested, but Honey convinced her to take it, knowing for Matt it was really no big deal. Except…it was.

Matt's next game was Saturday afternoon. Friday he again took her out for dinner, this time to an Irish pub near his apartment where, dressed in jeans and T-shirts, they sat in a back corner booth and drank Guinness and ate fish and chips.

"You know this isn't bad, for beer," she said, lifting the glass of dark brew.

Matt said nothing.

"So, tomorrow you play New York," she said, making conversation.

"Yeah."

"Are they any good?"

He blinked at her, his mouth tightening, then his gaze went unfocused.

She frowned. "Matt?"

He looked back at her and shook his head. "They have a few good players," he finally said. He looked down at his half-eaten dinner. He pushed it away. "You done?"

"Uh…no." It was not like Matt to not eat everything on his plate and then some of hers. "You?"

"Yeah." He picked up his cell phone, looked at it, set it down. He gazed around the restaurant.

"Okay. We could get this boxed up and take it home."

"Jesus. We don't need to do that." He rolled his eyes. "Fucking doggy bag — I don't think so."

She sat back. "Ooookay. Do you mind sitting there a few more minutes then, while I finish my dinner? Because you may be done, but I'm actually still hungry and still eating."

He gave a short nod. "Yeah, yeah. Sorry," he muttered.

But it turned out her appetite had in fact disappeared. "You feeling okay?"she asked quietly.

"Fine."

She nodded, forked up another piece of crispy battered fish, chewed it and swallowed it. She made herself do that a few more times, just because she'd made a point of wanting to finish her dinner. Then she took another swallow of her beer. "Okay," she said, Matt's attention on the television on the wall above the bar in the small pub. He glanced at her. "We can go now, if you want."

"I'll go pay the bill at the bar," he said, sliding out of the booth.

She watched him move through the tables, big and graceful. She narrowed her eyes a bit, worry curling inside her. Something was up with him. She opened her purse and touched up her lip gloss, checked her own cell phone needlessly, then waited for him to return.

They walked the two blocks to his apartment through the chilly evening. Fog was developing out over the ocean and the dampness made her shiver. Usually Matt would notice something like that and slide an arm around her, but tonight he walked beside her, not touching her, apparently lost in his own thoughts.

What was going on with him? Was he having second thoughts about them? Her heart landed in her throat, thinking that maybe he'd finally realized hanging around with her was not a good idea. She shoved her hands into her jacket pockets, shoulders hunched.

When they got to his apartment building, she paused at the door. "Maybe I should just go home."

He frowned. "What? Why?"

She eyed him. "You don't seem in a very good mood." She took a big breath. She had to ask. "Are you mad at me about something?"

He gave her a sharp look. "Fuck no!"

"Then what's wrong? You were all distracted and grouchy during dinner."

His eyebrows lifted. "Grouchy?"

"Yeah. Grouchy."

He rubbed his forehead. "Sorry. Didn't mean to drag you down."

"What is it?" She moved closer, more concern rising inside her.

"Let's go up to my place."

They rode the elevator up to his apartment in silence, questions buzzing in Honey's brain.

He went straight to his kitchen and grabbed a beer out of the fridge, then threw himself down onto his couch.

"Nothing for me, thanks," Honey said dryly. She kept her jacket on.

His head fell back. "Shit. Sorry, Honey. D'you want another beer? Wine?"

"I don't know. I guess I want to know what's going on."

"It's not you. Take your jacket off, for fuck's sake."

She gave him a narrow-eyed stare. "Whatever it is, you don't have to be an asshole. I'm going home. You can call me. If you want."

She turned to leave. She was at the door when she felt him behind her. He pressed her against the door with his big body. "Don't go," he murmured against her hair.

She closed her eyes. "Matt."

"I'm just on edge about the game tomorrow."

The game? *The game?*

He pressed deeper into her and she felt his heart thudding. One of his hands tightened on her hip.

"Why?" she whispered.

"I really don't want to talk about it. Can we just leave it at that? I'm sorry I'm being an asshole."

He moved back and she turned to face him, their bodies still touching. She gave him a searching look. "Are you hurt?" Oh god! "Is it your injury?" She bit her lip, her body going tense.

"No. I'm fine."

She let out a hard breath. Okay. "Talking about it might

help," she offered, although she still had no idea what the problem was.

"I'm just being an idiot," he said. "Come on. Let's watch a movie or something. You pick. It can even be *The Notebook*."

She gave him a crooked smile. "Gee, thanks. Seriously, Matt. Maybe you should just get a good night's sleep or something. I'll see you Sunday."

His mouth went tight. His throat moved as he swallowed. "Please. Don't go. I want you here, Honey." His eyes met hers. "Please."

Her heart melted and she let out another long breath. "Okay. But I want to watch *Die Hard*."

His eyes widened. "Yeah?" Then he shook his head with a short laugh. "Right."

"No, really." She knew he liked that movie. She pushed him back with a little shove to his chest. "Now let me in."

She took off her jacket as they walked back to the living room, dropping it on the back of a chair, and sat on the couch.

"Maybe I will have a glass of wine," she said to him before he sat again.

"Sure, babe, I'll get it."

Soon she was snuggled into his side with a movie on TV — a compromise in *Star Wars*, which she actually liked too.

An hour into the movie, Matt said, "We play New York tomorrow."

"Yeah. I know."

"That's the team I was playing when I got hurt."

She blinked into the dim room, going still. Her hand rested on his flat belly. "Oh." Her mind started working. "The guy who hit you...Fiero..."

"Yeah."

"Tell me what happened," she said quietly, keeping her cheek pressed to his chest. "When you got hurt."

"It was a dirty hit," he said, his voice rough. "It was late, it was from behind, his feet left the ice and he made direct contact with my head. Fiero got a five-minute penalty and a game misconduct. Then they reviewed the video, and he got a twenty-one game suspension. Almost the same number of games I missed," he finished bitterly.

"You don't think that was enough?"

"Hell. What's enough? That wasn't the first time he did something like that. I'd be happy if he wasn't allowed to play ever."

"Did you ever talk to him after?"

"No. He made some statement that he didn't think it was a bad hit, and he had no intention of hurting me, but he never apologized either."

She sucked in a shaky breath. "Are you mad at him still?"

He didn't answer for a long moment. His hand went into her hair and pulled through it, letting the strands slide through his fingers again and again. "I don't know."

"So… that's why you're on edge about tomorrow."

"Yeah. A little."

A little. Right. She smiled against his shirt. "Are you going to fight him?"

His body tensed against hers.

"I don't know."

"That wasn't a no."

"I want to punch his fuckin' lights out," he growled. "I seriously want to pummel him into a bloody pulp."

She tried to breathe. "So that's a yes. You are still mad."

He sighed. "Not as much as I was. Man, there was a time when the rage was just burning a hole inside me."

"Are you going to fight him?" she asked again.

"I'm not gonna back down if it happens. But I'm not stupid. I'm not gonna go out there and instigate something. I just got back to playing. I don't need a suspension."

"That's smart," she agreed.

"Fiero, on the other hand, *is* stupid," he said. "Who knows what the fuck he's going to do."

"Why would he do anything? He's the one who was in the wrong."

"Yeah, but like I said, he's stupid."

She smiled again. "Then you have an advantage over him."

"He's got twenty pounds on me."

Her stomach cramped, thinking of Matt fighting. Growing up around hockey and hockey players, that part of the game shouldn't bother her, but she hated the fighting, especially if it was Matt. The way they'd throw punches while on the ice, sometimes going down on the ice, both wearing sharp blades and equipment that was supposed to protect them but could actually cause an injury in that circumstance…it made her feel like she was going to throw up.

"I don't want you to fight," she said quietly. "But I know you'll do what you think you have to do."

They sat there in silence for long moments, the movie still playing, but Honey wasn't paying attention to it and she had a feeling Matt wasn't either.

Then his arms tightened around her and he pulled her up higher on his body. His hand went to her face, cupping her jaw. "Thank you, Honey," he whispered.

"For what?" She touched his cheek with her fingertips.

"Just for being here. Thank you for staying. Didn't wanna be alone tonight."

Emotion swelled in her chest and she found herself on the verge of saying something really, really stupid. Instead, she smiled and nodded, and touched her lips to his in a gentle kiss.

~

This time her dad didn't seem so surprised to see her when she showed up in his box.

Her insides were knotted, her throat dry, but she was trying to be cool and not let on how nervous she was for Matt.

"So, um…which guy is Fiero?" she asked her dad, looking at the players on the ice below them for the warm up.

Her dad gave her a long look. "Number seven."

She found him. Big guy. *Bastard*. She drummed her fingers on the counter.

"Is he a dirty player?"

"He's a repeat offender, yeah."

"Why do they let him play?" she demanded.

Dad snorted. "The suspension was intended to send a message that the league won't tolerate that kind of conduct." He shrugged. "I haven't seen him play yet this season. Hopefully he got it."

"Yeah. Hopefully."

She sensed Dad's amusement and glanced at him. "What?"

"You worried?"

She hitched a shoulder and turned back to the ice. "Nah."

"Uh-huh."

"You shouldn't have invited Matt for dinner that weekend."

"I thought you'd like it," he said.

"I did like it," she admitted quietly. "But please don't interfere, Dad. I'm trying to make it on my own. I don't know what exactly is happening with Matt and me. Probably nothing." That was an epic lie. "It was embarrassing when you got me that job that turned out to be just them doing you a big favor and making it look like I was working. I don't want you doing that with guys I date." Getting involved with one of the players on the team was undoubtedly a bad idea, but it was past too late for that. And it was *Matt*. "I worked hard at school so I could feel like I accomplished something on my own. Even though I had financial help from you."

"Lots of parents pay for their kids' education, Honey."

"I know. And I appreciate it. I made sure I didn't waste that opportunity. You got me my job, and I'm trying not to waste that opportunity too." And Matt? Was that an opportunity?

She felt like Matt was something so far beyond anything she could expect in her life, so good, so decent, so strong. It scared her. She could change her lifestyle, hit the books and graduate *summa cum laude*. She could take initiative at work and find things to work on even though they didn't expect her to. But could she try hard enough at a relationship to actually make it work? Did she even know how to do that?

Those questions terrified her. The longer this went on, the more she and Matt spent time together, the bigger the chance was that she was going to screw this up. The bigger the chance she was going to get hurt again.

"I just don't want Matt feeling pressure from you," she finally said to her father. "Especially if things end between us. I don't want you to treat him any differently."

She felt his gaze on her and she turned. They looked at each other for a long moment. "I didn't intend a dinner invitation to be any kind of pressure," he said quietly. "And of course I won't treat him any differently." He paused, looking uncomfortable. "Having a daughter is…Christ. The guys you used to date…we never really got to know them much, but most of them were assholes."

She choked on a laugh. It was true. "I know."

"And there were a lot of them," he continued, frowning.

Also true.

"All we wanted was for you to meet a nice guy and settle down."

"Yeah." Her chest constricted so tightly she could hardly breathe. These things were still so hard to talk about. Hard to admit. Even to herself. Because deep inside, that was all she'd ever wanted too. So eager to find someone to love her, she'd rushed into relationships with any guy who came along, even if he was a cokehead abuser who loved her for her money, or a spoiled rich kid like her, whose parents paid for his condo, his car, his parties, so he never had to work, or... Well, as Dad had said, there'd been a lot of losers.

"Matt's a decent guy," Dad said.

"I know."

Dad gave her another long, inscrutable look then nodded and turned back to the game.

She turned over all that in her head. Apparently Dad approved of her and Matt together. Which just made that scary, mixed-up feeling inside her even worse. She didn't need her parents' approval. She'd spent the last few years trying to get past that.

She focused on the game, sitting on the edge of her seat whenever Fiero and Matt were on the ice together. But nothing much happened between them. At one point, after a whistle, she saw them skate near each other. Her breath stuck in her throat, but all they did was apparently exchange words, which of course she couldn't hear.

Then she began to notice that nearly every other player on the Condors team was taking any opportunity to hammer Fiero into the boards. When she caught on to that, she started smiling. It wasn't until near the end of the second period that Matt leveled Fiero with a hit into the boards. She sucked in breath, but no whistle blew.

"Clean hit," Dad said beside her.

Every time Fiero got hit, the crowd cheered. Honey grinned.

In the end it wasn't Matt who fought Fiero, it was their

biggest d-man Jeff Bradley who took him on after Fiero skated into the crease and jostled the Condors' goalie. Fiero got a penalty for goaltender interference and it wasn't that bad a hit, and somehow Honey knew that Matt's team had his back all through this game. And she liked that.

CHAPTER 18

A week later, Matt's teammates were planning a night at Eden, a trendy upscale club in L.A.

"Want you to come with us," he'd told Honey Friday night back at his place after they'd gone out for dinner.

She'd made a face, sitting in his bed naked with sheets wrapped around her. "That scene doesn't appeal anymore."

"I want you to meet my friends," he said. "Want them to meet you. We're together. We can't hide from the world forever."

"I'm not hiding from the world." She frowned.

"Yeah, Hon, you are."

She crossed her arms over her breasts, still frowning. "I'm just not into that stuff anymore."

"I know you're not. And it's not like I'm all that fired up about it either. But they're my friends and I like hanging out with them. Sometimes it's just at the pool at my place shooting the shit, sometimes it's playing beach volleyball, sometimes it's a nice restaurant or a fun bar."

She sat there silently.

"Want you to be part of that," he said.

More silence.

"Babe. Honey."

"What?"

He reached for her face and cupped her chin so she had to face him. "Let me in," he said quietly.

She blinked. "What do you mean?"

"I mean, let me in. We've been spending a lot of time together. We go out just the two of us, but it always has to be somewhere people won't see us. My friends don't even know about us. That night your parents saw us, I thought you were going to hide under the table until they were gone. We're having a lot of hot sex, which, don't get me wrong, is great. But I want into your life. Let me in."

"You are in my life. You just said so."

"You know what I fucking mean."

They stared at each other. She felt a tight, burning sensation in her chest, rising up into her throat.

She knew it was a mistake. She'd known getting involved with him was a stupid thing to do. What had she been thinking? All this time she and Matt were spending together was drawing her deeper and deeper into this thing, whatever they had, and now he was pulling her in even further. Meeting his friends.

He wanted more. He wanted them to be a real couple.

Her lungs refused to expand and her skin went cold. She didn't want to end things between them, but... She closed her eyes briefly.

"Okay," she said. "We can go to the club."

"Got a VIP table," he said, leaning over to kiss her mouth. "It'll be fun."

"Right," she muttered.

Now they walked into Eden, big and dark, with colored flashing lights, occasional bursts of fog, and pumping house music. DJ Eric D'Angelo was at the front, mixing the music, his body moving, hands clapping above his head. Electronically generated funk, soul and pop recordings added to the foundation of kick drum beat and synth bass line. Honey felt the pulse of the music deep inside her body.

With his hands on her hips, Matt followed behind her closely into the crowded club, as a hostess led them to the VIP table his teammate Joe had reserved, up on a raised dais above the crowd, with its own bouncer guarding the steps and its own serving personnel.

"You look hot as hell," he said at her ear. "Golden girl."

She was wearing the strapless gold lace dress, her only other choice for the night other than the black sequined dress. She'd splurged on a pair of nude-colored stilettos she'd found on sale.

People crowded the dance floor, moving to the mid-tempo beat, arms swaying, hips shifting. Professional dancers on small raised stages also danced, girls in what looked like black lace underwear—skimpy bras and tiny boy shorts—and high heels. More people lined up around the long mirrored bar, holding drinks, laughing, talking.

The bouncer let them past him and they climbed the steps up to the small private area with a big round table with a curved padded bench seat around it. Joe Barzetti, Chris Dobie and Niklas Berglund were there, along with Joe's new girlfriend Bryn. Some shouted introductions were done, Honey smiling and shaking hands with everyone, then sliding into the booth followed by Matt.

A waitress was there immediately to take their order. Honey asked for a French martini and Matt ordered beer.

"Do you like dancing?" she asked in his ear.

He smiled down at her. "I don't mind it."

"Good. 'Cause I can't sit here and listen to this without wanting to move to it."

She was moving already, her shoulders and her head,

bopping a little to the beat. She looked around the bar, watched people dancing, accepted her drink from the waitress with a smile.

When Matt learned Joe had already started a tab, he held up his beer. "Thanks, dude," he yelled.

Joe grinned. "I'm not buying your fucking drinks all night."

Matt laughed. "Whatever."

Honey knew bar or dinner bills into four figures weren't unusual when Matt and his friends went out. They all had the money.

"Wait till Dobie and Nik start buying drinks for chicks," Matt said with a grin.

Joe rolled his eyes and slid his arm around Bryn.

"Great idea." Nik slid out of the booth. "Let's go mingle," he said to Dobie. And they disappeared down the steps and into the crowd.

That left her and Matt with the other couple.

"What do you think of this place?" Matt asked her.

"Haven't you been here before?" Joe said.

"No." Honey shook her head. "I was living in San Francisco the last few years. This place is new. I like it."

But she felt like she'd been there before, because it was just like every other club where she'd spent almost every night back in her wild partying days. Beautiful people dressed in expensive clothes, lots of them flirting and looking for hookups, lots of booze and no doubt lots of other substances.

"D'Angelo is a great DJ," Bryn said. "That's why the place is so packed tonight. Some of my friends are here somewhere too. We have to find them."

"They'll find us," Joe said.

"What do you do for a living, Bryn?" Honey asked.

"I'm an entertainment lawyer, at Warner Brothers."

Honey blinked. "Cool." She'd expected to hear "model" or

"actor". Bryn's long dark hair was straight and super shiny, her olive complexion smooth and perfect and her teeth gleamed the impossible bright white of expensive veneers.

"What do you do, Honey?" Bryn eventually asked.

"I'm a Programming Coordinator at the Condors Foundation."

"Foundation?" Bryn blinked.

"It's the charitable arm of the California Condors," she explained. "It's a way for the players, their wives and girl-friends and the coaches to contribute to the community."

"Oh, that's awesome," Bryn said. She glanced at Joe. "Didn't you say you did some volunteer work with a hockey camp?"

"Yeah." Joe nodded.

"You're so lucky you get to work with hockey players," Bryn said to Honey.

"Well, I don't do a lot of work directly with them," she said. "I'm mostly liaising with the community, but I have been working with Matt, getting him involved with a local school project. And I've been busy lately with a big fundraiser we're doing next weekend, actually, the Sweet Affair Ball."

"What are you raising funds for?"

"St. Clara Children's Hospital."

Bryn nodded. "That's so great. Are we going to that?" she asked Joe.

"Yeah."

"Oh good!" Then she shocked Honey by asking, "What could we do to help?"

Honey blinked. "Um…do you want to donate money?"

Bryn glanced at Joe. "I was thinking more about volun-teering somehow. I assume you already bought tickets?"

"Yeah." He looked bemused, watching Bryn. Then he looked at Matt and they exchanged glances, which Honey read as surprise.

"Well, if you want to help at the event, I can check my files at the office next week and see if there's anywhere we still need volunteers."

She expected Bryn to let it go at that, but Bryn insisted they exchange cell phone numbers so Honey could call her next week. Now Honey was a little bemused, but went along with it.

"Let's go dance," she said to Matt.

He made a face. "Okay."

She took the last sip of her martini and set the glass down on the table. They slid out of the booth and Matt held her hand as they walked toward the packed dance floor. Bodies moved to the beat of the music, hands in the air, pulsing lights illuminating them red and blue and purple. Honey turned to face him and started moving to the music. Their eyes met and she smiled.

"You're a good dancer."

She smiled her thanks. It had been a while, but she loved dancing. This was all familiar to her, the music, the bodies around her, the moves. She swiveled her hips, shook her hair, lifted her arms above her head. Matt's eyes were heated on her. She liked it.

She edged closer to Matt and draped her hands over his shoulders. In her heels, she was only a few inches shorter than him. Smiling back at her, he set his hands on her hips, and she bent her knees and starting rolling her hips.

"Hot," he said, watching her, bending his knees too.

They danced a few songs, her moves getting down and dirtier as she got into the music, then returned to their dais for another drink. Dobie and Nik had returned with some other people they'd invited to join them in their VIP area, everyone now standing by the table instead of sitting. It had turned into a small private party. Honey watched in amusement as some of the girls who'd joined them attached themselves to the players.

Their personal server approached and they ordered more drinks. A few cocktails, some dancing, Matt's teammates seemed like nice guys, even Bryn seemed nice—this was okay. They were joined by more people, the friends Bryn had mentioned, and Honey found herself enjoying some of the banter and laughter. Servers brought them trays of hot and cold hors d'oeuvres, thanks to their VIP status.

A few drinks later, she and Matt returned to the dance floor.

The music shifted into a slower mix, and now, holding his gaze as long as she could in a sultry connection, she turned her back to Matt. He set his hands on her hips. She bent her knees again, laid her hands on her thighs with her back arched, then looked at Matt again over her shoulder. She rolled her hips again, back into his groin. His lips parted and as they moved together, she felt him get hard.

They weren't the only ones dancing like this, not by a long shot. It was like sex on the dance floor, one girl bending over so her hands touched the floor, grinding her ass into her partner's crotch. Yeah, Honey may have done that a time or two and yeah, there were photos to prove it.

"Yeah," Matt muttered into her ear, pressing in deeper. She leaned a little to the side, knees bent, and he matched her knee bend, keeping his pelvis with hers as she started to move it around and around. He followed her movement, keeping his groin pressed to her ass. She leaned more to the side and he went the other way, and they looked at each other, eyes connecting in another heated exchange. Hands on her thighs, she deepened the knee bend, rolling her hips back and forth. His erection pressed into her ass.

"So. Fucking. Sexy," he muttered.

She smiled and lifted one arm to hook it around his neck,

shifting back in front of him. His fingers dug into her hips. Heat surrounded her. "Christ," he said into her ear. "You're killing me, Honey."

Well. Good. She gave him another grind and a roll of her hips to the beat of the music.

They finished that song then Matt said, "Need a drink. Now." He grabbed her hand and started dragging her off the dance floor.

"Hey," she said. "I was having fun."

He glanced at her and his lips tipped up as he caught her teasing smile. "Yeah," he growled. "You were having fun torturing me." He spun her around, into his arms, pressed front to front now, chest to thigh. "You want me to do you right there on the dance floor?"

She linked her arms around his neck. Her blood pulsed hotly through her veins, her body warm and aroused from the dancing. "That would be worse than anything I ever did in my wild days. I think you're corrupting me, hockey boy."

He choked on a laugh. "Oh babe." He dipped his head and gave her a hard fast kiss on the mouth.

And a camera flashed at them.

Honey paused and bent her head briefly. Her first reaction was "shit!" but wasn't this exactly what she'd expected? Might as well give 'em something good. So she lifted her head and kissed Matt again, this time deeper, with tongue.

"Honey," he muttered. "Come on."

They were moving toward their table, when Honey was attacked by someone hurling herself at Honey with a screech. "Honeeeeeeey!"

The other woman grabbed Honey in a tight squeeze and rocked back and forth.

Shock had Honey's eyes going wide. "Cressa!" She pulled back a little. "Hi!"

Her one-time BFF. She felt Matt stiffen beside her as he recognized Cressa.

Oh holy hell and shit fire.

"I can't believe it!" Cressa yelled. "You're here! You're back! Why didn't you call me?"

Matt's fingers on her hip dug in a little deeper. She glanced at him, which then made Cressa glance at him. Her eyes bugged out. "Matt! Omigod!" Then her gaze flickered back and forth between them. "You two are together?" A wrinkle appeared between her eyebrows.

"Um…" Honey stumbled.

"Yeah," Matt growled, sliding an arm around Honey's waist. "Hey, Cressa."

"Wow," Cressa said, eyes wide. Wide but unfocused. She was drunk. Or high. Or something. "Honey! I need to hear all about this!"

Honey rapidly tried to gather her scattered thoughts. Holy bajesus. "Who are you here with?" she asked. "Anyone I know?"

"Yes! Naarah and Jenni. You should totally come say hi! We need to do lunch, or go out some time. Next week is Jenni's birthday and we're having a big party at Octave. You have to come! Come on, let's go find them!" She started to lead Honey somewhere, but Matt's hand gripped her wrist.

"Hey babe," he said. "You're staying with me."

Honey smiled at him. "It's okay, Matt. I can go talk to them." She'd moved on past this scene but she didn't have to be rude.

Cressa gave him a blurry smile. "Matt. You're still so hot." She edged closer to him and slid an arm through his, grabbing his biceps. "Wow. You're even bigger than you used to be, I think." She giggled. "God. Remember? That night at the Four Seasons?"

Holy crapping crap. She had to bring that up. Honey's

insides burned and heat spread over her skin from forehead to toes. Well, there it was.

"That was so hot, that night," Cressa babbled on. "That was my first threesome." She gave Matt a coy, albeit drunken, look. "Not yours though. I remember. I remember you told us you once had three girls! Not just two!"

Honey kept her smile in place even as a sharp pain knifed through her.

CHAPTER 19

Fuck, fuck, fuck.

Matt couldn't stop the flashes of that night that exploded in his head. He and Honey and her best friend Cressa, all drunk and high and horny. He couldn't even remember whose idea the threesome had been. They'd gone to the Four Seasons and Honey'd paid for a room with the unlimited credit her parents provided her with. They'd shared another joint, drank some vodka. Two girls had been all eager at the time, and yeah, it was true, that wasn't the first time he'd done that. Honey was wild and hot, and at the time he'd been adventurous and horny and it had all seemed fun and studly. Yeah. Him and two girls. Didn't every guy dream of that? He'd been twenty years old, his judgment maybe not the best, but both girls were beautiful and sexy, Honey all blonde and long-limbed, Cressa curvy with dark waves flowing over her shoulders. Hormones had overtaken good judgment.

Another vision of Honey and Cressa naked in bed together flashed in his head. He closed his eyes briefly. Honey and Cressa both going down on him. Honey and Cressa touching each other, because they thought it turned him on. Him touching Honey. Him touching Cressa.

Mother of all fuckers.

His insides churned now. He didn't know what to do.

"I've missed you so much, Honey," Cressa said with a pout. "I'm glad you're back." Her gaze swiveled to Matt. "And you too, Matt." Her smile went sultry. "We had fun that night."

"Let's go," Honey blurted, and without even a glance at him over her shoulder, she linked arms with Cressa and disappeared into the crowd.

He'd hated himself for that night. But it had been so long ago. He thought he'd put it out of his head, thought Honey'd forgiven him for it, but hell, faced with a living breathing reminder in the form of Cressa, it all came roaring back.

Now he really needed a drink.

Dobie moved up next to him. "Dude," he said. "Honey Holbrook? Seriously?"

"I need a beer," he muttered. Dobie handed him his and he guzzled it down. "Shit."

"What up?" Dobie frowned.

"Nothing. Honey just ran into an old friend."

"Man, can't believe you're doing Steve Holbrook's daughter. Is she still as wild as she used to be?"

Matt shook his head, frowning. "Shut the fuck up. It's…" Whatever he said was going to sound lame, so he took his own advice and shut the fuck up. "I need another drink."

He looked around and caught the eye of the sexy blonde waitress who was looking after them. She strolled over. "What can I get you?" she asked with a flirty smile.

"Another beer."

"Right away."

He moved to the railing overlooking the club and looked for Honey.

It was impossible in the huge nightclub, in the dark with all the people there, the pulsing lights and fog. Finally he spotted her in a corner with a group of people, including Cressa. He watched her, music pounding all around him, inside him. She beamed a big smile as she talked and laughed, bending closer to listen to something one of the girls said, letting a guy put his arm around her waist and pull her against him in a hug. She set a hand on the guy's chest and smiled up at him, then laughed again.

She fit right in there at the club, no surprise, despite her reluctance to come. Gorgeous, golden, sexy. Her shiny blonde hair, lightly tanned skin and gold lace dress made her glow from head to toe. There were a lot of other hot girls in the club, but Matt's gaze was glued to her, had been the entire night. Now, his gut churned nastily, his muscles bunched, his jaw aching.

She'd wanted to go talk to her old friends.

Yeah, right. Were these the friends who'd used her for her money and let her go home with strangers when she'd outstayed her welcome and could no longer buy their drugs and booze? The people who'd let her take the fall for possession? Some friends. He recognized one of the guys as someone he'd met way back when. He'd hated the jerk then, hated his lazy, spoiled ass. He'd never got why Honey hung around with those people, couldn't understand why she didn't see them for who they were.

Now, he understood better why she had. Looking for all the love and affection that was missing from her home life.

He wasn't usually one to be critical of other people. Nobody was perfect, least of all him—he'd just had a very unpleasant reminder of that. He liked most people, and generally people liked him too. He wasn't one to judge. But he'd never liked these people Honey had called her friends, only when he'd tried to talk to her about it, it had just caused an argument, with her defending them even though he could see they were all losers.

She had to see that now.

He wanted to look after her. Protect her. Make sure these jerks didn't hurt her like they had before. But he had to trust that she'd grown up. He had to trust that she knew what she was doing, that she could deal with this. He knew she'd changed, he'd seen it in so many ways. She wanted to do things on her own—get her degree, make a success of her job. So, insides twisted into a hard knot, he accepted the beer from the waitress and went back to his friends and tried to pretend everything was good.

Honey left Matt, trying to ignore the disappointed frown on his face, letting Cressa drag her across the crowded club to where her friends were. The friends who'd lost interest in her when she'd no longer had money. Of course, she'd been trying to mooch off them, sleeping on their couches, eating their food, letting them buy the drinks for a change. She had to squeeze her eyes shut as a shudder of revulsion worked its way down her spine at the person she'd been.

But she could do this—say hi to these people, make some small talk and then get back to real people. Get back to Matt.

She was greeted with the same astonished squeals as Cressa had given her. Back in the day, Honey, Cressa and Jenni had been a tight trio of BFFs, having gone to the same high school together, grown up in the same affluent neighborhood with the same lifestyle and the same complete lack of ambition or goals for their lives. At one point Cressa had thought about being an actress, but seemingly had expected Hollywood to come knocking at her door instead of doing anything about it. Since Honey had left L.A., Jenni had done some modeling for Playboy and apparently had lived with Heff in the mansion for a while. Also there was Naarah, who Honey had also hung around with, who had done some acting, but her trips in and out of rehab had interfered with that. Honey was introduced to Lurlaine Arber, who she'd heard of but never met. She was the daughter of a famous show biz couple who'd appeared in an eighties sitcom and ended up married, and now their family had a reality show. Then there were the guys—Chandler Dunley, son of another Hollywood couple, Dene Williams, who Honey had dated for a while at one time, but she didn't catch what he was doing now, and two guys who turned out to be NBA players.

She answered questions about what she'd been doing for the last three years, what she was doing now, where she was living. She watched their puzzled expressions and changed the subject from her back to them, and she listened to them talk about so-and-so's latest party and the big birthday bash they were planning for Jenni and how another friend of theirs was out of rehab. Again.

Somehow Honey ended up on the dance floor again this time with Cressa and Jenni, just like old times. Honey almost had to laugh at how Cressa and Jenni were trying to outdo each other with their sexy dance moves, seeing how much attention they could attract. And they did attract attention, both of them beautiful and dressed in skimpy dresses and sky-high platform shoes. Cameras flashed again, and then Honey groaned as the two girls started grinding against each other, much as she and Matt had been earlier. She closed her eyes briefly, more memories coming back. A couple of hot girls practically making out on the dance floor had been a sure fire way to get attention.

And it worked for Cressa when Chandler shouldered his way through the crowd onto the dance floor, grabbed Cressa's arm and dragged her off. But Cressa just giggled and shot Jenni and Honey tipsy smiles as they left the dance floor.

Honey was done. But Jenni flung an arm around her shoulders. "I need a drink!" she said over the music. "Let's go."

Jenni danced her way off the dance floor and Honey reluctantly followed with a glance over her shoulder to scan the room for Matt. She didn't see him.

She soon had another French martini in her hand. Dene moved closer to her. "You look great, Honey," he said. "Can't believe you're back."

"Did you even notice I was gone?" she couldn't resist asking dryly.

He blinked, his eyes a little blurry from alcohol. Oh, who was she to judge? She'd been tipping back the French martinis all evening, trying to make this whole thing more bearable.

"Of coursh I notished," he said. "Missed you, Honey."

"Uh-huh. That's so sweet."

"Give me your number," he said. "I'll call you. We should go out some time."

That was the last thing she wanted. She should tell him she was seeing someone else. But they programmed each other's numbers into their phones. She didn't have to use it.

"Let's dance," Dene said, setting down his drink and grabbing her hand.

Back to the dance floor she went, this time with Dene. Her stomach churned a little, feeling…god, was that guilt? Yep, that's what that was. Guilt about leaving Matt to drink and dance with these loser people she really didn't care anything about.

Shit.

From the dance floor she spotted Matt up in their private VIP area, standing at the railing looking down. Looking right at her. It was too dark and he was too far away to really see his face, but she felt his gaze on her. She beamed him a big smile and waved, beckoning him to come down there and rescue her.

But he didn't.

Back at their table after one dance with Dene, Cressa and Chandler exchanged some pointed barbs and heated looks, and when he muttered something under his breath that sounded like, "Stupid cunt", Honey's jaw dropped. Her gaze snapped back to Cressa to see if she'd heard. Apparently she had. Her eyes filled with tears.

"Cressa," Honey murmured, sliding closer to her. "Are you and Chandler together?"

"He's my boyfriend," she mumbled. "We've been together about a year now."

"Is something wrong? You both don't seem very happy."

"Something's always wrong." She dragged the back of her hand beneath one eye. "Oh Honey. I missed you so much."

Um. Yeah. Honey'd never heard from Cressa all the time she'd been at school. Sure, she'd missed her. But whatever. Cressa was crying. Honey slipped an arm around her shoulders. "Let's go to the ladies' room."

Cressa let her lead her across the bar, down the hall and into the ladies' room, which was also huge and packed with girls all primping in front of the big mirrors, and some lined up waiting for toilets. One girl had a mini flat iron that she was using to touch up her hair. Honey rolled her eyes. Okay, maybe she'd done that. Once. A few times.

"Why would you stay with a guy who calls you a cunt?" she asked Cressa, once she'd established her in a quieter corner of the ladies' lounge.

"Because I love him."

Honey blinked. "Okay, I'll ask another way. How can you love a guy who calls you a cunt?"

"He doesn't mean it. He's just mad."

"What's he mad about?" Oh, she should not have even asked that question. Did it matter? He'd called her the c-word. Honey had no objections to that word when used in reference to female anatomy, despite her comments to Matt about his swearing, but when it was used as an insult—that was a deal breaker.

Or, it was now. There may have been a time she never really thought about it that much. A time when she laughed off guys' insults. Because she didn't want to think about it, or what that meant about her that she'd let a guy insult her like that.

Frack.

She didn't even know Cressa anymore and wasn't sure if she actually still even liked her, but the girl was upset and teary and she couldn't just ignore that.

"I don't know," Cressa whispered. "He's always mad about something."

"Dump his ass," Honey said.

Cressa blinked wetly at her. "You've changed."

"God, I hope so." Honey gave a faint smile. "Seriously, Cressa. You don't need that."

"I need someone." Cressa grimaced. "You know what it's like."

Yeah. She did. Her heart squeezed for Cressa. "Oh sweetie," she whispered. "It doesn't have to be like that."

She shouldn't let herself be dragged back into this. She shouldn't care. But Cressa was dissolving into tears, sobbing and wailing. Erm. Where were her other girlfriends, the ones she'd come with? Nowhere near, that was for sure, probably having a good time out on the dance floor or snorting coke somewhere. Honey let out a long breath and tried to get Cressa to calm down.

This took some time, and then doing makeup repair in

front of the mirror took even more time. Then they were finally ready to go back out and find their group again. She'd been gone a lot longer than she'd planned, dealing with Cressa's little meltdown. Was Matt looking for her? Wondering where she was?

The others were preparing to leave when she and Cressa got back to their table. "Come with us, Honey! We're going to a party. At Paul Azariah's."

She lifted her eyebrows at the mention of the movie star, a recent runner-up for *People* magazine's sexiest man of the year. "Sounds like fun. But I came with Matt."

"Where is he?" Cressa said, frowning. "Go get him! Bring him along. He's sexy. He's a hockey player," she told the others.

"We're here with some of his friends," Honey said.

"Bring them too!"

Yeah...no. Crashing a party with one extra person, maybe. With a whole entourage...well, that had never stopped her before, but now...just no.

"I can't," she said. "Tempting as it is! Wow! Paul Azariah!"

"I know! I'll call you!" Cressa called out as they left the club. She waved at Honey.

Honey just shook her head. Cressa. She didn't even have Honey's number. How would she call her?

She left the dance floor and found Matt up on the dais with his friends, standing talking to Joe and Bryn. He held a beer in a relaxed grip, laughing about something. She paused at the top of the stairs to watch him for a moment. He was so beautiful. So special and good.

When he saw her, his smile disappeared.

Not good.

Even so, he slid an arm around her waist and pulled her in close. "Decided to come back," he said in a low tone.

"Of course." She smiled with the relief of being back with him. "The others have left to go to a party at Paul Azariah's. Want to go?

"Fuck no."

"Just thought I'd ask." She was totally joking, but he didn't seem to get it.

He frowned. "*You* want to go?"

"He *was* almost voted sexiest man of the year."

Matt rolled his eyes. She gave him a nudge of her elbow. "I'm kidding. Although, Cressa wanted you to come."

He gave her a hard stare.

Shit. Was he angry at her?

Her insides went hollow and her chest ached.

But then heat flared inside her. What the fuck was he angry about? She hadn't done anything wrong. She'd talked to some old friends, danced a little…she'd stayed away longer than she'd intended but most of that time had been spent with Cressa crying in the ladies' room.

"Yeah," she said. "She wants another threesome. Just like old times."

His eyebrows jerked together and his gaze narrowed.

Shit. She'd crossed a line. She knew it as soon as she said it. "Let's go dance more," she said, trying to pull away.

"You've danced enough, babe," he said tightly. "I think we should call it a night."

"Already?" Truthfully, all she wanted to do was kick off her high heels, crawl into her bed, pull the covers over her head and stay there for about a year.

"Yeah. We're outta here." He pulled out his cell phone and called the car service to bring the car up front, then had a word with Joe and Dobie. Honey moved over to say good night to Bryn.

"I'll talk to you next week," Bryn said. "About the gala. And we'll see you there!"

At least Bryn had actually taken her number. But Honey knew exactly how that "I'll call you" line worked.

She and Matt collected their jackets from the VIP coat check then emerged out the front doors onto the sidewalk. Lights immediately exploded in their faces. Fuck! More cameras.

These were the paps who couldn't get into the club.

"Honey!" someone called. "We heard you were here! You living back in L.A. now?"

There'd been a time when she would have paused to strike a pose, smiling at the cameras, flirting with the guys. Now, she just wanted to run. But she didn't. She pulled out that smile again, tossed her hair back and started walking.

Matt stepped between her and the cameras, arm around her, hustling her along.

"You two dating, Matt?" someone called. "How long have you been together?"

"How are you feeling after your injury?" someone else yelled.

More flashes.

They kept walking. Fast. The car Matt had hired for them waited at the curb. They hurried over to it. The driver opened the door for them, and Matt handed Honey in. Her short dress rode up on her thighs as she slid in and to her shock another flash fired right in front of her, a photographer crouched low on the sidewalk.

"Fuck that bullshit," Matt growled, and he grabbed the photographer and lifted him up. Actually lifted him right off his feet. "You wanna get punched right in the face, dude? Delete that picture. Right fucking now."

The guy started to protest, but Matt gave another growl and backed him up against the fender of the car.

"Hey, hey, hands off," the guy cried, and a couple of other

photographers closed in. "I'll press charges for assault…or sue you—"

"Try it," Matt snapped. He yanked the camera away from the guy and peered at it. "Delete the fucking picture. Now. Or you'll be the one getting your ass sued. Not to mention nose broken and your expensive camera smashed on the sidewalk."

"This is a public place," the guy stammered. "I didn't do anything wrong."

Honey watched this all unfold like a dream, her eyes wide, her heart thudding in slow, painful beats.

Matt gave him a searing look.

"Fine," the photographer muttered. He showed Matt the picture, and deleted it. Matt shoved him away and climbed into the car. Honey scrambled across the seat to make room for him.

The driver jumped in and even as Matt slammed his door shut, they pulled out from the curb with a squeal of tires.

CHAPTER 20

Adrenaline punched through Matt's system. His hands curled into fists and he forced them to relax. He wanted to punch something. First of all that fucking photographer.

The fucktard had been going for a pussy shot as Honey got in the car. What he'd gotten had been pretty revealing. Thank Christ she was wearing panties.

"Fuck," he muttered, his jaw so tight it ached. He looked out the side window at the city lights passing by. "Fucking hell."

Every muscle tense, his face hot, he sat there willing himself to calm the fuck down.

He glanced at Honey, way the hell on the other side of the car, jammed into the corner, her eyes closed, lips rolled in. She held her little purse on her lap with both hands, knuckles pale.

What in the holy mother of fuckers?

He sucked in air through his nose and let out it slowly.

"Thank you."

He looked back at Honey at her soft words.

"And I'm sorry." She made a face.

He gave her a hard stare then turned back to the window. They rode the rest of the way back to his place in thick silence.

When the car pulled up in the curved driveway of Matt's apartment building, the driver jumped out and opened Honey's door. She didn't move.

"Do you want me to go home?" she asked quietly.

Matt paused with one leg out of the car. Christ, he was so furious he couldn't sort it all out. "I think we should talk about this in the morning."

He climbed out, went around and gave the driver Honey's address and a hefty tip, then walked into his apartment building.

Alone.

Honey leaned against the door of the town car, her head against the glass. The city lights were a blur of colors outside the window. The car was silent other than the noise of passing traffic.

Her throat ached and she closed her eyes at the squeezing she felt in her chest.

She hadn't wanted to go to the club and this was why.

One thing she did know now, she never wanted to go back to that life. She felt a tug of sympathy for Cressa and Jenni, and some of the others. They didn't want sympathy, and she supposed she didn't have to feel sorry for them. They were ultimately in control of their lives. It was certainly their choice if that was the life they wanted to live.

Of *course* that was the life they wanted to live. From the outside, lots of people would want that life—money, privilege, luxury. No worries about being able to afford a cell phone so their latch-key kid would be safer. No worries about having enough money for gas to get to work, or enough left after paying the bills to pay the babysitter. She kept thinking about Farrah and comparing her life to Cressa's. Farrah was strong and smart and loving, and trying to do her best at the most important job in the world—raising a child. Cressa's life revolved around useless bullshit that didn't matter. Just like Honey's used to.

The driver pulled up next to her building and jumped out to get her door. She had to sit up straight to avoid falling onto the sidewalk. She gave the guy a smile as he helped her out, and when she opened her purse for a tip, he held up a hand. "Mr. Heller tipped me already," he said. "No need."

"Take it anyway," she said, slipping the bills into his hand. She certainly didn't have money to burn like Cressa and her friends, or like Matt and his friends, for that matter, but she'd had a couple of pay checks now and she was doing okay. She appreciated that he watched as she unlocked the front door of the building and entered before getting back into the car and leaving.

In her apartment, she kicked off her shoes and padded barefoot into her dark bedroom. She stripped off her dress and headed to the bathroom, flicking on a light. She looked at herself in the mirror.

Tears slipped from the corners of her eyes. A fist squeezed her throat, and a sob escaped her. She'd known all along that when her past came back to smack them in the face like that, it wasn't going to be fun. Matt kept saying that he didn't care about that. But clearly he did.

Well, screw him. She couldn't change her past. It was always going to be there.

She washed the makeup off her face, brushed her teeth with weary strokes then returned to her bedroom in strapless bra and panties. She tossed them onto the chair along with the lace dress, and pulled on her big T-shirt nightie before slipping into her bed.

She and Matt had been spending most nights together, other than when he was on the road. Not enough for her to get used to sharing a bed with him. Not enough for her bed to feel empty. Not enough for her to miss him.

But she did.

She managed to avoid Matt on Saturday by heading to the beach with Farrah and Mia. They had lunch and spent the afternoon on the pier. Farrah asked her a couple of times if everything was okay, which meant she wasn't putting on a good enough act, but she denied anything was wrong.

Matt called but she didn't answer, and when he texted *"Where R U? Am at UR place"* she'd ignored that too. That resulted in several more increasingly angry texts until finally, *"Leaving for San Jose now, answer UR goddamn phone when I call pls"*.

She didn't.

She knew the schedule, knew he had games Monday and Wednesday, and would be home very late that night, as in early Thursday morning. She wasn't going to be able to avoid him forever. So Sunday evening she sat down with her computer on her lap to send him an email.

When she opened her browser, the first thing she saw was a picture of her.

Crapping crap.

It was a photo of her kissing Matt inside the club. There was another photo of her dancing with Cressa and Jenni, three of them laughing. She looked like she was having a great time. She couldn't stop herself from reading the story that accompanied the pictures, although there wasn't much, just a lot of innuendoes about her and Matt dating, and how after being gone for a few years, she was now back on the party scene. Then there was a whole lot of crap about her past escapades, including, dammit, that infamous skinny dipping picture of her and the two guys she'd been in the pool with.

She dropped her head back and stared at her ceiling. Well. This wasn't a surprise. She'd known people were taking pictures.

Matt did not deserve that. He was just trying to come back from his injury and prove himself, not get his reputation all trashed by being associated with her. No wonder he'd been angry that night. He had a right to be angry about it.

She pressed her lips together and went to her email site.

"Matt—I'm sorry about what happened Saturday night. I'm sorry about the pictures and the gossip that's out there now. That's why I didn't want to go out and that's why we can't be together. You don't need crap like that in your life. It's going to follow me around forever, I guess. But that's my issue to deal with, not yours. Play hard, stay safe. Love, Honey."

She looked at her closing. She should probably delete that. But it was true. She loved him.

Her nose started to sting and her throat ached again, but she wasn't going to let herself cry. She was going to be strong and do the right thing. She clicked "send" and then closed down her computer and went to bed.

Monday afternoon, Dulcie arrived at the office with her new baby. Everyone crowded around, and Dulcie handed the sleeping baby over to Celine. Honey approached with a reserved smile. She'd felt like crap all day, but she definitely wanted to see the baby. "Hi, Dulcie."

"Hi, Honey. How are things going?"

"Pretty good." As long as she meant work, that was. Her personal life was a whole different story.

Honey peeked at the bundle in Celine's arms and her mouth fell open when she saw that little Taylor was wearing the hat and sweater she'd made for her. The blanket was currently draped over the stroller. "Oh she's wearing her sweater," she breathed. She looked up at Dulcie.

Dulcie's smile was surprisingly warm. "Yeah. It's so beautiful. I can't believe you made that."

"You made this?" Celine asked. "Wow."

Honey shrugged. "Yeah. It's just a hobby of mine."

Warmth unfurled in her chest at the thought that Dulcie had made a point of dressing her baby in the little garments to bring her in there, and at the fact that Dulcie liked them.

"Is there anything I can help with while I'm here?" Dulcie asked. "Any questions for me?"

"Um…actually, not at the moment."

"Is everything set for the gala Thursday night?"

"It is." She hoped.

"Great. Um…do you guys mind keeping Taylor while I go talk to Trent for a few minutes?"

"Sure," Celine agree. "Unless she starts crying."

Honey grinned. "We'll deal with it if she does."

"*You'll* deal with it," Celine corrected as Dulcie moved away with a laugh. "I don't know shit about babies."

Honey touched a fingertip to the sweet, soft cheek. "I like babies. I have two nephews and a niece, and another one on the way."

"Then you can hold her," Celine said, handing off the baby.

Honey tucked the small, warm body into her arms and smiled down at her. "She's so pretty." She rocked her gently, just a bit. Taylor's mouth moved, but her eyes remained closed, her skin so thin and translucent tiny veins were visible in her eyelids.

Dulcie emerged from Trent's office a short time later and reclaimed her offspring. "I can't believe she's still sleeping. She should be hungry soon."

"Is she a good baby?" Honey asked. "Eating and sleeping okay?"

"She's pretty good. She wants to nurse about every three hours, which is good, and she's sleeping about five hours at night now."

"That's great."

"Um…" Dulcie hesitated, then said, "I just asked Trent if I could take a year leave of absence."

Both Honey's and Celine's eyes widened. "A year!" Celine said. "Without pay?"

"Yeah." Dulcie made a face. "We're fine for money, and I…can't bear the thought of leaving her."

"She's only a couple of weeks old," Celine said.

"Yeah. But I find I've fallen completely in love with her."

Honey smiled. "That's the way it should be."

"Yeah. Anyway, Trent said yes."

"What are we going to do without you for a whole year?" Celine demanded.

"Oh. You'll survive. And I'm around, if you guys need to call me about stuff, go ahead, I'm fine with that."

She'd told Honey that before she'd left, but Honey hadn't wanted to call her just when she had a new baby. She had enough on her plate. She'd been figuring things out on her own, so Dulcie being gone longer wasn't going to make much difference to her. She might not even be there that long anyway.

Taylor woke up, Dulcie used her old cubicle to nurse her, then went to the ladies room to change a diaper. "You like babies?" she said to Honey with a grin. "Maybe you want practice at diaper changing?"

Honey grinned. "I've done it," she said. "I'm good. You go ahead."

Dulcie had just walked away, murmuring to her daughter, when Trent appeared. "Honey."

She turned to him, smiling. "Yes?"

"Can I see you in my office?"

"Of course." Honey pushed away from the desk she'd been leaning on and followed him to his office. Crapsickle. Was this about all the stuff about her on the internet and tabloids?

He closed the door and gestured to the chairs in front of his desk. She sat and crossed her legs.

"Looks like Dulcie will be gone longer than expected," he said as he too took a seat.

"Yes. She mentioned that. I understand though. I'm sure it's hard to leave a new baby."

"My wife ended up taking twenty years off," he said with a wry smile. "Anyway." His gaze sharpened on her. "I'd like to extend the term for you until Dulcie's back."

She stiffened. "For the year?"

"Yeah."

She let that sink in for a minute, saying nothing.

"Control your excitement," Trent said.

"I'm sorry. I'm surprised. I didn't think you really wanted me here. If Dulcie's gone a year, you'd have time to find someone else."

He sat back in his chair. "We got off to a bad start," he said. "We...okay, I take responsibility...I underestimated you."

Honey's breath hitched. She didn't know what to say.

"I've noticed the things you're doing," he continued. "You stepped up even when people weren't all that supportive. The others have told me some of the things you've done — clearly you've won them over. You've showed a lot of initiative and determination. You've brought in money, and you've got great ideas. And that's only in a few weeks. I'd be happy to have you stay on for the year. And who knows after that." He shrugged. "I can only commit to the one-year term right now, but things can change in a year."

"Yes." She swallowed. "I'd planned on looking for something else when my three months here were done."

He met her gaze steadily. "If this isn't what you want to do, I understand."

"It's not that." She shook her head. "I like the work and I like working for the hockey team. To my surprise." She smiled then voiced the idea that had come to her in the middles of her sleepless night. "I'm actually thinking about moving back to San Francisco, though."

"Oh." His chin lifted. "Really."

She licked her lips. "I don't know if you saw the gossip column stuff about me on the weekend." If he hadn't, that might put an end to that job offer.

"I saw it." He shook his head. "Slimeballs. You'd think they'd leave you alone after all this time."

She sucked in a shaky breath. He was blaming the reporters, not her. "Yeah," she said slowly. "I'm afraid that might never go away. You need to know that."

He shrugged. "I don't see that having any impact on your work. If we get more press coverage for events because of you, that's a good thing. Not that I want you out there stirring things up." He held up his hands, but his eyes warmed. "You've used some of your connections to help us. And besides, a young woman should be able to go out with her boyfriend and have fun without getting swarmed by the press."

"He's…" Well, she would just leave that "boyfriend"

comment for now. Her boss didn't need to know any more about her personal life than was already spread out all over the internet and tabloid papers.

"San Francisco, huh. Well, anywhere else would be lucky to have you. But I mean it when I say, I hope you'll stay. You can think about it. Is a few days enough?"

"Yes. Yes, that's fine."

"Let me know by the end of the week. We'll still have time to look for a replacement if you decide to leave. I really hope you don't, though."

She rose from her chair and smoothed down her skirt. "Thank you."

Wow. Just…wow. She returned to her cubicle in a daze.

He'd noticed the work she'd done. And things had gotten better there, with the others actually talking to her and involving her in work discussions.

But last night, lying in bed, she'd thought about leaving when the three months was up. She probably shouldn't have come back to Los Angeles. Even though she'd had the job Dad had gotten her, and she'd been scared of not being able to find one on her own, she probably should have stayed away and made a new life for her somewhere else. She'd been stupid to think she could do it here, where her past would probably always haunt her.

It made her sad, for a variety of reasons. She'd miss being closer to her brothers and their kids. She'd miss Farrah and Mia. And she didn't even want to let herself think about how much she'd miss Matt, but that didn't matter because she was going to miss him even if she stayed.

She gave her head a shake as her phone rang. She picked it up.

"Hey, Honey, it's Bryn."

Huh. She hadn't really expected Bryn to call.

"Remember I offered to help at the gala. Just following up on that."

She'd come through. Wow. That was so nice.

"Yeah," Honey said. "I remember. So, um, I could use some help for about a half hour selling silent auction tickets, if you don't mind."

"Aw, that's nothing! I can do that. What time?"

They made arrangements, chatted a little about the evening at the club. Bryn didn't even mention the stupid tabloid coverage. Huh.

Weirdly, that made her feel sadder, because it would've been cool if Bryn and Joe and she and Matt could have hung out together as couples.

CHAPTER 21

Matt arrived at the Loews Hotel Thursday evening in another town car, all duded up in his tux. He fidgeted with the bow tie as he entered the hotel lobby, looking for the ballroom where the gala was to take place. Cocktails and the silent auction started at six o'clock, followed by dinner and entertainment at seven.

He still hadn't talked to Honey or heard dick from her other than that fucked-up email she'd sent him. He'd gotten back in the middle of the night and had headed home for some sleep in his own bed. He'd slept like crap all week. Weirdly he hadn't played like crap. Somehow his frustrations had turned into intensity on the ice and he was playing better than ever.

Although along with that intensity came a brutally physical game, meaning he was sore as hell. Whatever.

He was going to hunt down Honey and they were going to have that fucking talk he'd wanted to have last weekend. He'd been so wound up and furious that night he'd sent her home, thinking they'd talk the next day. Now he regretted it and wished he dragged her up to his apartment and had things out then and there.

He spotted a couple of the guys, Joe and Frankie, and headed toward them. "Hey, man," he said slapping Joe on the shoulder. "Nice monkey suit."

"You too."

The both rolled their eyes.

"Where's Bryn?"

"She's over there selling silent auction tickets. Come on, we have to drop some cash."

It was for a good cause. Matt tagged along as they went to survey the prize offerings. Which were fucking awesome. People were going crazy buying tickets and deciding what draws they wanted to enter.

He kept looking around, looking for Honey. He wasn't sure what she was wearing so he kept looking for her shiny blonde hair in the crowd. Of course, this was California and every other woman was blonde.

Not like her though.

Holy shit, there was Amanda Seyfried. And Shia Leboeuf.

Then he saw her. Across the room, standing talking to a small group of people. Like that night at Eden, she fit right in here. In an elegant black dress, black shoes with the highest, skinniest heel he'd ever seen, her hair pulled up into a stylish bun, she looked classy and gorgeous. Her smile beamed as she talked, and from there it looked like everyone there was hanging on her every word. Especially the old guys.

And yet, their attitude was respectful and attentive. Not salacious. And the women weren't much different, really. Honey touched one woman's arm in a gentle, friendly gesture as she said something, and then they both laughed.

She moved away from that group and moved on, only to stop to talk to someone else.

Working the crowd. And doing it like a pro.

Without even saying anything to his teammates, he started

shouldering his way through the crowd of people toward her. Only by the time he got there, she'd moved on. He followed her, but his gut clenched when he saw she had now stopped to talk to her parents.

Great.

He had no idea what they knew or didn't know about him and Honey and last weekend, and…fuckit. He forged on.

He touched the small of Honey's back as he approached her from behind. She turned to look at him, smiling. Her eyes flew wide and the smile vanished. "Matt."

"Honey." He looked at her parents. "Mr. and Mrs. Holbrook. Good to see you."

"You too, Matt," Steve Holbrook said. "Good road trip."

"Thanks."

Steve looked at his daughter. "Did you watch the games?"

"No."

"Huh," Steve said. "You've been coming to every home game, I thought you'd watch the away games on TV."

Every home game? Matt knew she'd been to a couple, but not every game.

She closed her eyes and sighed. "I don't really like hockey."

Steve laughed. Matt lifted his eyebrows.

"Honey never liked hockey," Mrs. Holbrook said. "She was never interested in any sports. In fact, she was never interested in anything. Except partying." She laughed. "Some things never change."

Matt turned his head and gave her a long look. "What does that mean?"

She blinked. "You should know. You were there with her. The pictures were all over."

One of the guys had helpfully showed him a tabloid with the picture of him and Honey plastered against each other that night in Eden. He hadn't been interested in seeing the rest of the pictures, but he'd looked, just to make sure that asswipe photographer really had deleted the crotch shot of Honey. He hadn't found it, but yeah, there'd been a few others, the same ones showing up over and over again on various blogs and websites along with the comments that made him burn.

"There's something wrong with going out to a club with friends?" he asked Mrs. Holbrook.

Her eyes slid sideways to her husband then back. "Uh, no, of course not."

"Honey did nothing that night except be there," Matt continued. "And she was only there because I wanted her to, because I wanted to go out with friends."

He caught the look on Honey's face, her mouth open, her eyes round. He still had his hand on her lower back and he felt the tension in her spine.

"Also," he continued. "I don't think you can say all she's interested in is partying, when she's holding down a challenging job." He smiled. "Looks like this event is quite a success. Congratulations, Honey."

"Th-thanks."

Mrs. Holbrook's eyes creased up at the corners. "Congratulations?"

"She's the one organizing this shindig," Matt said. Christ. Did her mother not even know that?

"Dulcie did most of the work before she left," Honey said. "And since they put it on every year, it was pretty easy to stick to the plan."

"I know how much work you've put into it," he said quietly. Which he did, from their many conversations about how her day had gone the evenings they'd spent together. He liked hearing her talk about her work, about the projects they were working on together and the other things she was involved in. Apparently her mother didn't enjoy that as much as he did. "So yeah, congratulations.

"She's the one who got some of these people here," he continued. "Shia Leboeuf. Wow. Smart to invite high profile people who are also hockey fans. The prizes are amazing. And people are spending a shitload of money here, which is great for the Foundation."

Mrs. Holbrook didn't look happy. Too fucking bad. Honey deserved better. Yeah, it was her mom, her family, but he wasn't going to stand by and let them continue to do a number on her confidence and self-esteem when she was working so hard to overcome the mistakes she'd made in the past.

He looked at Honey. "They need your help with something at the silent auction table."

"They do?"

"I said I'd come find you." He shot a smile at her parents. "Excuse us."

He eased her away from them and nudged her toward the tables set up to sell tickets. But when they neared the tables, he veered right and directed her firmly toward one of the doors to the hall.

"What—?" Honey tried to stop and looked up at him. "What are you doing? You said they needed something."

"I lied." He hustled her out the door and into the wide hall, then turned right and led her down the hall, past bathrooms, and into a small alcove with a table holding a floral arrangement and a couple of armchairs.

"What are you doing, Matt?"

"We never had that talk we were supposed to have last weekend."

"I emailed you—"

"Yeah, I got your bullshit email." He sat on a chair and pulled her down onto his lap.

"Matt!"

She felt so good there, in his arms, except she was tense and uncooperative. "We're gonna talk," he muttered. "But first…this…" And he caught her chin in one hand, turned her face toward him and kissed her.

She made a shocked little noise, then another noise that sounded like a half-hearted protest. He opened her mouth with his and slid his tongue inside, stroking over hers. His hand slid up her back, holding her close, and the hand on her jaw gentled, his fingertips sliding along her jaw, up behind her ear. His thumb put pressure on her chin to open her more to him, and then the soft noise that came from her throat was helpless arousal.

Her body softened against his and she kissed him back, so fucking sweet, so fucking hot, it made his blood surge through his veins, right to his dick. Which was pressed against her hip. She made another noise, no doubt because she felt him getting hard.

One of her hands pushed into his hair, the other resting on his chest. "Matt," she whispered.

"Yeah." He ended the long, deep kisses with several smaller, shorter kisses, still with lingering tongue on her bottom lip. They drew a little apart and her eyes fluttered open, heavy-lidded. "I missed you, Honey. You pissed me off, but I still missed you."

"I'm thinking about moving back to San Francisco."

He frowned. "What?"

"I think once my three-month term at the Foundation is up, I'll be better off starting over somewhere else."

"Huh? Why?"

"I know you were mad at me that night, at Eden. I—"

"Wait, what?" He jerked back. "I wasn't mad at you that night."

"Y-yes you were. You were furious."

"I was furious at those fucking photographers."

"No." She shook her head. "You were mad before that. You were mad because I was partying with Cressa and those others."

"Honey. No." His hand tightened on her jaw again. "I wasn't mad at you. I was pissed at myself. Guilty. Worried. A little."

"Worried?" Her forehead creased. "About what?"

"About you. With those losers."

She said nothing. Then, "Pissed at yourself?"

He closed his eyes briefly. "Fuck. Cressa had to bring up that fucking threesome."

"Oh yeah." One corner of her mouth kicked up into a rueful smile. "I kinda brought it up again, too."

"You were trying to piss me off, weren't you?"

Honey's heart pounded. Heat swept over her, and not just from Matt's scorching kiss. "What do you mean?"

She was totally stalling. She knew exactly what he meant. And he was right.

"Fucking don't play games, Honey," he said on a groan. "Just tell me what's going on with you. It felt like you were trying to push me away."

"I thought you were mad at me," she finally said. "For hanging out with my old friends. I know I was gone longer than I planned, but I wasn't doing anything bad. And it annoyed me that you were angry about that."

He lifted an eyebrow. "You still consider them friends?"

She made a face. "Not really. But...Cressa and Chandler are together and he called her a...he was really mean to her. We ended up in the ladies' room with her crying her eyes out."

"Huh." He blinked.

"I was trying to tell her she doesn't have to put up with that from any guy. That she deserves better. God!" She closed her eyes. "It reminded me so much of me."

"Baby. That's what you were doing?" His eyes softened.

"Yeah. That was why I was gone so long. I just wanted to get back to you but she was really upset. I thought you might come rescue me, but you didn't."

"You went off with them on your own free will," he muttered. "After Cressa brought up our threesome. Also, I didn't go find you because I trusted you. I was worried, but I trusted you."

"Oh." She swallowed hard. "When I came back and you were acting all pissed and I said that…I knew I shouldn't have. I knew I was pushing a button."

"Uh…*yeah*." He groaned. "I did not want you to be reminded of that."

"Okay, we both made mistakes," she said. "You're always telling me to just let it go. You need to do that too."

"Fuck." His jaw tightened. "Okay, I'm sorry you thought I was pissed at you."

"At first I was hurt," she whispered to his throat, playing with a button on his shirt. "That you were mad at me, when I didn't do anything wrong. Then *I* got mad. And I said that. I'm sorry. But really…" She sighed. "That whole night just proved my point."

"And what point would that be?" His voice was low and edged with anger.

She shivered. "That we don't belong together."

"Bullshit," he bit out. "Oh my fucking god." He tipped his head back, eyes closed, jaw tight.

"I knew that was going to happen eventually," she insisted. "The reporters, the cameras, my old friends trying to drag me back into that life. You don't need that in your life.

At first I was angry because you'd kept saying you didn't care about that stuff, but that night, you were pissed off and it seemed like you did care."

"Honey." He tipped her chin up with his fingers so their eyes met. "You thought that little of me?"

She bit her lip, her eyes burning. "I'm sorry. You'd have the right to be angry about that. I know you said you don't care about what people think, but you're a professional athlete, with a public image, and it *does* matter. So I sent you that email."

"Which was utter bullshit. You know I don't give a fuck about any of that shit. Fuck yeah, Honey, we belong together."

Her heart went soft and warmth spread through her body.

"I was definitely pissed off at you this week, though," he growled. "When you wouldn't answer my calls or my texts. What the fuck?"

"I just thought it was better to end things."

"Yeah…no. I don't think so. I wasn't just mad, though. Fuck." He closed his eyes again. "I was terrified."

"Uh…"

"That I'd lost you," he explained. "But I wasn't giving up."

"Oh, Matt." She leaned her forehead against his. She'd screwed up again, pushed him away, even hurt him.

"I love you, Honey."

She went very still. Did he really just say that?

Oh god. Oh god.

"Honey?"

She nodded.

"You've gone to every home game?"

"Yes."

"You signed your email, 'Love, Honey'."

She nodded again. Her throat had closed up and her heart

was once again cracking and melting. "I love you too," she finally whispered back.

"I know."

She snorted a little laugh. "Han Solo."

He grinned.

"Why do you love me?" she asked. "I've screwed up so much. Even with you. I was so worried I didn't have it in me to have a real relationship, and I was right."

"No." He lifted his chin and kissed her mouth softly. "We both screwed up. I love you because you're beautiful, Honey—on the outside and the inside. You have such a warm heart. You're generous and caring. With Cressa, who did nothing to deserve that from you. She abandoned you as a friend, but you still care. You care even when you don't want to admit it, like with Mia. Seeing you with kids is awesome—you let yourself just relax and be yourself, and it's so amazing. You're smart and determined. Yeah, you made some bad choices, but you picked yourself up and moved on, and that's not easy to do. Which means you're also strong."

He really saw those things inside her. It amazed her. Humbled her. And if she could get past the huge mistakes she'd made in the past, she could get past this. Especially with him there offering her unconditional love and acceptance. He made her feel as if she really was worth all the trouble.

Along with her boss recognizing her contributions at work and asking her to stay on...her friendship with Farrah and Mia...Dulcie accepting her and helping her...hell, she *was* worth it. "I'm sorry, Matt."

"Eh. We both screwed up. We admitted it. Now we move on."

She stared at him. "Just like that?"

"Yeah. Just like that."

This kind of honest, open communication was not something she was used to. Nor was she used to making a mistake and being immediately forgiven for it.

"You really love me?"

His lips curved. "Yeah. I really love you."

She'd screwed up and he loved her anyway.

Her heart nearly exploded in her chest.

She'd never known anyone so accepting of her and who she really was, ugly baggage, past mistakes and all. "Thanks for sticking up for me with my mom."

"Any fucking time," he growled.

Her heart expanded even more. "I need to get back in there," she said in a shaky voice.

"Yeah. I guess you do. And it's almost dinner time. I'm hungry."

"What else is new?"

He gave her butt a little tap, gave her lips a smooch then lifted her easily off his lap. He took her hand to walk down the hall back to the ballroom.

"You're coming home with me tonight," he said.

She met his eyes and nodded.

"Did I tell you how hot you look?"

She smiled. "Hmm…no."

"Well you do. Nice dress."

"Thanks." She glanced down at the Marc Jacobs dress she'd bought on sale at TJ Maxx for the gala.

"And *really* nice shoes."

"Again, thank you."

"Wanna fuck you wearing those shoes."

Her stomach did a little flip and heat washed down through her. "Um. Okay."

He grinned, lifted her hand and kissed her knuckles, then led her into the ballroom.

~

Four hours later Matt got his wish. Honey's legs, still wearing those fuck-me shoes, wrapped around his waist as she came, her sweet pussy rippling around his cock, his face buried in the side of her neck. "God yeah," he groaned as his own orgasm roared through him. "Love you, Honey. Fucking… love…you."

Her hands roamed over his back, up the back of his neck into his hair, hugging him tightly. "Love you too, Matt. So much."

They lay there, panting for air, hearts thudding together. Then he rolled to his side, bringing her with him, holding one leg up on his hip, still buried deep inside her. He gave a couple more slow slides in and out while he was still hard.

"Mmmm." Honey let out a sexy sigh.

His hand curved over her ass. "Yeah."

She snuggled in closer, if that was even possible. "I want to talk about what happened last time we were together, that summer."

He grimaced. "Okay."

"Hey. You're the one who wanted to talk."

He grunted. "Go."

He felt her smile. "I was in love with you. Back then."

His heart clenched and his arms tightened around her. "Honey."

"It's okay. I know you didn't feel the same."

"Oh yeah. I did."

Her head lifted and he met those gorgeous eyes. "You did?"

"I was crazy about you, Honey. You were amazing—so beautiful and sexy and fun."

"I thought you ended up hating me."

"Nah. I never hated you. I just didn't understand why you hung around with those people. They were losers. Users."

"You were willing to jump into bed with one of them. And me."

He groaned and slid a hand up into her hair to press her face against his chest. "I knew that was going to come up. Did you hate me for that?"

"It was my fault."

"Don't actually even remember whose idea it was. We were all hammered that night."

"Yeah. But I wanted to do it. It was hot and wild and wicked. And I thought it would impress you and make you happy."

"I was twenty years old and horny as hell. Yeah, it made me happy. Two hot girls all over me? Hell yeah. Until I sobered up and realized what we'd done. I cared about you, Honey. Didn't want to hurt you."

"Yeah, I discovered I did not like thinking about you and Cressa."

"Know what? Hot as it was, I felt the same. You and Cressa…that was just wrong."

"I was so stupid."

"We both were. Young and stupid. People are allowed to make mistakes, Honey."

"I'm learning that. Thanks to you. God…" She burrowed closer into him and her body quivered with emotion against his. His hand threaded through her hair, rubbed her neck.

"You don't have to be perfect to be loved," he said quietly. "I love you, Honey."

"I always felt like that, growing up. But I couldn't be perfect, so I just tried to be bad."

"Nobody's perfect."

After a short silence, she said. "I was mad at you for leaving."

"When? The other day?"

"No." She smiled. "Years ago."

"Honey. I had to go."

"I know. But it hurt. You were the only guy who ever gave me the kind of attention I craved. You paid attention to me in a way I'd never had in my life. I let myself care about you and then you rejected me because I was hanging around with people you didn't like. You were the least judgmental person I'd ever met, but I felt like you were judging me and I wasn't good enough."

"I wasn't judging you. I already told you. You were hanging around with stupid people, and I couldn't figure out why."

"Then you went and told my dad about the stuff my friends and I were doing. That felt like betrayal. Rejection."

"I know." He rubbed her neck again. "I'm sorry. I only did it because I cared about you. I was worried about you. I didn't reject you."

"It felt like it. When we had that big fight about my friends and why I hung around with losers like that. I felt like you were just being critical like my parents. I hated that. It made me just want to rebel even more. They were my friends. They were more like family to me than my own family. I know you didn't get that."

"No," he admitted, giving a tug to her hair to once again pull her head back so their eyes could meet. "Didn't get it then. But I do now. Now I know you better."

"I had to be forced to stand on my own feet and figure out who I was. And I did. I mean, I still am. But I'm getting there." She smiled, her gaze roaming over his face. "I admired you. I loved you back then for being so strong. You're always so calm, so sure of yourself, so easygoing and open."

"Maybe too easygoing. I went along with things for a long time too—played hockey because that was what was expected of me. Getting into the NHL was a given, because of my brothers, and I never fully appreciated the opportunities I got."

"You don't get into the NHL just because you have three brothers who were in the NHL." She fixed a frowning stare on him. "You got into the NHL because you're a great player. *You.*"

He smiled. "Thanks, babe."

"It's true."

"Yeah, okay. But I pretty much coasted along until I got injured. That changed my outlook on life. And that's why I was *not* going to let you go—something that good doesn't come along very often and I'm not missing out on that because I was just going to be easygoing and let it go. I'd fight every two-hundred-fifty-pound goon in the NHL every night for you."

"Or a one-hundred-fifty-pound photographer."

He grinned.

"I love that you did that for me. I never ever had anybody who looked out for me in situations like that. Although, sometimes I created those situations. But not always. Sometimes I hated it but I had to pretend I loved it."

He gathered her closer again. "Always got your back, babe."

"I know. And Matt…me too. I mean, I've got your back."

He remembered the night he'd been so on edge about the game against Fiero. She had been there for him. He never could've told anyone else about that, for sure not the guys he played with. It made his chest ache. When he'd walked into that meeting room weeks ago, he hadn't wanted the distraction of Honey Holbrook, but now he knew…he needed her. "I know. Thanks, Hon. And," he growled, "you're not fucking moving back to San Francisco."

She smiled. "Um yeah. About that. Guess what? Dulcie's going to take an extended leave, for a year. And Trent asked me to stay on. He said he's noticed the things I've been doing and other people have too. They really want me there."

"That doesn't surprise me." He smiled back at her. "So you're *not* leaving?"

"I asked Trent for a few days to think about it." Their eyes met, hers soft and warm, and her mouth curved. "But no. I'm not leaving. Not now."

"Thank Christ."

"But I don't want you fighting."

"What?" His eyebrows pulled together.

"I don't like fighting. It scares me."

He grinned. "I can't promise that. I can't even promise you and I won't fight sometimes. But I will promise that I'll keep it clean. No dirty fighting. On the ice or off."

"Okay. But dirty is okay sometimes."

"Ha. Dirty sex.

She laughed. "Yeah. I'm good with that."

"Me too, babe." He kissed her mouth. "Me too."

"There is no fucking way we're staying in that house with all those kids."

Honey laughed and leaned in to Matt where they sat in first class on the jet making its approach into Winnipeg's James Richardson International Airport. "I thought you liked kids."

"I do, but Jesus Christ, Jase and Remi keep poppin' em out, they have three now and one is a baby who probably screams all night, and Logan and Nicole are staying with my parents too, with Chris. Tag and Kyla obviously have their own place, but when they're over, there will be *six kids there*, and *three* of them are *three years old*. It's insane."

"It sounds like fun to me."

"Yeah, you think you love kids, just wait. You'll want to go home and get your tubes tied."

She laughed again. "As if."

"Believe me, I've considered a vasectomy when I've left here."

Honey's smile faded. "Uh. You're not serious, are you?"

Matt's grin went crooked and he leaned in to kiss her. "Nope."

A soft exhalation escaped her. "Okay. Good."

"Don't worry, Hon, I have every intention of knocking you up. Some day."

His words sent a little shiver through her. "I don't get any say in that?"

"Babe. You know you want kids."

She did.

"Anyway, I was going to book us a room at a hotel, but Kyla convinced me we should stay with them. At least there are only two kids there."

Honey bit her lip and nodded as the wheels touched down on the runway, and then her seatbelt dug into her hips as the jet slowed. They were in Winnipeg.

Matt and his brother organized a charity golf tournament every summer to raise money for the children's hospital. Usually he spent most of his summers home in Winnipeg, but this year he'd chosen to stay in Santa Monica with her. Luckily her boss had given her two weeks off to accompany him on this trip to help with the tournament.

She was about to meet the entire Heller family in one fell swoop.

Eeep.

Remi took a huge swing with the golf club, with impressive form…and completely missed the ball.

After a beat of silence, Kyla yelled, "Fore!"

All four women collapsed into giggles. Remi leaned on her club. "Damn. I was sure I was going to hit it that time."

"Your swing looked really good," Honey offered.

"Where's that beer cart when you need it?" Remi asked with a grin.

"Do over," Nicole announced. "Go ahead."

"Thanks," Remi muttered, straightening her stance again. "Who's counting, right?"

"It's not like we're going to win the tournament," Kyla added.

The four women were on hole seventeen at Twin Pines Country Club, and the whole afternoon had been like this. Honey's face hurt from laughing.

This time Remi hit the ball and they all cheered her.

Nicole went next and hit a long high ball straight down the middle of the fairway.

"I am so jealous of you," Remi sighed.

"Me too," Honey said.

Kyla teed up her ball and at that moment her husband Tag zoomed up on a golf cart with his brother Logan.

"Babe," Tag called to Kyla. "Spread your legs and lift your head."

She lifted her head and tried to give him a reproving look but ended up dissolving into laughter again along with everyone else. "I think I've heard that before."

He grinned, leaning an arm on the steering wheel. "Oh yeah." He winked. "How's it going?"

"Awesome." She bit her bottom lip and focused. And waited. "I can't do this with you watching. My hands are so sweaty I can't get a good grip."

"Oh, your grip is just fine," Tag murmured.

Honey laughed as color washed into Kyla's cheeks.

"Okay, okay." She swung and hit the ball, a decent shot in Honey's opinion.

"Nice stroke," Tag said.

She walked toward him, eyes on him, lips twitching. "Thanks." She leaned into the cart and kissed him.

"Hey, Remi, are those kids' clubs you're playing with?" Logan called.

Remi grinned. "Shut up." She lifted her club as if to swing it at her brother-in-law, but they both laughed. "I know I'm short, no need to rub it in."

"Let's go," Logan said to Tag.

"Are you guys even golfing?" Kyla asked.

"Of course we are."

"I think you're just driving around in that cart and distracting everyone."

"We're entertaining them," Logan said. "We don't want to try too hard, because, you know, we'd just end beating everyone embarrassingly."

The girls all hooted at that.

Logan and Tag left before Honey took her shot, and then the four women climbed into two carts and headed down the fairway.

On the putting green a short time later, Remi pressed her hands to her breasts. "Damn," she muttered. "I need to go feed that baby."

Honey blinked, but smiled. "Oh-oh."

"We're almost done, Rem. One more hole."

"The way I golf we could be here several more hours."

"Take the cart and go if you want," Kyla said. "I'll catch a ride with Honey and Nicole."

But then Jase and Matt arrived in their cart.

"Ladies!" Jase called. "Almost done?"

"I need a ride back to the clubhouse," Remi said, walking toward them over the close-clipped grass. "I need to feed our son."

Jase's face softened. "Sure. Come on."

"I can't believe you have three boys," Honey said to her as Remi dropped her putter into her golf bag.

"We wanted a girl." She grinned. "We may still try again."

"Are you crazy?" Kyla demanded. "Four kids? I wasn't even sure I wanted one kid," she told Honey. "We got pregnant by accident. But something weird happened after Josh was born. It didn't happen immediately, but I fell in love with him. So we went for two. But that's it."

"At least you got your girl," Remi muttered.

"I foresee the same future for Amy as I had," Kyla said. "All these boys. I have two brothers and then growing up with these Heller boys, I was always the only girl."

"At least you understand," Honey said.

Remi added, "We'll make sure the boys don't leave her out."

"Also make sure Grandma and Grandpa Heller don't spoil the heck out of their little princess," Nicole said with a grin.

"Plus," Kyla added, "the odds of ending up with a girl are not in your favor after three boys. You'll end up with four boys, like Laura and Doug did."

"It'd be crazy if they all ended up playing in the NHL," Honey said with a grin.

"Ha! Crazy is right. Could that even happen again?"

"Sure!" Remi climbed onto Jase's lap in the cart. "We'll have our own hockey team, between all of us. See you back at the clubhouse." She waved as they took off.

Nicole, Kyla and Honey finished off the last hole, took their carts back and walked toward the clubhouse. Honey turned her face up to the warm sun. What a great day. She'd had so much fun getting to know Matt's sisters-in-law better.

People were milling around the terrace behind the clubhouse. The smoky scent of hot dogs on the grill wafted toward them. The last few foursomes were finishing up and volunteers were preparing to award prizes. Some old-timer NHL players were there for the event, and apparently a lot of prominent Winnipeg businessmen, including Kyla's lawyer bosses and the owners of the Jets hockey team. Honey'd already fielded numerous questions about her father and teasing inquiries as to why he wasn't there.

Wow, she could really score some major brownie points next year if she could convince her dad and her pro-golfer brother to come. Hell, both her brothers. Oh yeah.

She mingled through the crowd, this kind of environment familiar to her though she didn't know many people, but it was easy for her to make conversation about how folks had golfed, the weather, the silent auction and donations, and of course hockey.

There was a lot attention from the media on her, which she didn't think was warranted, but she had to appreciate the distance and discretion they showed, unlike the aggressive paparazzi in California. She found the local photographers oddly respectful, asking her permission to photograph her, getting some shots of her with the Heller wives and some with Matt.

The day wasn't about her, but heck, if it helped increase interest and attention on the event, she could handle it.

She went into the clubhouse to freshen up. When she came back outside, Matt and his brothers were all involved in conversations, and Nicole, Kyla and Remi had disappeared. Laura and Doug were talking to some people over by the outdoor bar on the patio.

Honey looked around, feeling momentarily lost, and spotted a boy in a wheelchair on the edge of the stone patio. She tipped her head and moved toward him, drawn to him out of interest in what his story was, and curiosity about why he was there alone. She paused beside his chair and dropped to a crouch. "Hi," she said. "I'm Honey."

"Honey Holbrook," the boy said immediately. "Steve Holbrook's daughter. Your dad was the greatest hockey player ever."

She grinned. "Wow. You must be a big hockey fan."

"I love hockey."

She took in his bald head, pale complexion and thin frame, and something inside her squeezed. "What's your name?"

"Ryan."

"Pleased to meet you, Ryan. What brings you here today?" She gave a teasing smile. "Were you golfing?"

He grinned. "No. I came to see my favorite hockey players, the Heller brothers."

"Do you play hockey?"

"Not anymore." His straightforward reply made her insides tighten even more. "I love hockey. I used to play goal. But I got too sick to play."

"Well, I hope you'll be well enough to play soon."

"I won't get better," he replied, still matter-of-factly. "I'm dying. I have cancer."

Honey blinked and her throat constricted. "Oh." Shit. Shit shit shit. "I'm sorry to hear that." What the fuck were you supposed to say to that? "How old are you, Ryan?"

"I'm twelve."

The corners of her eyes stung and she fought for composure.

Oh god. She was going to lose it. She'd dealt with a lot of kids who'd had rough lives, but this was…unthinkable. Unbearable. She sucked in a long breath and fought for self-control. "Did you meet the Heller brothers yet?"

"Not yet. My mom and dad are here, and they're going to try to see if I can meet them."

"How about if I introduce you? I know them."

His eyes lit up. "I know you do. You're dating Matt."

"I sure am."

"I'd really like to meet them." His expression became more animated, his eyes wider.

"Should I take you over to them? Or bring them over

here?" She didn't want to wheel him away and have his parents come back looking for him.

"You can take me to them. Holy cow! This is cool!"

She figured out the brakes on the chair and pushed him over the patio toward the group of people where Matt and his brothers stood talking and laughing. When she was close, she stepped from behind the chair and touched Matt's arm. He looked down at her and smiled, his eyes warm and bright. "Hey, Hon."

She tipped her head toward Ryan in his wheelchair. "There's someone here who wants to meet you and your brothers."

She watched Matt take it all in quickly, immediately excusing himself to the group and clapping a hand on Tag's shoulder to get him to join them. Logan and Jase clued in too and soon they were all hunkered down around Ryan's chair.

The look of delight on Ryan's face as he talked to his favorite hockey players was too much for Honey. She tried to stay and listen, but her throat hurt so bad, and she had to give a huge sniffle and turn away so they didn't see her lose it.

She hastened back to the clubhouse, just trying to get away, to get somewhere private to regain control. She made it inside, turned and found a quiet alcove, covered her face with her hands and burst into tears.

Arms came around her and she found herself enfolded in a hug from Laura Heller.

Honey turned into the older woman's arms. "I'm sorry," she sobbed. "I just…I can't…"

"It's okay, Honey." Laura rubbed her back. "It's okay. I overheard you with that boy."

"He's…d-d-dying. And he's only twelve." Her chest burned and she couldn't stop the tears from flowing.

"I know. It's so sad." Laura's voice trembled too.

"And h-he's so brave," Honey sobbed, hanging on tighter.

Laura's arms rocked her a little, stroked her hair. "God. God. I have to go back out there, but I don't know if I can."

"You can. Take a minute. If Ryan can do it, you can too."

She sniffed again. "Oh my god. Yes. Yes."

"Matt loves you."

Honey gave a hiccup. "Um. Yeah. I love him too."

"I was concerned," Laura continued, arms still holding her. "When he said he was dating you."

"Be-because of my reputation."

"Yes. Just being honest. I wasn't sure what you were going to be like. I was picturing a spoiled, rich princess. But that didn't make sense. For Matt. I trusted his judgment. But I wanted to meet you myself."

Honey gave a jerky nod, embarrassed now, her face wet, her makeup probably wrecked. "I understand."

Laura drew back and used her thumbs to gently stroke away tears from Honey's hot cheeks, smiling at her. "You're beautiful. Inside and out. I watched you with all our grandkids at the house. They love you. Kids are a good judge of character. I watched you today, having so much fun with Remi and Kyla and Nicole. They like you too. I saw you talking to people out there, charming everyone, including the news people. It's not your event, but you threw yourself into it wholeheartedly, helping get things organized last week, letting reporters interview you even though you clearly didn't want to."

"Um…"

"Then I watched you with that boy. Oh, Honey. I can see how big your heart is. And I know why Matt loves you."

"Frack," Honey muttered, squeezing her eyes closed. "You're making me cry even more."

Laura laughed softly. "I'm sorry. Here." She handed her some tissues.

"Thank you."

Honey wiped her eyes and blew her nose, but still felt that tight ache inside her chest that threatened to turn to tears again. She bent her head and took some deep breaths. "I need to use the ladies' room again. I probably look scary."

"Let's both go. Some cold water on your face will help."

They took a few more minutes to clean up. Luckily Honey was wearing waterproof mascara, but her nose and cheeks were bright pink. Oh well.

"Okay?" Laura asked.

"Not really." Honey gave her a smile. "But I'll fake it. Wow. Sometimes we take so much for granted, when we should feel so, so blessed."

"That is so true." Laura paused. "Thank you, Honey."

"For what?" Her eyes widened.

"For loving my son. For making him happy."

They looked into each other's eyes, smiled, and Honey reached for Laura's hand and squeezed it. "Thank you," she said. "For raising such a great guy. And for being so nice to me when I was losing my shit." She covered her mouth, eyes wide.

Laura laughed and waved a hand. "Don't worry, I've heard it all, raising four hockey players."

"I bet you have."

They strolled back out.

They paused outside on the patio and Honey took in the four brothers still crouched down talking to Ryan, all of them so big and gorgeous, healthy and tanned from the afternoon in the sun, with wide smiles and sincere interest in Ryan, and Honey's heart swelled up so big she thought it might burst.

Matt looked up at her and caught her eye and his eyes crinkled up with warmth and love. When she'd fallen in love with Matt, and him with her, she'd thought that was enough, more than she'd ever hoped to have, but now being a part of his family made her feel even more incredibly lucky. As a kid she'd dreamed about warmth and laughter and hugs and happiness. Unconditional love. A mother who cared and comforted her, siblings who were interested in her and teased her, people she could open her heart to and love, and trust them to take care with her feelings and love her in return.

Now she had that. She had it all.

AUTHOR NOTE

Thank you so much for reading Offside! Make sure you're on my mailing list for news about my next releases. If you enjoyed Offside, please consider leaving a review at the retailer of your choice or at Goodreads to help other readers find my books.

I've been so thrilled and gratified that readers have loved my Heller brothers so much. Every email I get asking about Jason's baby, or when the next book is out, or when Matt would have his story, made me feel like you all think of these guys as real people as much as I do! I am incredibly blown away by the response to this series. I was always told nobody would be interested in hockey or hockey players, but I wrote these books anyway and I'm so glad I did. Thank you!

And never fear, dear, dear readers, although this is the end of the Heller brothers series, I *will* be writing more hockey books!

OTHER BOOKS BY KELLY JAMIESON

Heller Brothers Hockey

Breakaway

Faceoff

One Man Advantage

Hat Trick

Offside

Power Series

Rule of Three Series

San Amaro Singles

Windy City Kink

Brew Crew

Aces Hockey

Last Shot

Bayard Hockey

Stand-Alone Books

Dancing in the Rain

Three of Hearts

Loving Maddie from A to Z

Love Me

Friends with Benefits

Love Me More

2 Hot 2 Handle

Lost and Found

One Wicked Night

Sweet Deal

Hot Ride

Crazy Ever After

All I Want for Christmas

Sexpresso Night

Irish Sex Fairy

Conference Call

Rigger

You Really Got Me

How Sweet It Is

ABOUT THE AUTHOR

Kelly Jamieson is the bestselling author of over thirty romance novels and novellas. Her writing has been described as "emotionally complex", "sweet and satisfying" and "blisteringly sexy". If she can stop herself from reading or writing, she loves to cook. She has shelves of cookbooks that she reads at length. She also enjoys gardening in the summer, and in the winter she likes to read gardening magazines and seed catalogues (there might be a theme here…) She also loves shopping, especially for clothes and shoes.

Subscribe to her newsletter for updates about her new books and what's coming up.

Find out what's new…
www.kellyjamieson.com
info@kellyjamieson.com

www.ingramcontent.com/pod-product-compliance
Lightning Source LLC
Chambersburg PA
CBHW032027310726
48972CB00002B/568